THE OPTICIAN

Detective Jason Smith book 35

Copyright © 2025 Stewart Giles

For Claire Grange:
An incredible human being who displayed an
early aptitude for violence in school plays.

CHAPTER ONE

"Open your eyes."

Detective Sergeant Jason Smith wasn't listening. He'd drifted off and he was lingering in the limbo between sleep and wakefulness. His mind was bringing a dream to the surface - a dream with a soundtrack to it. It was a familiar song, but Smith couldn't recall the title. A man was speaking over a background of guitars.

What we have here is failure to communicate.

"Please, open your eyes."

Smith was aware of the woman's voice now.

"I don't know how good you think I am," she said. "But if I'm to finish examining your eyes, you really need to keep them open."

Smith obliged. "Sorry, I think I fell asleep for a moment there."

"That has to be a first."

Stella Read had come highly recommended. Smith had been having trouble with recurring migraines, and his wife DS Erica Whitton had suggested that he get his eyes tested. It was possible that the migraines were caused by the strain he was putting on his middle-aged eyes. Smith had been reluctant to see a specialist at first, but during a particularly nasty migraine he'd admitted defeat and agreed to make an appointment.

"What's the diagnosis, doc?" he said.

"I'm not a doctor," Stella said. "And the diagnosis is this – you should have come to me a long time ago."

"I can see OK."

"That's like saying a one-legged man can walk OK. You're long-sighted."

"That's a good thing, isn't it?"

Stella didn't comment on this.

"It's quite common with the onset of middle age," she told him. "I see from your file that you're forty."

"Not for another nine days," Smith said.

"You've done well to go this long without help. You mentioned migraines?"

"I've suffered with them for years," Smith said. "Some are worse than others."

"It's possible that the strain you've been putting on your eyes is a trigger for the migraines. We'll see if the glasses can help."

"Glasses?" Smith repeated.

"Glasses," Stella said.

"Can I get a second opinion?"

Stella smiled and rolled her eyes. She stood up and walked towards the door.

"Mandy," she shouted. "Could you come in here for a moment please?"

Shortly afterwards, a woman who didn't look much older than Smith's seventeen-year-old daughter came into the room.

"Mandy," Stella said. "Mr Smith would like a second opinion. The tests show that he suffers from hypermetropia – his left eye is considerably weaker than the right, and he also has astigmatism."

"You're half-blind, sir," Mandy said.

With that, she left the room.

"That's quite a double act you've got going on there," Smith said. "Glasses, you say?"

"I'll make you up a prescription," Stella said. "It shouldn't take more than a few days."

"I feel old."

"It happens to the best of us," Stella said. "You've already left it too long. You shouldn't mess around with your eyesight. You don't realise how precious it is until it's gone."

CHAPTER TWO

"Do you see?"
Gemma London didn't. In fact, the familiar sensation of opening her eyes had been replaced with something she couldn't comprehend. The nerve endings in the eye sockets were telling her brain that her eyes were open, but Gemma thought there surely had to be a communication error somewhere down the line. No matter how hard she concentrated, all she was aware of was a thick wall of blackness.

"The anaesthetic will wear off soon."
Anaesthetic, Gemma thought. *Where the hell am I?*
She recalled nothing that could explain her current situation. She wanted to find out some answers but there was something wrong with her vocal cords too. She could detect a strong odour – her sense of smell appeared to be functioning as it should, but as she breathed in the pungent reek, Gemma wished that it wasn't. It was a metallic stink, mixed with something chemical.

"You'll soon see."
Gemma tried to move her arms, but something was stopping her. Her legs were also immobile.
"The sensations will come back in waves. It will be unpleasant at first, but it's nothing you don't deserve. You don't like me, do you?"
Gemma had no idea what the voice was talking about.
"People like you will never actually *see*. I'm going to fix that."

The first indication that the anaesthetic was wearing off arrived with a prickling sensation on the outside of Gemma's cheeks. The pins and needles spread upwards to her eyes and then there was pain. Gemma was unable to scream – there was something in her mouth stopping the sound from escaping. Flashes of light exploded inside her head and her vision slowly returned. But there was something terribly wrong with it. The sensation was disorientating, and Gemma thought that she might be sick. She sensed that she was sitting upright with her chin raised, but the pieces of information that her eyes were sending to her brain didn't corroborate this. She was facing forwards, but her eyes were looking at her legs. Gemma noticed that one of her stockings was torn at the knee.

"What we have here is a perfect globe luxation."
Gemma could now hear her heartbeat in her ears. It was beating dangerously fast.
"The optic nerves and the surrounding muscles have not been damaged. Soon, you'll see clearly for the first time. It hurts, doesn't it?"
Gemma managed to nod. She still had no idea why this was happening to her.

Something appeared in her periphery, and she moved her head instinctively. The effects of the anaesthetic were gone now, and Gemma was aware of the pressure on her left eyeball. She felt every touch as it was squeezed back into the eye socket. The process was repeated with the other eye.
"You'll soon see who you really are."

Gemma London couldn't see anything. Both eyeballs had been replaced in their sockets, but they'd been inserted with the corneas and pupils facing inwards.

CHAPTER THREE

"What's the prognosis?"

Whitton didn't offer Smith any pleasantries when he got back to work after his appointment.

"What did the optician have to say?" she added.

"I'm old," Smith said. "And I need glasses."

"I told you so. Where are they?"

"Apparently, she has to make up a prescription," Smith said. "It's going to take a few days. I can't believe I'm going to have to wear glasses. There's nothing wrong with my eyes."

"You're half blind."

"That's what the optician's assistant told me," Smith said. "Can we talk about something else?"

"You realise what time of year it is, don't you?" Whitton said.

"Apart from my impending fortieth birthday?" Smith said. "I reckon a midlife crisis is on the cards."

"Stop being such a baby," Whitton said. "No, it's the Super's favourite week of the year."

"Crime stats," Smith guessed.

At the end of January every year, Superintendent Smyth bored the pants off everyone in the employ of York Police with his crime statistics presentation. Years ago, he'd devised a points system, and he took great pleasure in torturing the men and woman of York Police with it. For hours he would rattle on about the crimes that they'd dealt with over the past year. Everyone, without exception dreaded the presentation, and everybody was expected to attend.

"I'm thinking of giving it a miss this year," Smith said.

"How are you planning on doing that?" Whitton said.

"I'll figure something out. I may be sick that day."

"You won't get away with it. At least the Super has something to be pleased about – the crime stats for the past year are pretty good. You might even get another award."

"It'll end up the same place as the last one," Smith said. "At the bottom of the bin in the canteen with the rotten tomatoes. When is it happening?"

"Didn't you get the email?"

"Nope."

"It's next week, Monday. And you're going to be there."

Smith's phone started to ring. The screen told him that it was a number not stored in his list of contacts, but he answered it anyway.

"Smith."

"Jason Smith?" a woman asked.

"That's me. Who is this?"

"My name is Mandy. We met earlier at Mrs Read's practice."

"The optician?" Smith said.

"That's right. I was asked to contact you to let you know that your glasses will take longer than initially promised."

"No worries," Smith said. "I've managed this long without them. I'm sure I'll cope for a few more days. What's the delay?"

"The manufacturers we use are experiencing a backlog of orders. I apologise for the wait."

"It's fine," Smith said.

"As a token of our gratitude for your patience, could I offer you some prescription sunglasses at half the usual price?"

"Sunglasses?" Smith said.

"They'll be the same prescription as your glasses."

"I'm good, thanks," Smith said. "The last time I checked I was living in Yorkshire, and there isn't much call for sunglasses. Thanks for the call."

Bridge came into the canteen with the DCs King and Moore. Bridge had been suffering from a cold and even though he'd recently recovered, he still didn't look well. His nostrils were raw from the continuous blowing, and he had dark bags underneath his eyes.

He got some coffee from the machine and joined Smith and Whitton at their table.

"God, I'm sick of this winter."

"It's January." Smith stated the obvious. "What's your point?"

"Well, it's been colder than usual this year – I'm sure of it."

"Stop moaning."

"You're in a worse mood than usual today," Bridge said.

"My darling husband needs glasses," Whitton said.

"I don't *need* glasses," Smith corrected. "I've been advised to wear glasses – there's a big difference."

"What glasses are you getting, Sarge?" It was DC King.

"Whatever the optician gives me, I suppose," Smith said.

"You usually get to choose the frames," DC Moore joined in.

"She didn't ask," Smith said. "What difference does it make?"

"It depends," DC King said. "If you're not bothered whether you look like John Lennon or Harry Potter, then it doesn't really matter, does it."

"I don't think either of them would suit him," Whitton said.

"I'll let the optician decide," Smith said. "I really couldn't care less."

PC Baldwin came into the canteen and made a beeline straight for their table.

"I was wondering where everyone was," she said.

"We're just discussing Smith's optical woes," Bridge said. "He's going to be wearing glasses soon."

"It's no big deal," Smith said.

"It doesn't sound like it," Whitton said.

"Is something up?" Smith asked Baldwin.

"I don't know," she said. "A distraught woman just came in to report a missing person."

"And?" Smith said.

"Her housemate didn't come home last night, and apparently it's out of character for her."

"Get her to go through the motions," DC Moore said. "If she hasn't been seen since last night, she's not officially missing, is she?"

"The housemate thinks something has happened to her," Baldwin said. "She's convinced of it."

"I'll have a chat with her," Smith offered. "It's not like I've got much else to do right now."

CHAPTER FOUR

Smith decided to speak to the housemate in his office. The woman's name was Hillary Twain, and she shared a house with Gemma London in Heslington. Hillary looked to be in her mid to late twenties and she was wearing a pair of glasses with lenses so thick they made her eyes look enormous. She reminded Smith of a bushbaby. Her hair was mousy brown, and it looked like it hadn't been washed for a while. Smith offered her something to drink.
"I've got coffee or coffee."
"I don't want coffee," she said. "I want you to do something about finding Gemma."
"OK," Smith said. "Let me get some details. You share a house with Miss London, is that correct?"
"I told all this to the woman on the desk."
"And now you can tell me."
"We share a house in Heslington," Hillary said.
"How long have you lived together?"
"Almost two years."
"Are you and Gemma students?"
Hillary shook her head. "We both work. We rent a student house because it's cheaper, and the vibe is good in that part of town."
"Where's that accent from?" Smith said.
"Scotland. What difference does that make?"
   "When did you last see Gemma?" Smith asked.
"Yesterday evening," Hillary said. "At around half-seven. She left to go to a new pub on the Hull Road. I was supposed to go with her, but I wasn't feeling well."
"Are you feeling better now?"

"What has that got to do with anything?"

"I like to get all the details," Smith said. "What's the name of the pub?"

"*The French Connection*. It's a dumb name, I know but it was somewhere new."

"Do you know if Gemma had planned to meet anybody there?"

"I don't think so."

"Was she in the habit of going out on her own?" Smith said.

"It's not against the law, is it?"

"No," Smith said. "Look, if I'm going to be able to help you, I have to ask these questions. Is it possible that Gemma could have stayed over with someone? Does she have a boyfriend?"

"No, and no. She would have let me know if she wasn't coming home, and she doesn't have a boyfriend."

"I'm sure there's a perfectly logical explanation for this," Smith said. "Perhaps she hooked up with some friends and spent the night with them. Her phone battery could have died."

"She'd never let the battery die. Something has happened to her."

"Have you tried calling her friends?" Smith said. "What about her family?"

"They're all in Birmingham. She doesn't have any family in York?"

"And her friends?" Smith said. "Did you call any of them?"

"I don't know all of them. But I called her work, and she didn't turn up this morning."

"Where does she work?"

"At the gym in Holgate. She's a personal trainer. And she never misses a day of work."

"We don't usually follow up on missing persons until at least twenty-four-hours has passed," Smith said.

"You have to take this seriously," Hillary said. "This isn't like Gemma."

"If you'd allow me to finish," Smith said. "But I can see that you're extremely concerned, and I want to help to put your mind at ease. I'll see if I can retrace her movements last night and take it from there. I'm going to need her mobile number."

"Of course," Hillary said.

She handed him a business card.

"Jim's Gym," Smith read. "Really?"

"I think it's got a certain ring to it," Hillary said.

"You said the pub was *The French Connection*?"

"That's right. It's on the Hull Road, not far from the sports village. I think it used to be an Irish place."

"I'll find it," Smith said. "Do you have the details of Gemma's family?"

"I told you," Hillary said. "They all live in Birmingham."

"I'm just looking at all possibilities. She may have been in contact with a family member. Do you have a recent photograph of Gemma?"

Hillary took out her phone and swiped the screen. She tapped a few times and showed the photo to Smith.

Gemma London was extremely attractive, and Smith got the impression that she knew all about it. She was posing for the camera in what looked like a much warmer place than York. The sun was shining, and she was dressed only in a swimsuit, covered by a thin sarong.

"That was taken in Tenerife last month," Hillary said.

Gemma was tall and slim with long black hair. She reminded Smith of an actress he couldn't put a name to. Her eyes were a peculiar shade of green, and Smith wondered if she was wearing contacts.

"She's not someone you'd easily forget," he said.

"What's that supposed to mean?" Hillary said.

"It means it's likely that people will remember her, and that should help us. What was Gemma wearing when she went out last night?"

"I'm not sure."

"Can you try to remember?"

"I think it was a black skirt, black stockings and a red shirt. It probably was. Oh, and she has blond hair now. Do you think something has really happened to her?"

"It's too early to say," Smith said. "But in the majority of cases like these, the people reported missing turn up, safe and sound, and I'm sure this case will be no different. I don't think you have anything to worry about."

"You don't sound convinced."

"Like I said, it's too early to say. Could you forward that photograph to this number?"

He handed her one of his cards.

"And we'll take it from there."

"Will you let me know if you find her?" Hillary said.

"Of course," Smith said. "We've got your details."

Hillary tapped her phone and soon afterwards, Smith's phone beeped. He opened the attachment and looked at the photograph of Gemma London. He was instantly drawn to her green eyes. They really were beautiful eyes. Smith didn't know then that he was going to look into those eyes again very soon, but the sight of them was going to repulse him when he did.

CHAPTER FIVE

"What's French about it?" DC King wondered.

She and Smith were waiting for someone to open the door at the pub on Hull Road. *The French Connection* was where Gemma London was supposed to have gone last night, and Smith hoped that someone there would remember her.

All of the windows on the side of the pub facing the street had been painted with scenes from what appeared to be a gangster movie. Men in black, holding machine guns were staring out. Smith wondered if the landlord was a fan of old films.

"I think it's named after a movie from the seventies," he said. "The name rings a bell."

"I've never heard of it," DC King said. "Are you sure there's someone here? The place looks locked up to me."

The door opened and a short man in his fifties looked up at Smith. He had to raise the rim of his felt porkpie hat to do so.

"James Norton?" Smith said.

"Call me Jimmy," the man said. "Get yourselves inside. It's cold and we don't know who might be watching."

He was speaking with a terrible American accent.

Smith and DC King shared a curious glance and went inside the pub.

Inside, there were more indications that the theme of the pub was based on the movie. Promotional posters for *The French Connection* were plastered all over the walls. Smith thought it was incredibly dark in there. The man who'd introduced himself as Jimmy suggested they talk at the bar. The bar area was adorned with more memorabilia from the old film. Smith read the list of cocktails on the board next to the bar. He wondered what was in the *Hitman* and the *Pontiac*, but he didn't ask.

"What's with the hat?" he asked instead.

"I like to stay in role," Jimmy said.

"Is it something from the film?" DC King said.

"Is she being serious?" Jimmy asked Smith.

"Perhaps you should ask her that." Smith said.

"Surely you've heard of Popeye Doyle?"

"Nope."

"I strongly suggest you check out the movie. It's probably the finest example of Film Noir of the twentieth century."

Smith wasn't interested in old movies.

"Are you the landlord here?" he said.

"I own the place," Jimmy said. "It's always been a dream of mine to have a joint like this. It used to be an Irish pub, but those bars are so old hat nowadays. What's this about? You didn't really explain on the phone."

"Were you working here last night?" Smith said.

"Of course. It was opening night."

"On a Wednesday?" DC King said.

"Best night to have an opening. The students are back from the Christmas break, and the turnout last night proved me right."

"Was it busy?" Smith said.

"We made a killing," Jimmy said. "Which is appropriate, given the concept."

Smith took out his phone and found the photograph of Gemma London. He showed it to the Popeye Doyle wannabe.

"Do you remember seeing this woman in here last night?"

"She was here, yes," Jimmy confirmed. "She's not someone you're likely to forget, is she? What's she done?"

"We're trying to find her," Smith said.

"Do you remember who she was with?" DC King said.

"How am I supposed to remember that?" Jimmy said.

"Do you have CCTV here?" Smith said,

"I've got cameras, but they're not operational yet."

"What's the point of them then?"

"I don't know how much you know about running a bar," Jimmy said.

"Nothing at all," Smith said.

"We only opened our doors last night, and there are still a few things we need to sort out. The CCTV wasn't a priority. Are you going to tell me what this woman's done?"

"We're going to need a list of the people who were working here last night," DC King said.

"Not until you tell me what's going on," Jimmy said.

"The woman has gone missing," Smith said. "We're trying to find her, and this place was one of the last places she was seen, so you can now understand why we need to ask you these questions."

"Why didn't you just tell me that at the beginning?"

"Who was working here last night?" DC King said.

"I'll get their details. What do you think has happened to her?"

"We're going to find out," Smith said. "In cases like these, the missing person usually turns up within twenty-four hours, but we need to follow it up anyway."

The main door opened and a woman who looked to be in her early twenties came in. She was a tall woman, and she was wearing an excessive amount of makeup in Smith's opinion. He wondered how long it took her to get ready in the morning. She rubbed her hands together and made her way over to the bar.

"Holly," Jimmy said to her. "These detectives want to talk to you. Holly is the bar manager here."

"Were you working last night?" Smith asked.

Holly nodded. "What's going on?"

Smith showed her the photograph of Gemma London.

"Do you remember her?"

"How could I forget her?" Holly said. "Drop dead gorgeous and fully aware of it."

"What time did she get here?" DC King said.

"Probably around eight. The place had filled up by then, but I remember her. She's the kind of woman who makes sure she's noticed."

"Was she alone?" Smith said.

"I think she came in on her own, but that didn't last long."

"Do you know the people she met up with?" DC King said.

"Students, I think. They looked like students anyway."

Smith wasn't sure if they were going to get anything useful from *The French Connection*. A busy pub and an opening night meant that they could rule out regulars, and it was going to be impossible to track down anyone who might know where Gemma went after she left. He was running out of questions to ask.

"This is a long shot," he said. "But do you remember if the woman hooked up with anyone?"

"A bloke?" Holly said.

"It's not unheard of."

"I don't think so," Holly said. "It's possible, although most of the people in here were way out of her league, weren't they?"

"What do you mean?" Smith said.

"Student types. What's the old saying – fighting above your weight class, that's it. What do you think has happened to her?"

"She probably spent the night with a friend," Smith said. "Had a bit too much to drink and bunked off work because of it."

"What is it with the world today?" Holly said.

"In what respect?" Smith said.

"I don't know how these things usually work," Holly said. "But I've never heard of the police putting so much effort into a missing person after only a few hours. Would you be here asking your questions if the woman who'd gone missing was a proper minger?"

"Minger?" Smith repeated.

"Let me make myself a bit clearer," Holly said. "Things are done differently where beautiful people are concerned, aren't they? The normal rules don't apply."

"We're just doing our job," DC King said.

"Get real," Holly said. "I'm not stupid. And I know for a fact that if this woman doesn't show up, her face is going to be staring at us from all over the media in no time. That's just the way of the world these days."

The young bar manager had hit the nail on the head. Before long, Gemma London's pretty face would be famous. There wouldn't be many people in the city who would forget it when they saw it. Smith was never going to be able to put it out of his mind either when he understood what had been done to her.

CHAPTER SIX

Their next port of call was the gym where Gemma worked. DC King voiced her concerns to Smith on their way there.

"You think something has happened to her, don't you?"

"I don't know, Kerry," Smith said. "I've got this terrible feeling, and when that happens, I get antsy. Something doesn't feel right."

"How many people are reported missing each year?"

"Thousands," Smith said. "And ninety-odd percent of them turn up pretty soon after they've been reported missing, but something feels *off* about this one. I don't know what it is."

"I don't get that feeling, Sarge," DC King said. "It seems to me that Gemma London is slightly in love with herself."

"What's your point?"

"I've met people like her," DC King said. "Men *and* women. They think the world revolves around them and they don't spare a thought for anyone else. I reckon she hooked up with a bloke at the pub, she went back to his place and didn't bother getting up for work."

"According to the housemate, she never misses a day of work."

"There's always a first time for everything."

"What's a minger?" Smith asked out of the blue.

DC King laughed. "Are you serious?"

"That bar manager didn't really explain."

"It's a derogatory term for an ugly woman," DC King said. "And Holly had a point."

"Bullshit. I take all missing persons seriously. It makes no difference whether they're catwalk material or if they have a face like a bush pig, I'll investigate them the same way."

"That's just you, Sarge," DC King said. "It doesn't apply in the real world. Beautiful people really do get all the breaks – it's a fact of life. And, subconsciously, we care more about what happens to attractive people." Smith had never really thought about this, and he didn't feel like dwelling on it now.

The gym was an ultra-modern affair and Smith thought it was drastically at odds with the name of it. *Jim's Gym* suggested a place that someone had set up in their garage – a makeshift fitness centre filled with second-hand equipment, but the place where Gemma London worked looked like it must have cost a fortune to fit out. Smith had never been much of a fitness freak, so he had no idea what most of the equipment was.

The woman behind the reception desk stood up as soon as she spotted them. She offered them a smile and asked if they were interested in membership.

"Not today," Smith said. "I'm DS Smith and this is DC King. We're here about one of the employees here. Gemma London."

The receptionist rolled her eyes at the mention of Gemma's name. Smith saw from her name badge that she was called Jazz.

"Did I say something wrong?" Smith said.

"Gemma isn't here," Jazz said.

"We're aware of that. Do you know Gemma well?"

"I suppose so."

"How long has she worked here?" DC King said.

"Nine months," Jazz said. "When she's here, that is."

"Does she work part time?" Smith said.

"She may as well do. What's she done?"

"She's been reported missing," DC King said.

"Is there someone else we can talk to?" Smith said. "Is the owner of the gym here?"

"He's rarely here," Jazz said. "Hold on – I'll see if Paul is available."

She left the reception area and Smith watched her walk towards a room at the back of the gym.

"Gemma's housemate told me that she never missed a day of work," he said.

"That's not what the receptionist implied," DC King said. "Do you think we could be wasting our time? It seems that the lovely Gemma is no stranger to skipping work. I still think she got together with a bloke last night, and she didn't bother to let her housemate know about it."

"I don't know why," Smith said. "But I get the impression that something else is going on. I could be wrong – I'm getting on a bit now and I could be losing my touch, but something just feels wrong."

Jazz returned with a man who looked to be in his thirties. He was dressed in a tight tracksuit and the tan on his face didn't look like it was the result of the Yorkshire sun.

"I'm Paul," he said. "We can talk in my office."

He led them to a tiny room next to the reception area and asked them to take a seat.

"You're here about Gemma," he said.

"Her housemate has reported her missing," Smith explained.

"It must be serious if two police detectives are here," Paul said.

"We're just trying to get an idea of who she is," DC King said.

"She's worked here for nine months," Smith said. "Is that right?"

"More or less," Paul said.

"What is it you do here?"

"I manage the place."

"And what does Gemma do?" DC King said.

"She's a personal trainer," Paul said.

"What does that entail?" Smith said. "I'm not much of a gym bloke."

"I can see that. Perhaps you ought to consider hiring a personal trainer. A lot of people think they can get fit on their own, but there's a lot more to it than that. If you want to do it properly you need to follow a strict regime, and most people find that having a trainer to push them helps."

Smith wasn't the slightest bit interested in joining a gym.

"When I spoke to Gemma's housemate," he said. "I was told that Gemma never missed a day of work,"

"The housemate is misinformed," Paul said.

"She made a habit of it?" DC King said.

"If it was up to me, she wouldn't still be working here. Our clients pay a lot of money for membership here, and they expect professionalism. I've lost count of how many times I've had to step in when Gemma hasn't turned up for work."

"That must be annoying," Smith said. "Why haven't you taken any action against her? Surely, as the manager it's your job to keep your employees in check."

"Try telling that to the owner," Paul said. "He thinks the sun shines out of Gemma's backside. It's no secret that he's smitten with her."

"Do you associate with Gemma outside of work?" Smith said.

"Never," Paul said. "We're not really into the same things, and I don't really measure up to her high standards."

"What's your opinion of her?" Smith said. "You can be brutally honest now."

"My opinion of her? I think she's a conceited bitch. Is that honest enough for you? She thinks she's God's gift to humankind. She was born with advantages, and she exploits those advantages to the extreme."

"Where do you think she might have gone?" DC King said. "I know you two don't socialise, but do you have any idea where she could be?"

"All I know is she's not where she's supposed to be," Paul said. "She's probably flaunting her beauty to extract God knows what out of some rich guy."

"Where is the owner of the gym now?" DC King said. "Jazz said he's rarely here."

"Hardly ever. He has a number of other businesses in the city. If I see him four times a year, it's a lot."

"Where can we find him?" Smith asked.

"He'll probably be at his new place on Hull Road," Paul said.

Smith and DC King exchanged a glance.

"What place is this?" Smith said, although he had a very good idea.

"A new pub," Paul said. "*The French Connection.*"

CHAPTER SEVEN

"What we have right now is a whole load of confusion."
Smith had insisted that they hold a briefing as soon as they'd returned to the station. The team was now gathered in the small conference room to hear what he had to say.

"When we spoke to the owner of *The French Connection*," he said. "He told us he'd seen Gemma there last night, but he neglected to mention that she worked for him at his gym."

"We didn't twig," DC King said. "His name is James Norton – he introduced himself as Jimmy, and to look at him, you wouldn't think he would own a gym in a million years."

"*Jim's Gym*," Bridge said. "What a terrible name for a gym."

"What does it all mean though?" DI Smyth asked.

"Something strange is going on, boss," Smith said. "Why would James Norton not tell us that Gemma works for him?"

"Is it possible that he isn't aware that she works at the gym?" Whitton put forward. "If he owns a load of businesses in the city, he might not know all the people who work for him."

"No," Smith said. "The receptionist at the gym reckoned that Mr Norton thought the sun shone out of Gemma's arse. That's why she's got away with bunking off work so much."

"What does he have to say about it?" DC Moore said. "Have you questioned him again?"

"He wasn't at the pub when we went back there," DC King said.

"We'll speak to him again soon," Smith said. "I want to know why he kept this information from us."

"Where is this actually leading?" DI Smyth said. "We've got a woman who was reported missing by her housemate. She was last seen at a pub on

Hull Road, and we now know she works for the owner of the pub, but what are we planning on doing with this information?"

"There's more, boss," Smith said.

"I thought you might say that."

"The housemate gave her name as Hillary Twain. She claimed to have lived with Gemma for two years in a house in Heslington. When I called her on the number she gave me, I was informed that the number didn't exist. She sent me a photo of Gemma from that number, but it's no longer in service. And this is the interesting part. There is nobody by that name at the address she gave us."

"I'm not following you, Sarge," DC Moore said. "Are you saying that Gemma doesn't live with Hillary Twain?"

"I'm saying that neither Gemma nor Hillary are residents at the address Miss Twain left when she filed the report this morning."

"Who the hell is she then?" Bridge said. "Hillary, I mean – if that's even her real name."

"And why did she make up such an elaborate story?" DC King said.

"We're not in the habit of corroborating the stories of people who file missing persons reports," Smith said. "Why would we doubt them?"

"But what would someone stand to gain from lying like that?" Whitton said. "It makes no sense whatsoever."

"Are we still treating Gemma as missing?" DC Moore said.

"I don't know what we're treating her as, Harry," Smith said. "But something weird is going on, and I want to know what that is."

"Let's go through the timeline," DI Smyth said. "I'm inclined to agree that something strange is happening here, but the info we have is somewhat garbled. None of it is very clear."

"According to the mystery housemate," Smith said. "Gemma left for the pub at seven-thirty last night. This may or may not be true, but we do know that she was seen at *The French Connection* shortly afterwards. Unfortunately, the pub doesn't have operational CCTV yet, so we won't be able to see if we can find her that way. The clientele of the pub will be difficult to track down too. It was opening night, and therefore we don't have any regulars to look into."

"Gemma hasn't been seen since," DC King said. "She's not answering her phone, and she hasn't been seen on social media since last night."

"Do we even know if we've got the right number for her?" DC Moore said.

"It's the number on her business card from the gym," Smith said. "So, it's safe to assume it's Gemma's."

"She seems to have disappeared into thin air," DC King said.

"Leaving behind a web of confusion in her wake," Smith added.

"Let's not get too dramatic now," DI Smyth said. "What can you remember about this fake housemate?"

"Not much," Smith admitted. "She was pretty average looking. A bit of a plain Jane. And she had a Scottish accent. Hold on."

"Here we go," Bridge said. "The Smith brain is about to astound us all again."

"The camera over the front entrance is working again," Smith said. "I know it is – I give it the middle finger every time I go out for a sly cigarette. It will have caught the phony housemate going in and out. We need to take a look at the footage."

"You really must stop giving the CCTV the finger," Whitton said.

"I can't resist it. Who monitors the cameras?"

"I don't think the footage is monitored round the clock," DI Smyth said. "We know what time she was here, so it shouldn't be difficult to find her, but what then? What is she even suspected of?"

"Wasting police time?" DC Moore suggested.

"I don't give a hoot about that, Harry," Smith said. "She's involved in this – I know she is."

"What exactly is *this*?" Whitton said.

"I have no fucking idea," Smith said. "But it's something."

DI Smyth's phone started to ring. The sound of it made Smith smile. He'd changed his ringtone, and it was a somewhat inappropriate one for a detective inspector. The Police classic, *Don't stand so close to me* was cut short by a blushing DI Smyth.

The conversation didn't last long, and DI Smyth's parting words told everyone inside the small conference room that there was work to do. *On our way.*

"It looks like you were right, Smith," DI Smyth said. "Something has happened. The body of a woman has been found on the patch of open ground between the A64 and the sports village. The description matches that of Gemma London."

CHAPTER EIGHT

The first thing that occurred to Smith when he got out of his car on the east side of the car park at the sports village was this was a risky place to dump a body. It was midweek in the middle of winter, so the area wouldn't be as busy as it got in the summer, but there were always people around here. Clients used the sports village all year round, and the cycle circuit to the south was a popular spot too. The cars on the A64 to the east could be seen from the car park, and Smith wondered why Gemma had been left here. He could think of better places to dump a dead body in the city.

The sight of Grant Webber's Suzuki told him that the Head of Forensics was here already, and Smith expected nothing less. He could see the white-cladded technicians getting to work about fifty metres away. A tent had already been erected, and Smith knew that the body of Gemma London was concealed within. There was no ambulance, and Smith wondered why. Only one police car was parked there too. Surely a dead body warranted a bigger presence at the crime scene than this. A cordon had been set up at the edge of the car park but there was nobody manning it. Smith spotted the PCs Griffin and Bowler on the far side of the car park. He walked over to them. Someone needed to make sure that nobody went anywhere near the body.

As he got closer, he saw that they were talking to a man and a woman. "Can I have a word?" Smith said to PC Griffin.
"This is John and Gaynor Flood, Sarge," the piggy-eyed PC said. "They're the ones who called it in."
"I need you by the outer cordon," Smith said. "There are people here, and that police tape is like a red rag to a bull to a rubbernecker."
"But Sarge…"
"Do it now please," Smith said.

PC Griffin opened his mouth, but no words came out. He turned around and headed for the edge of the car park.

"Do you need me there too, Sarge?" PC Bowler said.

"Walk with me," Smith said.

He put a few metres between them and the couple who'd found the body.

"You stay here and make sure nobody else enters the car park. It's Angie, isn't it?"

PC Bowler looked like her favourite film star knew her name. The smile on her face widened and Smith was worried she was going to hug him.

"Could you get onto it please," he said, before she actually did embrace him.

"Am I to stop everyone from driving in, Sarge?" she said.

"Everyone," Smith said. "It's likely the body was transported here by car, and there might be something for the forensics team to look at in the car park itself."

"You don't think she was killed here, Sarge?" PC Bowler said.

"I don't think anything right now," Smith said. "I'm going to have a chat to the couple who found her."

"I'll make sure nobody comes anywhere near the car park, Sarge."

"Great," Smith said. "And could you do me a favour?"

"Anything, Sarge."

"You don't have to end every sentence with a *Sarge*," Smith said. "It's not necessary."

He walked back towards the man and woman.

"You must be someone important," John Flood said.

Smith guessed his age to be around the same as his.

"Of course he is," Gaynor said. "He's the one that's been on the tele. Smith, isn't it?"

"That's right," Smith said. "Are you alright? Do you require medical attention?"

"The fella with the face like a slapped arse already asked us that," Gaynor said. "I would have thought there'd be rules about employing coppers who looked like that."

"They're not allowed to discriminate these days, love," John said. "They've got fat, spotty, short-arsed, repulsive police officers all over. Equal opportunity, I think it's called. Some of them don't even know how to read."

Smith wondered which century this couple had crawled out of.

"Someone will be along shortly to take a statement," he said. "But I'd like to ask you a few questions now."

"It's not the first time our John has found a stiff," Gaynor said.

"Is that so?" Smith said.

"That was different," John said. "It was a bloke in the flat below us and he was ninety if he was a day. It's not the same."

"Dead is dead," Gaynor said.

"What were you doing here?" Smith asked.

John pointed to the A64. "Car ran out of petrol just over there. We came to see if we could borrow some from someone here."

"We don't have a jerry can," Gaynor said. "We were hoping to borrow one of those too."

Smith didn't think people still ran out of petrol.

"What time was this?" he asked.

"Two minutes before we found her," John said.

"I phoned you lot straight after," Gaynor added.

"Did you see anyone hanging around?" Smith said.

"There were some people in the car park," John said. "That's why I came up with the idea of trying our luck here. There's a petrol station about half a mile up the road, just past the Grimston Bar roundabout, but this was closer. Is there a problem with that?"

"No problem," Smith said. "Like I said, someone will be along to take a statement. Are you sure you don't need medical assistance?"

"It was no big deal," Gaynor said. "The crows had already had a good go at her eyes, but apart from that, it was no big deal."

CHAPTER NINE

"Are you here alone?" Billie Jones asked.

Webber's assistant had intercepted Smith before he'd even made it halfway towards the tent that had been erected.

"Whitton and Kerry are speaking to the people at the sports village," Smith said. "And Harry and the love of your life are seeing if the cyclists down on the circuit saw anything."

"Love of my life is going a bit far," Billie said. "I'm still open to offers. I seem to recall that you and I shared a moment not so long ago."

"Stop fucking around, Billie," Smith said. "You can't do things like this."

"Relax. I'm messing with your head."

"I'd appreciate it if you didn't. Is it Gemma London?"

"The driving license in her purse says it is."

"The couple who found her mentioned something about her eyes," Smith said.

"You have to see it to believe it."

"That's what I was planning on doing. Do you have a spare suit?"

Billie looked him up and down. "Not bad. Have you lost some weight?"

"Billie," Smith warned.

"Alright," she said. "You used to have a sense of humour, once upon a time. I'll grab you that suit."

Once he was suitably attired, he walked over to the inner cordon. Webber spotted him before he got there. The Head of Forensics shook his head, and Smith didn't know what it meant. Webber eased himself under the tape and carefully stepped to the side. He continued walking in a wide arc and Smith knew he was expected to do the same. They met up about ten metres from the tent.

"How long has she been here?" Smith asked.

"Good afternoon to you too," Webber said. "I don't think she's been here long. Although it's difficult to tell with this weather. She's definitely not been dead long."

"She was last seen at a pub not far from here. Any indications of how she died?"

"Nothing obvious," Webber said. "Nothing external anyway. But whoever killed her didn't like her eyes."

"The couple who found her mentioned something about them. They reckoned the crows had a go at her."

"Do you see any crows around here?"

"You probably scared them away," Smith said.

"The injuries to her eyes were definitely not caused by birds."

"Can I take a look?"

"Follow me," Webber said. "Walk in my footsteps. We've tracked the possible path that whoever brought her here took, and we haven't finished examining it."

Smith walked closely behind. Webber walked slowly and carefully, and Smith had to concentrate so he didn't collide with him. They stopped next to the tent and Webber did the honours with the flap at the side.

Smith prepared himself for a whiff of something unpleasant, but nothing came. The only smell inside the tent was a subtle hint of deodorant mixed with BO and Smith assumed that Pete Richards was the cause of that. Webber's technician was sweating even though it was only a few degrees above freezing.

"This is exactly how she was left," Webber said.

Smith observed the woman on the ground and two things occurred to him immediately. The black skirt, black stockings and red shirt were exactly what the woman claiming to be Gemma's housemate had said she was wearing. And even though she'd lied about the housemate thing, it was clear that she'd come into contact with Gemma last night. The second thing he registered was Gemma's hair. The housemate had made a point of informing him that she now had blond hair, but Smith could see that she'd lied about that too.

Even in death, Gemma London was strikingly attractive. Her black hair was fanned out on either side of her face and Smith wondered if she'd been displayed like this. Her fine nose and high cheekbones lent her an elfin aspect, but the eyes didn't complement it. They were too big and when Smith's own deficient eyes focused harder he realised why that was. They were nothing like the eyes he recalled from the photograph of Gemma. These white orbs were all wrong. If Smith had to compare them to anything he would say they resembled the cue balls used in snooker. But these cue balls had strings attached. Smith asked Webber about it.

"Those aren't strings," the Head of Forensics told him. "Dr Bean will be able to confirm it, but I think what we can see are the retinal vessels and the optic nerve."

"I don't get it," Smith said.

"It looks like her eyeballs were removed and pushed back in."

"Why? Why would someone choose to do that? I know that's not your department. I'm just thinking out loud. Surely that wouldn't be enough to kill her."

"I doubt it," Webber said. "It will probably have been extremely painful, but I doubt it would have been fatal. Have you seen enough?"

"No," Smith said. "Why do that to her?"

"I'm sure you'll figure it out. We still have a lot of work to do."

Smith took the hint. He turned to leave and turned around again. His eyes focused on the hideous picture that was Gemma London's eyes. "That is fucked up. I don't know much about the anatomy of the eyes, but surely that's not easy to do."

"We really have a lot of work to get through," Webber said. "And I would prefer to do it while we still have daylight. It'll be dark in a couple of hours."

"I appreciate that," Smith said. "But I need to look at her for a moment longer."

"Do I need to be concerned?"

"No more than usual," Smith said. "What kind of a sick fuck would do this to a beautiful young woman? They've left the rest of her face alone. What is it they didn't like about her eyes?"

Webber placed a hand on his shoulder.

"That's enough now. This is not doing you any favours."

"I'm going to find out who did this to her," Smith said.

"Take a few deep breaths," Webber said.

Smith looked at him. "What?"

"You've stopped breathing."

Webber was right. Smith had held his breath without realising it. He inhaled a lungful of air and breathed out. His eyes found the part of Gemma London's face where her eyes had been violated, then he turned around and left the tent.

CHAPTER TEN

Smith walked back to the car park at the sports village and took out his cigarettes. He lit one and inhaled deeply. He could still see Gemma London's face in his mind, and he knew he would see it for quite some time. Whitton and DC King walked over to him.
"You look like shit," Whitton said.
"Thanks," Smith said. "We've got a seriously deranged individual on our hands."
"You got your wish then," DC King said.
"I wish I hadn't wished for it, Kerry," Smith said. "If that makes any sense. She had her eyes removed and replaced the wrong way round."
"That is sick," Whitton said.
"Why would someone do that to her? I don't understand it."
"Don't try to understand it."
"No," Smith said. "I need to understand it. I have to know why he did that to her if I'm to stand a chance of catching him."
"It's a bloke then?" DC King said.
"Almost definitely. A woman isn't capable of brutality like that. We're looking for a man."
"We might have a witness," Whitton said. "A woman thinks she saw a couple walking in the direction of where she was found about two hours ago."
"Thinks?" Smith said.
"She'd just arrived at the sports village," Whitton said. "And she spotted them when she was getting out of her car."
"You said she saw a couple?" Smith said. "As in two living people?"
"That's what the witness said."

"There's nothing to indicate that she was killed where she was found," Smith said. "In fact, she has no obvious injuries apart from the damage to her eyes. If the witness did see the killer and the victim, he was taking a risk in killing her and dumping her during the day. Did the woman give you a description?"

"Not a very good one," Whitton said. "She only saw them for a split second, and she didn't pay them much attention. Two people – that's all she could tell us."

Smith's cigarette had gone out, so he relit it.

"Do you think she knew him?" he asked. "Do you think she knew the man who did that to her?"

"It's possible," DC King said. "Perhaps she was taken by surprise."

"No," Smith said. "This is all wrong. I don't know much about eyes, but I reckon that kind of mutilation would take time. The optic nerves were still intact, and the vessels of the retina were still attached to the eyeballs. That won't have been easy to pull off, and it's certainly not something you could do in the middle of a patch of ground during the day. I think she was dumped here during the night."

"What about what the witness saw?" Whitton said.

"It wasn't Gemma London and her killer. She was left on display. On her back with her hair fanned out around her. Whoever did this to her wanted her to be seen. That too isn't something you'd do in broad daylight."

"What now?" DC King said.

"Now we try to trace her movements," Smith said. "Where did she go after she left the pub last night? She was last seen in *The French Connection*. Where did she go after that?"

"The DI has got some uniforms looking into the businesses close to the pub," DC King said. "We might get lucky with CCTV footage."

"Does the sports village have cameras?" Smith said.

"Only inside the main complex," Whitton said. "Nothing pointing at the car park."

Smith scanned the area. The hum of the cars on the A64 was never-ending. It was a busy road, and the volume of traffic was high. Beyond that were open fields for miles.

"This is a really weird place to dump a body," Smith said.

"What do you mean?" DC King said.

"If I was going to dispose of a body in the city, I would choose somewhere more isolated. The chances of being seen are high here."

"Perhaps the location was chosen for a reason," Whitton suggested.

"I think it was."

Smith turned his head and observed the sports village. Behind it was the road that fed onto the main Hull Road.

"How far would you say it is to the pub where Gemma was last seen from here?"

"As the crow flies," DC King said. "Probably no more than a few hundred metres."

"She wasn't brought here by a fucking crow, Kerry," Smith said.

He threw his cigarette butt onto the ground and walked back to his car.

"What's got into him?" DC King said.

"Don't ask," Whitton said. "He's been really grumpy since the reality of his fortieth birthday has dawned on him, and the optician's diagnosis didn't help. He'll probably have a midlife crisis and get it out of his system."

"I don't know how you live with him. No offence."

"None taken. I know how his mind works, and I've learned to handle it. Between you and me, I switch off most of the time when he's talking to me."

"You deserve a medal. I have the utmost respect for him, but there is no way I'd be able to live with him."

"He takes things too personally," Whitton said. "He takes it as a personal affront every time someone is killed in this city."

"Where is he going?" DC King pointed to the red Ford Sierra that was exiting the car park at a snail's pace.

"He's probably retracing the route to *The French Connection*," Whitton guessed. "Who knows?"

CHAPTER ELEVEN

Smith decided to retrace the route from the sports village to the pub where Gemma London was last seen. He wanted to get an idea of the distance involved and the properties on the way. He was convinced that Gemma was abducted close to *The French Connection* and killed somewhere nearby. She was killed, her eyes were mutilated, and she was brought to the patch of land next to the sports village afterwards, probably in the dead of night.

There was only one road in and out of the sports village and there wasn't much on the way to Hull Road. The university nursery was the first thing Smith passed and the small car park for Diamond Woods was a further hundred metres along the road. That was it. There were no residential properties here, and Smith didn't think Gemma was killed anywhere close to the road.

He turned left onto Hull Road and followed the road until he got to *The French Connection*. He was surprised to find it open. He debated whether to stop and see if James Norton was there, but another idea came to him as he was considering it. He passed the pub and drove straight for the city centre. There were some questions that needed answering, and Smith needed the advice of an expert.

After an internal debate about whether to get a ticket from the parking meter in the Monk Bar car park, Smith walked the short distance along Monkgate to the opticians. He decided against the ticket. He would take his chances. He was on police business after all, unofficial or not.

The young woman who Smith knew was called Mandy was sitting behind the reception desk.

"Is Stella here?" he asked her.

"She's busy with a client," Mandy said. "Is there anything I can help you with? Is it something regarding your glasses? Stella said that you'd be back

– you left before we gave you the opportunity to choose which frames you'd like."

"I couldn't care less about that," Smith said. "No, this is about something else. How long will she be?"

"Not long. I don't see your name in the appointment book."

"It's not," Smith said. "This is an impromptu visit."

"You can take a seat if you like. You're in luck – Mrs Read doesn't have another appointment until four."

Smith had a look at the frames on offer while he waited. He was amazed by the variety available, and he wondered if he should pick his own frames after all. Some of them were rather radical and he didn't think top brass would appreciate it if he came to work wearing a pair of glasses that made him look like Elton John. It took him five minutes to select some suitable frames. He made Mandy aware of his choice.

Stella Read appeared ten minutes later. Smith told her he needed her advice on something unrelated to his eyes and she invited him into her office.

"Can I trust you?" he asked.

"Of course," Stella said.

"This is strictly confidential," Smith added. "And I need your word that it's not going to go any further."

"As an optician, I'm not bound by doctor, patient confidentiality, but you have my word, nevertheless. I'm curious."

Smith decided not to tell her too much.

"How easy is it to remove a human eyeball?" he said.

Stella's eyes opened wide. "I was not expecting that."

"Perhaps I should have warned you first. I imagine it's quite a tricky operation to remove an eyeball."

"Not really. With a bit of pressure in the right places, it's relatively simple."

"How would you go about it?"

"I presume this isn't strictly hypothetical?"

"It's not," Smith said. "I attended the scene of a murder earlier today and the victim had both of her eyeballs removed and replaced facing inwards."

"Interesting."

"I'm glad you think so," Smith said. "Our Head of Forensics believes the optic nerves and the retinal vessels were still attached. Would that make it trickier?"

"I really don't think I can help you. You'd be better off speaking to a surgeon."

"You're familiar with the anatomy of the eye, aren't you?" Smith said.

"I am. But without more information, I can't really offer you an opinion."

Smith thought for a moment. Then he took out his phone and sent a short message to Grant Webber. The reply came less than a minute later. Smith knew that Webber would have taken lots of photographs of Gemma London's eyes. Smith clicked on the photograph and handed the phone to Stella.

"Oh my," she said.

"I apologise," Smith said. "It's not pretty, is it? I really need you to keep this to yourself."

"I've already promised that I will. Your forensic technician is correct."

"About the optic nerves and the blood vessels?"

Stella nodded. She enlarged the photograph so that Gemma London's left eyeball filled the screen.

"This is a textbook globe luxation," Stella observed.

"A what?" Smith said.

"It's an operation to remove the eyeball," Stella explained. "When the purpose of the operation is to replace the eyeball afterwards."

"Why would someone do that?"

"There could be issues with the socket where the position of the problem necessitates the total removal of the eyeball. In order for the eyesight of the patient to be unaffected, the optic nerve and the blood vessels feeding the eye have to be undamaged."

"How easy is it to do that?" Smith said.

"It's a complicated operation," Stella told him. "The optic nerve and the vessels are delicate, and they're easily damaged. I'd say this was performed by someone with a high degree of experience. This is not something you learn from the Internet."

Smith nodded his head and sighed deeply.

"That's what I thought. I won't take up any more of your time."

CHAPTER TWELVE

James Norton didn't give much away when he spotted Smith next to the bar in *The French Connection*. Smith was on one of his one-man missions again and he decided to stop off at the pub on his way back to the station. He'd missed no fewer than six calls from DI Smyth, and he'd ignored all of them.

The owner of the pub walked over to Smith. He wasn't wearing his Popeye Doyle hat now.
"Can I get you something to drink? You look like a guy who could use one."
"I'm not here to drink," Smith told him. "Why did you lie about Gemma London?"
"I didn't lie about anyone."
"When we spoke to you earlier you said you'd seen her in the pub last night, but you neglected to inform us that she worked for you."
"Strictly speaking," James said. "That's not the same as lying."
"You lied by way of omission. It's the same thing in my book."
"We'll have to agree to disagree on that."

"Gemma didn't show up for work this morning," Smith said. "We've now learned that this is nothing new."
"I don't know what you want me to tell you," James said. "I have very little to do with the operations of the gym."
"You don't take an interest in a business you own?"
"I own several businesses. I can't be active in all of them."
"OK," Smith said. "Let's start again. How well did you know Gemma?"
"*Did*?" James said. "As in past tense? Are you telling me she's dead?"
Smith regretted the slip instantly. He knew the news of Gemma's death would get out soon anyway, so he opted to tell James Norton the truth.

"I'm afraid Gemma is dead," he said. "Her death is suspicious."
"Murder?" James said.

"It's suspicious. And this puts a different perspective on things. Your earlier omission is also suspicious."

"Am I a suspect?"

"Until we have the culprit locked up," Smith said. "Everyone is a suspect, especially the people who knew her. You were here at the pub last night, is that correct?"

"It is."

"You told us that Gemma came in around eight," Smith said. "But you don't recall when she left."

"Also correct. It was packed in here and I was working flat out."

"What time did *you* leave?"

"Probably around midnight."

"Probably?"

"It was after twelve. I like to do the cash up straight away, and I also like to lock up."

"You're involved more in the pub than the gym then?" Smith said.

"I make a point of being hands-on in the early stages of the businesses."

"Can anybody confirm what you've just told me?" Smith said.

"I was here alone from half-eleven until I locked up," James said.

"It's unfortunate that you haven't bothered to set up your CCTV yet."

"Do I need to contact my lawyer?"

"That's up to you," Smith said. "Where did you go after you left the pub?"

"I went straight home," James said. "I was dog-tired."

"Can anyone corroborate this?"

"I live alone. It's not a crime, is it?"

"Nope," Smith said. "I think that's all for now. We'll probably need to speak to you again."

"I didn't kill her," James said.

Smith nodded. He didn't think the owner of *The French Connection* killed Gemma London either, but he didn't share this with James.

"I'll let you get back to work," he said.

He was halfway to the door when something occurred to him. He turned around and walked over to James.

"Do you know someone by the name of Hillary Twain?"

"The name doesn't ring a bell," James said.

"Are you sure?"

"I have a good memory for names," James said.

"Do you know if Gemma lived alone?"

"We didn't have that kind of relationship."

"What's that supposed to mean?" Smith said.

"Gemma worked for me," James said. "That's as far as our relationship went."

"You liked her though, didn't you?"

"Who wouldn't? She was a beautiful woman."

"She was," Smith agreed. "We'll be speaking to you again."

His phone started to ring as soon as he got outside. Elvis Costello was telling him that Oliver's Army was here to stay and it meant that DI Smyth was trying to get hold of him again.

This time Smith answered the call. "Boss."

"Where the hell have you been?" DI Smyth said.

"I wanted to retrace Gemma London's movements last night," Smith said. "And I popped in *The French Connection* to ask the owner a few more questions."

"You are not the only detective on the team, Smith."

"I'm aware of that, boss," Smith said. "Was there something you needed from me? You've called me half a dozen times."

"If you'd bothered to answer your phone the first time I called," DI Smyth said. "You'd be aware that we have another dead woman. A German tourist found her at the golf club in Fulford."

"That's not far from where I am now," Smith said. "What do we know about her?"

"Whitton and Kerry are there now," DI Smyth said. "Looks like the same MO as Gemma London. Both of her eyeballs have been removed and replaced facing inwards."

CHAPTER THIRTEEN

Smith was experiencing mixed emotions as he drove the short distance to the golf club. He'd half-expected this – he didn't think the murder of Gemma London would be a one-off, and he wondered how many more women would fall victim to the latest killer in the city. DI Smyth had informed him that his presence wasn't required at the crime scene – it was all under control, but Smith had a disturbing desire to see what had been done to the unknown woman. He knew that this wasn't exactly healthy, but he needed to look at her. He needed to see her eyes.

The golf club wasn't open for business. It was the middle of winter, and it wouldn't be operational for another few months. Smith wondered what the German tourist was doing there. Something else occurred to him. Gemma London had been left in a part of the city where it was inevitable that her body would be found quickly. Why was the latest victim dumped somewhere where it was unlikely anyone would go?

Smith pushed all of these questions to the side as he parked his car next to Whitton's VW. It was starting to get dark, and Smith knew that Webber and his team would be forced to work by the glare of a spotlight. The Head of Forensics hated it when that happened. Smith lit a cigarette and looked around. The only access road to the golf club was via Heslington Lane. The university campus could be seen to the north and south of the road was open fields. Smith wondered if the location the killer had chosen was significant.

"You really shouldn't be smoking at a crime scene."
It was Billie Jones. Smith hadn't heard her approach.
"We need to stop meeting like this," she added.
"What do we know?" Smith got down to business.

"No ID. Could be intentional, or she may just be one of those people who doesn't bother carrying ID. She looks to be in her early twenties. Another supermodel type."

"What about her eyes?" Smith said.

"Same as the other one," Billie said. "Eyeballs removed and replaced the wrong way round. What do you think it means?"

"I haven't figured that out yet."

"I assume you want to take a look."

"Of course," Smith said. "But I want to talk to the bloke who found her first."

"It was a German tourist."

"What was he doing here?" Smith asked. "The golf club isn't open."

"Apparently he was taking a stroll, and he ended up here."

"Where is he?"

"I think Kerry is with him by the clubhouse.

"I'll find them."

"Is everything alright?" Billie said.

"Never better," Smith said.

"Because if you ever need to talk, you know where to find me. Perhaps we could grab a drink sometime."

"Perhaps not," Smith said. "I don't know what your game is, Billie, but you need to stop it."

"I don't play games."

"Glad to hear it."

Smith walked away from her. He found DC King on one of the benches outside the clubhouse. She was sitting next to a man who looked to be in his fifties.

"Kerry," Smith said.

"Sarge," DC King said. "This is Bert Unger. Herr Unger, this is DS Smith."

"Please," the German man said. "Call me Bert."

"Are you OK?" Smith said. "Do you need medical assistance?"

"No."

"Fair enough. What were you doing here? The golf club is closed for the winter."

"I came across the place," Bert said. "I was out for a walk, and I came to take a peek."

"Are you here on holiday?" Smith said.

"Of course."

"Someone will be with you shortly to take a statement," Smith said. "But I want to ask you a few questions too. Are you here alone?"

"Yes."

Smith didn't know if it was a language thing, or if the German tourist was a man of few words.

"Can you talk me through what happened?" he said. "What time did you arrive here at the golf club?"

"Five minutes before I found her," Bert said.

"Herr Unger phoned us immediately," DC King said. "That was at five past three."

"Did you see anyone else around?" Smith said.

"No. I did not."

"Where did you start your walk?"

"I'm staying at the Pavillion."

"It's on Fulford Road," DC King said.

"It's not far," Bert said.

"So," Smith said. "You will have walked along Heslington Lane."

"Correct."

"Did you see many people around?"

"No."

"None at all?"

"A few."

Smith didn't think he was going to get anything useful from the monosyllabic German. He thanked him for his time and told DC King that he wanted a word in private.

"What is it, Sarge?" she said next to one of the greens.

"I want to apologise for earlier," Smith said. "I was a bit rude."

"A bit?"

"I'm sorry. I don't know what it was about Gemma London's murder, but it affected me somehow."

"I thought all of them affected you."

"Not like this," Smith said. "You'd think you'd become immune, wouldn't you?"

"I don't think that's possible, Sarge. What do you think it's all about?"

"Right now," Smith said. "I haven't a fucking clue. Two beautiful young women have been killed and both of them have had their eyes violated. There's a damn good reason for that, but I'm struggling to see what it is."

"It'll come to you," DC King said. "It always does."

"I hope it does. I'm going to take a look at her."

CHAPTER FOURTEEN

Two hours later the team gathered in the small conference room for the final briefing of the day. Gemma London's name had been written on the whiteboard, but the identity of the second victim still remained a mystery. There was little doubt that the murders were connected, so DI Smyth didn't even bring it up for discussion.

"Any thoughts about a possible motive?" he put forward instead.
"Someone does not like beautiful women," DC Moore said.
"That's pretty obvious," Bridge said.
"The violation of their eyes is important," Smith said. "I spoke to an optician earlier and she confirmed that the operations that were carried out are not easy to pull off."
"You consulted a civilian?" DI Smyth said. "You divulged details of an ongoing investigation with this woman?"
"Relax, boss," Smith said. "It won't go any further. What the women were subjected to is something called a globe luxation. It's a complicated operation and it requires a high level of surgical skills."
"Talk us through this operation," DI Smyth said.
"I don't know the exact details," Smith said. "But a globe luxation is a process where the eyeball is removed from the eye socket without damaging the optic nerve and the blood vessels attached to the retina. It's a very delicate process."
"What's the purpose of such an operation?" DC King asked.
"It's when there's no option but to remove the eyeball, but the surgeon is able to ensure that the eyesight remains fully functional."
"Are you serious?" DC Moore said. "Are you saying it's still possible to see with your eyeballs popped out?"

"As long as the optic nerve and the vessels supplying blood to the eyes are undamaged, yes."

"Are we looking for an eye surgeon?" Whitton said.

"We're looking for someone with extensive knowledge of the anatomy of the eye," Smith said.

"We still haven't discussed why this was done to them," DI Smyth said. "Any theories there?"

"It seems like an awful lot of work for nothing," Bridge said. "What's the point of preserving their eyesight if they're dead? It's pointless."

"It isn't," Smith disagreed. "There is a very good reason for it. I just haven't figured it out yet."

"And why bother to remove the eyes if you're just going to put them back in?" DC Moore said.

"They were replaced facing inwards, Harry. There is a reason for that."

"Such as?"

"I told you," Smith said. "I haven't figured that part out."

"Until we have an ID for the second victim," DI Smyth said. "We won't speculate on a possible link between the two women."

"They were both incredibly beautiful," Smith said. "That's the connection."

"You could be right," DC Moore said.

"I'm right. We've got a bloke who likes to kill attractive women."

"We still don't know if it is a man," Whitton said.

"I think it is. I know we've dealt with some murderous females before, but this strikes me as the work of a man. And we need to ask ourselves how he's choosing them."

"Apart from their beauty?" DC King said.

"Apart from that. He doesn't simply decide to kill a woman after bumping into her one night. He watches his victims for some time beforehand. I don't know how he abducts them, but nothing we've seen so far suggests that these murders are spur of the moment acts. He's put a lot of work into getting it right."

"How soon before we have the post-mortem results from Gemma London?" Bridge asked.

"Dr Bean will make it a priority," DI Smyth said.

"Neither victim had any visible injuries," Smith said. "Apart from the obvious damage to their eyes. It's possible they were killed with the help of some kind of drug."

"If that's the case," DI Smyth said. "Pathology will confirm it. We managed to get lucky with some CCTV footage close to *The French Connection*. The wine bar opposite has cameras looking out onto the road outside the pub. We've got officers sifting through the footage and it's possible that Gemma London was caught on camera when she left the pub."

"He abducts them," Smith said. "And he takes them somewhere to carry out the operations on their eyes. That kind of thing can only be carried out in private. My optician said that, in Gemma's case the operation was a textbook globe luxation, and specialist equipment would have been necessary. It looks to me like the women were drugged throughout the operation. You do not carry out such a delicate task with your victim kicking and screaming. Once the operation is complete, he transports them to a pre-selected location, and he dumps them. And that brings me to the choice of locations."

"The sports village was risky," DC King said. "Even at this time of year there are always people around."

"Not in the middle of the night," DC Moore pointed out.

"I've been thinking about that too," Smith said. "I think Gemma was left there in the daytime, not long before she was found."

"How did you come to that conclusion?" Bridge said.

"If she was dumped during the night, why wasn't she found sooner? She was left not far from the car park. She was wearing a bright red shirt, and it wasn't difficult to see her. It was risky, but I still think the killer dumped her not long before she was found."

"The golf club isn't far from the sports village," DC King said. "No more than half a mile. As the crow flies."

She dared to turn to Smith and offer him a smile. He smiled back.

"What are you thinking, Kerry?" he said.

"The golf club is closed for winter," DC King said. "The likelihood of someone going there is slim, so why was the second victim left there?"

"That's a good question," Smith said. "The positioning of Gemma London's body suggested that she was put on display. The killer wanted his work seen, but if that's the case, why leave the second victim where the chances of her being found quickly were very low?"

Nobody had a theory about this.

The door to the room opened and Baldwin came in.

"Sorry to interrupt," she said. "But you need to see this."

She placed her tablet on the table and tapped the screen.

"What is it?" Smith asked.

"The murders of the two women have gone viral," Baldwin said.

"That was quick," Smith said. "I suppose it was bound to happen."

"This is bad, Sarge."

Smith looked at the screen of the tablet. It was a Twitter feed.

"The comments are already running into the thousands," Baldwin said. "And the identity of the first victim is already out there, along with a load of photographs of her."

"Some of these comments are not nice at all," Bridge said. "Look at this troll. *Serves the conceited bitch right.*"

"*Give the man a medal*," DC King read. "This is sick."

"That's not the worst of it," Baldwin said.

She scrolled down to one of the latest tweets.

"Fuck," Smith said. "Where the hell did they get this?"

On the screen was a photograph that had been posted within the hour. Smith recognised the woman in it immediately.

"How was this not taken down by whatever admins they have on here?" he said.

"There's not much you can't post on Twitter," Baldwin said.

"How did they even get this photograph?" DI Smyth said.

"The shit is going to hit the fan when this reaches top brass," Bridge said.

The photograph on the screen had already attracted almost a hundred comments, most of them malicious.

"*Not so pretty now, is she*?" Whitton read one of them.

"We don't even know who she is," Smith said. "What if her family or friends see this?"

"How can these people be so cruel?" DC King said. "The general consensus here is that beautiful people will get what's coming to them."

"Have you seen what they're calling him?" Bridge said.

"The Optician," Smith read. "It's gaining traction. They're calling this sick fuck *The Optician*."

CHAPTER FIFTEEN

Smith couldn't read any more. He'd left work behind him, but he wanted to keep abreast of the activity on social media. Whitton's mother had phoned, and Smith knew that their phone calls could last for hours. The Twitter posts were now running into the tens of thousands, and someone had set up a Facebook page for the two women. The comments varied. A few of them expressed sympathy for the victims, but the majority were downright cruel.

The killer the public had dubbed *The Optician* was mentioned in most of the posts, and it made Smith's blood boil. Two women were dead, and the people of the city were treating them as though they were characters in a twisted psychological thriller. It really did make him sick to the stomach.

A renowned psychologist Smith had never heard of was not holding back with her opinions. Dr Vanessa Sweetman had recorded a podcast, and it had already been viewed more than six thousand times. Smith dared to add to the number of views.

Dr Sweetman was clearly very comfortable in front of the camera. The podcast showed her sitting at a desk looking like she was made up for a photo shoot. She was an attractive woman with flawless skin. Her brown eyes stared out behind a pair of lilac framed glasses. Smith wondered if she actually needed them. After explaining who she was and outlining her extensive experience she went on to offer her *insight* into the recent murders.

In her opinion, Gemma London and the mystery woman found by the golf club were victims of a killer suffering from some kind of God complex. The murderer was almost definitely a man, and it was highly likely he'd suffered extreme rejection sometime in his life, possibly at the hands of a beautiful woman.

Dr Sweetman carried on to offer a profile of sorts of the man York Police was looking for. He would be in his mid-twenties to early-thirties and he would probably live alone. His life would be mediocre, and he would be of below average intelligence. A man for whom life had offered nothing but disappointment, he would probably watch a lot of pornography, and the few people who were acquainted with him would consider him slightly odd.

Smith turned the podcast off. He'd never heard such drivel in his life. There was nothing in Dr Sweetman's diagnosis of the man the city was calling *The Optician* about the reasoning behind the mutilation of the victims' eyes, and Smith wondered if the pretty shrink was some kind of charlatan. She was supposed to be famous in her field, but he'd never heard of her. And surely any psychologist worth their salt would latch onto the damage to the women's eyes before anything else.

Whitton was still on the phone to her mother. He could hear her muffled voice in the living room. Whitton's dad was in the final stages of cancer, and he was now bedridden most of the time. The cancer had spread from the prostate to the liver, and it had spread quickly. Harold Whitton didn't have long left.

Smith wanted to know more about Dr Vanessa Sweetman. He brought up his list of contacts and found a number he hadn't dialled for a while, and after a brief internal debate, he pressed call.
"Jason," Dr Vennell answered straight away. "I was just thinking about you."
"I need to ask your opinion on something," Smith said.
"I'm fine, now you ask."
"Sorry," Smith said. "How are you?"

Dr Fiona Vennell and Smith shared a history. The young psychologist had given him a clean bill of mental health after a near death experience and the two of them had entered into a relationship of sorts. Smith found her to be a highly competent psychologist, but there were times when she made him uncomfortable. She was a little bit in love with him, and she made no effort to hide the fact.

"Have you got a minute to talk?" he asked.

"I've always got time for you, Jason," Dr Vennell said. "You know that. What's on your mind? I assume it has something to do with *The Optician*."

"Could you please not call him that. But yes, that's partly why I'm calling. What do you know about Dr Vanessa Sweetman?"

"How long have you got?"

"Is she the real deal?"

"If you mean, is she a genuine Doctor of Psychology, the answer is yes."

"Have you seen her latest podcast?" Smith said.

"No. Should I have?"

"She's gone in front of the camera spouting a whole load of crap about how the sicko the city is calling *The Optician* is some kind of loser who watches porn. She's so far off the mark, it isn't even funny."

"Who do you think he is?"

"It's too early to tell," Smith said. "But he is definitely not someone of below average intelligence. What I've seen so far is the work of someone who is clearly driven and motivated. He's left very few clues behind, and he's planned the murders meticulously. This isn't some anorak who was once rejected by a beautiful woman. And the lovely Dr Sweetman didn't even touch on the most important aspect of the murders. These women had their eyes removed and replaced facing inwards. That has to be significant."

"Hold on a second."

Dr Vennell didn't offer any explanation for the silence that followed.

"Sorry about that," she said half a minute later. "I thought someone was at the door, but there was nobody there. Do you want to meet up?"

"I'm not sure," Smith said.

"You phoned me, remember? It sounds to me like this one is affecting you. Let me help."

"OK," Smith found himself saying. "What does your day look like tomorrow?"

"I have patients in the morning only. It's Friday and I was planning on working half day. But I'd be happy to see you. Can you come here at two?"

"I'll make time for it," Smith said. "I don't think this guy has finished yet – not by a long shot, and I still have no idea why he does that to their eyes."

"I'll see you tomorrow," Dr Vennell said. "Somebody is ringing the doorbell again."

Whitton came into the kitchen and the expression on her face told Smith the phone call with her mother wasn't pleasant.

"My dad has taken a turn for the worse," she said. "I don't think we've got long left."

Smith put his arms around her. "I'm sorry."

"Can we go round there?"

Smith nodded. "Are you sure you want me there too?"

"My dad asked for you. I think he'd prefer to have another bloke there. You know what me and my mum can be like."

"No worries," Smith said. "I'll pop next door and ask Lucy to come and keep an eye on the girls."

CHAPTER SIXTEEN

Smith was surprised when the door opened at Whitton's parents' house and Harold greeted them with a smile. There was no disguising the fact that he wasn't well, but at least he was up and about.
"You know you don't need to ring the bell," he said.
"I know, Dad," Whitton said. "It just seems wrong to barge in."
"Get inside out of the cold," Harold said. "Your mother has baked some of her ginger biscuits, if you're interested. Between you and me, I'd give them a miss if you value your teeth."

They sat in the living room. Harold brought Smith a beer, but he didn't get one for himself.
"I can't even taste the stuff anymore," he explained.
Harold had lost a lot of weight. Whitton had told Smith that he had virtually no appetite, and most of the food he did manage to eat came straight back up again. Harold's skin was sunken, and it had taken on a sickly yellow hue. There was little doubt that this man was dying. He moved slowly, and Smith sensed that he was in a lot of pain.

"Come and give me a hand with the biscuits," Jane said to Whitton. Whitton got up and followed her to the kitchen.
"How are things, son?" Harold asked Smith.
"Not great," Smith said.
"I've been following the Optician thing on Twitter."
"I didn't think you went in for social media," Smith said.
"I've got nothing much else to occupy my time. I haven't got the energy to potter around in the shed like I used to, and it's too damn cold anyway. I feel it more now, you know – the cold, I mean. I look like hell, don't I?"
Smith nodded. "I've seen you look better. Are you in pain?"

"Most of the time," Harold said. "I've got strong painkillers – morphine, I think it is, but it messes with my head. I'm not afraid of a bit of pain."
"You should really take the painkillers."
"I do when it gets too much, but the pills turn me into a zombie. And I get peculiar dreams when I take them."
"What kind of dreams?" Smith said.
He took a long drink from his beer.

"Have you ever had a dream more than once?" Harold asked.
"Recurring dreams?" Smith said. "I used to get them all the time."
"Well, in this particular dream, I'm right here in this room, looking down on the proceedings. There are a load of people here, and I'm not one of them. They're talking about me, and the way they're speaking tells me it's the wake after the funeral – my wake."
"That must be terrifying."
"That's not the half of it," Harold said. "I'm watching the whole thing play out, and at the same moment each time, our Jane blurts out over the other people talking – *where's the urn*?"
Smith started to laugh.
"It's not funny, lad. There's a moment of silence, and then all hell breaks loose when they all start hunting for my urn. Jane says she can't remember where she left it – where she left me. It's not anywhere to be found in the house, and nobody seems to know what happened to it. It's at this point that I always wake up. And I always call out – *where's the urn*?"

"That is some dream," Smith said.
The smile on his face wouldn't budge. Harold was grinning too now.
"I've tried to figure out what it means," he said. "They say that dreams happen for a reason, don't they? A shrink would probably psychoanalyse me and suggest that it's my subconscious sending out some kind of message, but whatever it's all about, it's not pleasant. Any thoughts?"

"None at all," Smith said. "I'm not a dream expert. It's probably just the morphine playing tricks with your head."

"It's more than that, son," Harold said. "Maybe I'm coming to terms with my own mortality and wondering whether I'll be missed when I'm not around anymore."

"Of course you'll be missed," Smith said.

"I've only been dead and burned to ashes five minutes," Harold said. "And already, Jane's gone and lost the bloody urn. It doesn't sound too promising, does it?"

"It's a dream, Harold," Smith said. "It's not real."

"It feels real enough."

"Where do you think it is?" Smith asked. "The urn I mean?"

"God knows. All I know is it's not where it's supposed to be."

"You should write this down," Smith said. "It would make a great short story. Where's the urn? Brilliant."

"Where's the urn?" Whitton repeated.

She and her mother had come back into the room.

"It's a private joke," Harold told her.

"It sounds like a pretty sick one, if it is," Jane said.

Smith raised his glass to his lips, mostly for something to do.

"Just do me a favour, son," Harold said. "I've heard about those tracking devices you can buy these days. When the time comes, I want you to attach one to my urn to make sure it doesn't get misplaced."

Smith had to use every ounce of self-restraint not to spit out the beer in his mouth.

Harold grinned again. "I'm pulling your leg, lad. It's neither here nor there to me what happens to it. I'll be dead, won't I?"

"What sort of conversation is this to have?" Jane said.

"Boys," Whitton said and shook her head. "How are you feeling, Dad?"

"I'm having one of my better days, love," Harold said. "I had a bit of a turn earlier, but it seems to have passed. What about you?"

"Everything's fine at home, but the case we're working on is taking its toll on us already."

"Your dad has been following the Optician crap on social media," Smith said.

"I didn't think you were a big fan of that," Whitton said.

"I'm not usually," Harold said. "But this thing has piqued my interest."

"You're not the only one," Smith said. "We've got a twisted killer out there and the people of the city are treating him like some kind of hero."

"I have no idea what you're talking about," Jane said.

"They're calling him *The Optician*," Smith said. "I won't go into detail about what he does to his victims, but he's killing beautiful women. The trolls are lapping it up. People are making out like these women deserve it because of how they look, and it's really starting to irritate me."

"Can we please talk about something more pleasant?" Jane said.

"On one condition," Harold said.

"Anything. You name it."

"When it's time," Harold said. "I want you to promise you'll not take your eyes off my urn."

"Harold," Jane said.

"Dad," Whitton added.

"I'll take that as a yes then," Harold said. "Let's talk about football."

CHAPTER SEVENTEEN

"We've had a number of breakthroughs overnight," DI Smyth began the briefing the next morning. "We have an ID for the second victim of the killer the city has colourfully dubbed *The Optician*."

"Can we not call him that?" Smith said.

"It's what everybody is calling him, Sarge," DC Moore said. "And I think it's quite catchy."

"I don't give a shit what you think," Smith said. "We're not calling him that."

"Unfortunately," DI Smyth said. "The woman's identity was discovered as a result of the photograph that was posted yesterday."

"Do we know where the photo came from?" Bridge asked.

"That's not important," DI Smyth said. "Her name is Casey Plant, and she was twenty years old."

"Who ID'd her?" DC King said.

"A friend," DI Smyth said. "He saw the photograph on Twitter, and he recognised her. Her identity has been broadcast far and wide."

"Her poor family," Whitton said. "What a terrible way to discover someone you love is dead."

"The person responsible for posting the photo should pay for this," Bridge said.

"It can only have been the bloke who found her," DC Moore said. "The German tourist. We should have him arrested."

"What's done is done," DI Smyth said. "Arresting him is not going to achieve anything."

"We have enough to deal with," Smith said. "We need to retrace Casey's movements. What do we know about her so far?"

"Very little," DI Smyth said. "And that's the focus for today. We'll speak to Casey's family and friends."

"What else did you have to tell us?" Smith said. "You mentioned a number of breakthroughs."

"I did," DI Smyth said. "Dr Bean has the post-mortem results for Gemma London and the conclusions he came to are rather interesting. Gemma had a cocktail of drugs in her bloodstream. She was given a large quantity of a benzodiazepine, probably intramuscularly. There was evidence of needle marks in her neck and shoulders."

"That won't have killed her though," Smith said.

"No," DI Smyth said. "Dr Bean is not one to speculate, but he believes that the sedative was administered prior to the operation on the eyes. This is by no means conclusive, but Dr Bean is ninety percent certain that this is the case."

"That's good enough for me," Smith said.

"It's also been confirmed that Gemma was still alive when her eyes were violated," DI Smyth said. "There is evidence of this in the tissues inside the eye socket."

"Why operate on her eyes when she's still alive if he's planning on killing her afterwards?" DC King wondered. "Why do that?"

"It's important," Smith said. "He wanted her to know what was being done to her."

"Why?" DC Moore asked.

"We find the answer to that, and we get closer to catching him."

"A high quantity of something called succinylcholine was also found in her system," DI Smyth continued. "And this is where I'll need to quote directly from the report."

He opened up the file in front of him.

"This particular drug is what's known as an NMBA. It's a neuromuscular blocking agent most commonly used to facilitate intubation. It is rapid acting and its effects are short-lived. Gemma would have been paralysed within a minute of the drug being administered."

"How long do the effects last?" Smith said.

"No more than ten minutes," DI Smyth said.

"Is there any way to determine which drug was administered first?" Whitton said.

"Unfortunately, not," DI Smyth said.

"The muscle relaxant was first," Smith decided.

"What makes you so sure of that?" DC Moore said.

"It's the logical assumption to make. Gemma is given the NMBA to render her unable to put up a fight. She's abducted and taken somewhere close by. Somewhere no more than ten minutes away. She was probably tied up and then the benzo was administered, prior to the murderer violating her eyes. But we still don't know what killed her. She was given something else afterwards, wasn't she – something lethal?"

"It appears so," DI Smyth said. "Dr Bean detected a high enough dose of cyanide salt in Gemma's bloodstream to prove fatal. It will have killed her within minutes."

"We're looking for someone with a medical background," Smith said.

"I'm inclined to agree," DI Smyth said. "The substances found in Gemma's body are not drugs you can buy at Boots. Very few people will have access to them, and that leads me to believe that our killer is a medical professional."

"He could have got them on the black market," DC Moore put forward. "We know very well that if you've got enough cash, you can get your hands on just about anything. And you can do it anonymously."

"It's worth considering," Bridge agreed.

"No," Smith said. "The drugs, coupled with the skills he's displayed suggest someone in the medical profession."

"We won't waste time on speculation," DI Smyth said. "I want you to get straight to work retracing Casey Plant's movements before she was abducted and killed. Casey was in her second year of a business degree, and she lived in a house with two other students. Speak to the housemates first, before you tackle the family. They're justifiably distraught, and the social media stuff is not helping things. And speaking of which, I have the unpleasant task of discussing the matter with the officers with the pips."

"Is there a press conference on the cards?" Smith said.

"It's inevitable," DI Smyth said. "The Tweets are still piling up, and the general consensus is we need to counter the speculation with a press conference to give the public something concrete."

"We don't have anything concrete," Smith pointed out.

"They don't know that. You know what it's like."

"Damage control?" Smith guessed.

"Got it in one. And there's a rumour that a certain celebrity psychologist will be invited to the party."

"Vanessa Sweetman?" Smith said. "You have got to be kidding me. The woman doesn't know her arse from her elbow. I watched her podcast thing, and it was like watching a bad seventies serial killer movie. She practically used every cliché in the book. She doesn't have a clue. If she paid more attention to the psychology behind the murders and less on her appearance, she might be able to contribute something, but I don't think that's going to happen."

"It's not my decision," DI Smyth said. "Top brass wants a face that people know and trust."

"She's supposed to be a celebrity shrink," Smith carried on. "But I've never heard of her. I happen to have an appointment with a bonafide psychologist this afternoon – someone who might actually be able to help us?"

"Dr Vennell?" It was Whitton. "Since when?"

"I was going to tell you," Smith said.

"I bet you were."

"We need help," Smith said. "And I think Dr Vennell can help us to get inside the head of this maniac."

"Harry," DI Smyth said. "I've got a job for you."

"Sir," DC Moore said.

"I want you to examine the CCTV footage from the wine bar across the road from *The French Connection*."

"I thought we had uniforms working on that."

"We do, but I need your eagle eye. The officers tasked with the job think there's some footage of a woman matching Gemma's description getting into a car outside the pub, but I want you to do your thing and get it confirmed."

"No problem, sir," DC Moore said.

"This briefing is over," DI Smyth announced. "Get to work. Speak to Casey Plant's housemates first."

"The press conference is a bad idea, boss," Smith said.

"Aren't they always? My hands are tied."

"Kerry," Smith said. "You're coming with me. Today, we're going to get some answers. This one is really starting to get under my skin."

CHAPTER EIGHTEEN

DC Moore had always been comfortable analysing CCTV footage on the screen of a laptop. When he was two years into his career in Wimbledon, he'd been selected to take part in an advanced training program specialising in CCTV surveillance and he'd spent six months doing very little else afterwards. He knew the ins and outs of CCTV and he'd been trained to spot the miniscule details that most people couldn't see.

It wasn't yet clear what time Gemma London had left *The French Connection*, but the officers who'd gone through the footage from the wine bar believed the woman getting into the car at eleven minutes past ten was definitely Gemma.

DC Moore didn't take that as a given, and he decided to watch the footage from the time Gemma arrived at the pub. Two minutes in, he paused it and concentrated on the woman standing outside on the street. A quick glance at the photograph on the tablet next to the laptop confirmed it – he was looking at Gemma London. DC Moore resumed the footage, frame by frame to be absolutely sure, but it didn't take long to determine that this was indeed the woman who had been found in the field close to the sports village. She was dressed in a black skirt, black stockings and a shiny red shirt. Her black hair fell halfway down her back. This was definitely her.

People came and people went. At just after half-nine a woman of similar appearance to Gemma's came outside, but it didn't take long to establish that it wasn't her. This woman was shorter, and her hair wasn't as long. DC Moore didn't just focus on the people who could be Gemma, he looked for anybody acting suspicious outside the pub. It was possible that the person responsible for abducting and killing her was lurking, waiting for her to emerge.

The pub was situated on a main road and cars on both sides of the road drove past continuously. DC Moore paid close attention to the vehicles too. They were convinced that Gemma had to have been picked up by someone in a car. It was the only possible explanation. A lot of the cars were public transport vehicles. Taxis from local companies competed with Uber drivers for business. Some of them stopped close to the pub, but all of them drove off soon after depositing their passengers.

When the clock on the bottom of the screen told DC Moore that it was 10pm he slowed the footage down and watched carefully. It was a quiet time outside the pub and not much happened. Nobody exited the pub, and nobody went inside for three minutes.

Then, at seven minutes past the hour a vehicle coming from the direction of the city centre appeared in the shot. Even though the footage had been slowed down, DC Moore could see that the car was driving extremely slowly. A pedestrian walked past and overtook it. The car stopped directly outside the pub. DC Moore paused the footage and got to work.

He zoomed in until the vehicle was the only thing in the shot, then he cropped it, so he could analyse it in more detail. He cursed the program he was using as the pixelation blurred the more he zoomed in. He tried another approach. It had raised a few eyebrows back in Wimbledon when he used it, but he didn't care.

The magnifying glass had been a gift from his grandmother when he made the announcement that he was going to join the police, and he was planning on joining the ranks of the CID. She'd given it to him and explained that every good detective needed one. A magnifying glass was an essential tool in every self-respecting sleuth's kit. DC Moore had accepted the gift, and he'd treasured it, even though he didn't think he would ever need it.

He was wrong. And as he reduced the still shot of the vehicle outside *The French Connection* to its normal size and placed the magnifying glass over the screen he smiled when he thought about his grandmother's unusual gift.

"Uber," DC Moore read.

The vehicle was an Uber taxi. Unfortunately, the direction the camera was facing meant he couldn't make out the registration number, but he had plenty of information right in front of him. It was a black saloon car – possibly a VW or an Audi and there was a distinct scratch on the back right side fender. The driver wasn't in view, and no matter which angle DC Moore angled the magnifying glass he couldn't make out who was sitting in the driver's seat. The tinted windows didn't help matters.

The Uber was still there two minutes later, and DC Moore could feel his heartbeat quickening in his chest. He was onto something here. He resumed the footage and watched it, frame by frame from 22:09. The black Uber was parked almost directly in front of the entrance to the pub, and this made DC Moore think he definitely had the right vehicle. There was a downside to this though – it was going to be difficult to see the people coming out of the pub. The car was blocking the view of the door.

At 22:10 something on the screen caught DC Moore's attention. It was a subtle change in the footage, but he spotted it. A light came on inside the car and soon afterwards he could see a small puff of smoke from the exhaust. The driver had started the engine. The winter temperatures had helped. The cold air resulted in condensation and there was more visible water vapour from the exhaust. DC Moore watched, unblinking. Something was about to happen – he could feel it.

Something did happen. At 22:11 there was movement behind the car and DC Moore caught a glimpse of something red. He rewound the footage and watched it again.

"You're going to get into the car," he said. "Aren't you, Gemma?"

Frame by frame, DC Moore watched as the woman he knew to be Gemma London approached the black Uber. She looked left and right and for a split second she appeared to be staring right at the camera on the opposite side of the road. DC Moore could feel goosebumps creeping up his arms. He was looking at possibly the last footage of Gemma London while she was still alive.

It was all over in less than ten seconds. Gemma disappeared from the shot, and the black car drove off in an easterly direction. DC Moore didn't stop there. As the vehicle was almost off the screen, he paused the footage and got to work with his magnifying glass again. He was determined to get a look at the vehicle's registration plate.

He was about to be sorely disappointed. The plate on the rear of the car was now clearly visible, but it was blank. DC Moore knew beyond a shadow of doubt that this was the car that had driven Gemma London to her death.

CHAPTER NINETEEN

"The problem as I see it," Superintendent Jeremy Smyth said. "Is the general public is getting all of its information from an unreliable source." DI Smyth was sweating even though it was rather chilly in the office. Meetings like these always made him feel uncomfortable. So far, the man whose office it was hadn't spoken a word. Chief Constable Robin Cartwright had seemed somewhat disinterested from the onset.

"I agree that we need to put out the fire that appears to be growing in size," DI Smyth said. "But we're up against something we can't beat. We're fighting a losing battle with social media. The news is instant, and the average man in the street takes it as gospel."

"The information is wrong," Superintendent Smyth pointed out. "And we need to rectify that."

"How are you proposing to do that?" Chief Constable Cartwright spoke for the first time.

"A press conference of course. I'm a firm advocate of absolute transparency. We cannot be seen to be withholding information from the people who, in essence, pay our salaries."

"With respect, sir," DI Smyth said. "What you're suggesting is not only unrealistic, but it could be detrimental to the investigation."

"Are you suggesting that a press conference is a bad idea?"

"I'm suggesting we come up with an alternative," DI Smyth said. "We've been here before, and we've been burned before."

"I assume we have a presence on social media," the CC said.

"Of course, sir," Superintendent Smyth said. "We have a Twitter account, and I think there's a Facebook thing too."

"Why not make use of those instead?" DI Smyth said. "You said it yourself that the news that's put on social media is instant, and this way we'll be in control of the narrative."

"I still believe the celebrity psychologist could be beneficial," Superintendent Smyth said.

"What do we actually know about her?" DI Smyth said.

"Dr Sweetman has close to half a million followers on Twitter."

DI Smyth thought about pointing out that Donald Trump had fifty times that, but he didn't think his uncle would see the relevance.

"How exactly do you think we can benefit from bringing Dr Sweetman on board?" he asked instead.

"People listen to her," Superintendent Smyth said. "She's more likely to get people's attention than some middle-aged man in a uniform. This is the modern age, Oliver and we need to embrace it."

"We don't know anything about her," DI Smyth said. "This isn't a reality competition – this is a real-life murder investigation, and I'm concerned that by involving a celebrity psychologist, we'll be turning it into a circus. Two young women have been brutally murdered, and it's possible that more women are going to die. This isn't the way forwards."

"Do you have a better suggestion?" Superintendent Smyth said.

"We cannot control what's posted on social media, but we can choose to ignore it. Twitter feeds are the modern version of newspapers – today's news is tomorrow's fish and chip wrappers. People will soon get bored of it."

"Fish and chip wrappers are thrown in the dustbin," Superintendent Smyth said. "Twitter posts aren't. We live in an age where news is not forgotten – it's perpetual, and we have to keep up with the times. I want Dr Sweetman involved."

"And I've given my opinion on the matter," DI Smyth said.

"OK," Chief Constable Cartwright said. "I'm going to leave this in your capable hands. Could you give me a run down on the progress thus far."
"It's early days, sir," DI Smyth said. "Gemma London's body was only discovered yesterday, and we've been working tirelessly ever since."
"Do you have any theories?"
"We're looking into a few. Like I said, it's early days."
"Is this monster the city has dubbed *The Optician* likely to strike again?"
"It's possible," DI Smyth said.
"That's precisely why we need to think out of the box, Oliver," Superintendent Smyth chipped in. "This case is not going to be cracked in the conventional way."
"I really don't know what that means, sir," DI Smyth said. "Where murder is concerned, there is no convention involved. There is no one size fits all with a murder investigation."
"I have every confidence in your team," Chief Constable Cartwright said.
"What about the general public, sir?" Superintendent Smyth said.
"What about them? Like I said, I'm going to leave the publicity in your more than capable hands. I have an appointment in the capital this evening, and I have a car waiting, so if there's nothing else."
"There's nothing else, sir," DI Smyth said before his uncle decided to say otherwise.

He got to his feet to emphasise the fact. Superintendent Smyth reluctantly did the same. They said their goodbyes to the big boss and left the office.

"You do realise what time of year it is," Superintendent Smyth said as they were making their way downstairs.
DI Smyth sighed. So, this was why his uncle was so keen to take drastic measures.
"Crime statistics," he said.

"And everything was on track for another spectacular victory," Superintendent Smyth said. "Before your Optician came and threw a spanner in the works. Jack Jones in Leeds must be rubbing his hands together in glee. This is going to knock me back into second place."
"You?" DI Smyth said this much louder than he intended.
"I meant York Police," Superintendent Smyth said. "Of course I meant York Police. With two unsolved murders, and the possibility of more on the cards, it's not looking good for this year's presentation."
"I couldn't give a fuck about your crime stats presentation," DI Smyth said. "I really couldn't. I have work to do."
He marched off towards his office. He didn't need to look behind him to see his uncle's gormless mouth open wider.

CHAPTER TWENTY

Smith was dealing with two wailing women, and he wasn't sure how to handle it. He and DC King were sitting opposite Casey Plant's housemates, and both women hadn't stopped crying since their arrival. Ella Snow and Ingrid Lee were hugging on the sofa and Smith looked to DC King for help.

"We appreciate that this must be a difficult time for you," she said. "But we need to ask you some questions and we need to do that now. There will be plenty of time for emotions, but that time is not now. Do you understand?"

She received a couple of nods in reply.

"Good," she said. "Because in a murder investigation, time is of the essence. It's essential we ask our questions while the information is fresh in the heads of the people with the answers. So, could you please stop your sniffing and crying and pay attention to what we have to say?"

This wasn't quite the assistance Smith had in mind when he'd given DC King the nod, but it seemed to have the desired effect. Both women blew their noses simultaneously and turned to face them.

"How long have you known Casey?" Smith asked.

"We met during Fresher's Week," the blond woman said.

Smith couldn't remember if it was Ella or Ingrid.

"Ingrid ended up snogging her for a bet," the other woman said.

Ella is the redhead then, Smith thought.

"It wasn't a bet," Ingrid said. "It was a stupid drunken thing."

"Whatever," Ella said.

Smith wasn't interested in this.

"How long have you lived here?" he asked.

"Since the start of term last year," Ella said. "We were in Halls in the first year."

"When was the last time you saw Casey?" DC King said.

"Wednesday," Ingrid said.

"When on Wednesday?" Smith said.

"We went out to this new pub on Hull Road," Ella said. "And we went on to a club afterwards."

"On a Wednesday?" Smith said. "Did you not have classes the next day?"

"What difference does that make?"

"Fair enough. We're going to need the names of these places."

"The pub was pretty dire," Ingrid said. "It was one of those new theme places, but the theme was something I'd never heard of."

"*The French Connection*?" Smith guessed.

"How did you know that?"

"It's the only new pub on Hull Road," Smith said. "What about the club?"

"*Blast*," Ella said. "It's over in South Bank."

"Did you all go there together?" DC King said.

Ella nodded. "We got bored of the pub, so we got an Uber to the club."

"What time was that?" Smith said.

"About eleven," Ella said. "Hold on."

She retrieved her mobile phone from the table and swiped the screen. After a few taps she read from the screen.

"We left *The French Connection* at 22:59. Can you believe I was asked how it was three minutes later? Then we were moving, and we arrived at *Blast* at 23:14."

"And your phone told you all that?" Smith said.

Ella observed him as though he was an idiot.

"Miss naive there keeps her location on permanently," Ingrid explained. "She doesn't realise how dodgy it can be."

Something occurred to Smith. They hadn't found Casey Plant's phone.

"Did Casey have her phone with her when you went out on Wednesday?"

"Really?" Ingrid said. "What kind of question is that?"

"We'll take that as confirmation that she did," DC King said. "We haven't been able to locate it. Do you know if she had *Find my device* activated?"

"More than likely," Ella said.

"She was always losing her phone," Ingrid said.

"Did you ever help her find it?" DC King said.

"Sometimes," Ella said. "But we don't know her passwords."

"You've lost me there," Smith said.

"*Find my device* is an app you use when you've misplaced your phone, Sarge," DC King explained. "You can log into another device, and the app will give you a location."

"But you need a pin or a password," Ella said. "And only Casey had those. I can't believe she won't be coming back."

Smith was worried that the waterworks were about to be switched on again, but the tears didn't come.

"Tell us what you did at the nightclub," he said.

"It was OK," Ingrid said. "Not too busy. We danced a bit, had a few drinks and Casey said she wanted to go home."

"Why was that?" DC King said.

"She wasn't feeling too good."

"Did she have a lot to drink?" Smith said.

"No more than usual."

"That wasn't what I asked."

"We had a few drinks at the pub," Ella said. "And a couple more at the club. We can't afford more than that. Casey wasn't drunk, if that's what you're asking."

"Did she leave on her own?" Smith said.

"We offered to go with her," Ingrid said. "But she said it was fine. She'd called an Uber, and she said she would wait outside for it. She said she needed some fresh air."

"And you let her go by herself?" DC King said.

The tears came then.

"I know," Ella sobbed. "We should have gone with her."

"She might still be alive if we had," Ingrid said. "I don't think I'm ever going to forgive myself for that."

"It's not your fault," Smith said. "What time did the Uber get there?"

"I don't know," Ingrid said. "We got chatting to a couple of blokes and Casey wasn't there when we went back to the table."

"Give us a rough time," Smith said. "It's possible that she was caught on CCTV."

"Around one," Ella said.

"But she won't have been caught on camera," Ingrid said. "The club doesn't have CCTV. The cameras were vandalised a few nights ago. One of the bartenders was moaning about it."

Smith glanced across the room, and his eyes fell on the clock on the wall. "Shit."

"Sarge?" DC King said.

Smith got to his feet. "I need to go. I'm late for an appointment. I'll drop you off at the station on the way."

"Who is *The Optician*?"

Ella's question caught Smith off guard, and he didn't really know how to reply.

"We're going to find out."

"Why did he do that to her eyes?" Ingrid asked.

"I really don't know," Smith said.

"She had the most beautiful eyes," Ingrid said. "She really was a beautiful girl. People who met her couldn't help falling in love with her. Men and women alike."

CHAPTER TWENTY-ONE

"Do you think I've put on weight?"
Rachel Gold was observing her backside in the full-length mirror attached to the door of the bedroom.
Her boyfriend Wayne didn't bother looking up from the game he was playing. "Don't be daft."
"I have," Rachel said. "It was all that food you made me eat over Christmas. You knew I was trying to keep my weight down."
"You're not fat," Wayne said.
"You're not even looking," Rachel said. "You're more interested in that fucking Xbox than you are me. Is it because I'm getting fat?"
"You are not fat."

Wayne paused his game and got off the bed. He walked over to her and wrapped his arms around her.
"You're creasing my dress," Rachel said. "I haven't got time to iron it again."
"I give up. What time is the thing with the agency?"
"It's not a *thing*, Wayne," Rachel said. "Do you even listen to what I tell you?"
"I don't really have much choice, do I?"
"What's that supposed to mean?"
"Well," Wayne said. "You're always talking, aren't you?"
"One of us has to. I can't even remember the last time we had a conversation – a proper one, I mean."
"I sort of give up when you start rattling on about your favourite topic."
"My favourite topic?" Rachel said.
"*You*, sweetheart," Wayne said. "You yourself and you."
"That's not fair."

"It's the truth. If you ever went on one of those highbrow quiz things, your specialised subject would be Rachel Gold."

"There's nothing wrong with being confident," Rachel said. "Self-belief is important if you want to survive as a model."

Wayne sighed. "You're going to do great. You're gorgeous and everyone with a pair of eyes in their head can see that. What time do you have to be at the agency?"

"Half-two. Shit, it's already five to. Can't you give me a lift? What if the Uber doesn't get here on time?"

"I told you," Wayne said. "The brakes on the Golf are shot. It's too dangerous. I've got a mate coming to look at it later. The Uber will be here. Those cars are reliable. Knock 'em dead."

Rachel sucked in her already non-existent stomach and pouted at the mirror. "I intend to. I'd better go."

"No kiss goodbye?"

"You'll mess up my makeup. I'll see you later."

The Uber was waiting outside, and Rachel took this as a good sign. Today was the day. Friday 28 January was going to be the day that her life changed forever. She bent down to admire her face in the wing mirror and got in the back. She wasn't going to travel in the front. She was better than that.

"Badger Hill, isn't it?"

Rachel was surprised by the driver's voice and when their eyes met in the rearview mirror she smiled.

The driver's eyes smiled back. "Has anyone ever told you that you're obscenely beautiful?"

"It has been said," Rachel said. "Can we get going? I'll leave a bad review if you don't get me there on time."

* * *

The first thing that caught Whitton's attention when she was invited into Casey Plant's parents' house was the photographs in the hallway. Every inch of wall space had been covered in them. Some were framed, and others weren't. The subject matter in all of them was the same. A girl in various stages of her life was staring at the camera, smiling. In some of the photographs she was holding trophies and rosettes and Whitton deduced that this was Casey Plant.

"She's been modelling since she was small," Casey's father said. He'd introduced himself as Bill and he was very short man. Whitton wasn't tall, but she stood a good few inches above Bill Plant. He asked Whitton and Bridge to take a seat in the living room and told them he was going to check on his wife.

"Is it just me," Bridge said. "Or are those photos a bit weird?"
"It looks like they're very proud of Casey," Whitton said. "There's nothing weird about that. You don't have kids, so you wouldn't understand."
"I have nephews and nieces," Bridge said. "And none of my brothers have shrines like that to their kids."
"We won't talk about that with Mr and Mrs Plant. They must be devastated."
Bill came into the room.
"Our Janice isn't up to speaking to you. The doc came round earlier and gave her something to calm her down, and she's out of it. Can you make this quick?"
"We won't take up too much of your time," Whitton said. "We're very sorry for your loss. Has someone been round to see you? A family liaison officer, I mean?"
"A bloke popped round," Bill said. "But I sent him on his way. He probably meant well, but the last thing we need right now is some stranger pretending to help us."

"We realise that this must be difficult for you," Bridge said. "But we need to ask you a few questions about Casey. Is that alright?"

"I suppose so."

"Was Casey a professional model?" Whitton said.

"Not really," Bill said. "She did a load of pageants when she was little, and she still did some photo shoots on and off, but she had her head screwed on. She knew that models had a shelf life, so she decided to study so she had something to fall back on. She was doing a business studies degree."

"She was a beautiful woman," Bridge said.

"Aye, she was."

Neither Whitton nor Bridge were expecting what happened next. Bill Plant shot to his feet so quickly Whitton thought he was going to attack them. He marched over so he was only a couple of feet from them.

"Do you know what it feels like to see your baby girl on display like that?"

"Could you sit down please, Mr Plant?" Whitton said.

He ignored her. "For the whole world to see. Can you imagine what that does to a parent? The bastards that posted those photos of her like that should be shot. Are you going to do something about it?"

"Our hands are tied where social media is concerned," Whitton said.

"It's disgusting. We had to find out that our daughter had been murdered from Twitter. Can you imagine what that feels like? I've deleted my account now."

"Please, Bill," Bridge said. "Sit back down."

He obliged but he kept his eyes on Whitton's.

"When you catch him," he said. "When you catch the monster who did that to my baby girl, can you promise me one thing?"

"If I can," Whitton said.

"Will you kill him?"

"You know I can't make a promise like that. When we catch him, he will face the full might of the law."

"You'd better kill him before I do," Bill said.

"Please calm down, Mr Plant," Bridge said.

"Do you have kids?" he asked Whitton.

She nodded. "Three girls."

"Then you might understand what I'm about to say. When you do catch him, he won't be safe from me. I will make it my life's mission to end him. I'll do it – I don't give a damn about the consequences. I'll take him when he's in court, and he won't see it coming. I'll visit him in prison and do it there if I have to, but I will terminate him."

"I appreciate that this is an extremely difficult time, Mr Plant, but you can't talk like this."

Whitton had never experienced a reaction like this from a grieving parent.

"What would you do if you came face to face with the monster who'd killed your little girl?" Bill asked her.

Whitton didn't reply, but she could empathise with him. If she were in the same position, she wasn't sure whether she would be able to stop herself if she was left alone with the killer of one of her children.

"I will not rest until the bastard is dead and buried," Bill said. "That's a promise. What he did to my baby will come back tenfold when I get hold of him."

CHAPTER TWENTY TWO

Smith arrived at Dr Vennell's practice to find it locked up. He checked the time on his phone – he was fifteen minutes late, but he didn't think she would have left already. He brought up her number and before he got the chance to call her a figure appeared in the doorway and the door was opened.

"I thought you'd stood me up," Dr Vennell said.

"Sorry I'm late," Smith said. "Why was the door locked?"

"I keep it locked when I'm here alone. There are a lot of strange folk around these days."

"You of all people should know," Smith said. "Are you going to let me in?"

"I think I'll be safe with you. Come on then. I'll make us some coffee."

"I took the liberty of watching the podcast that the lovely Dr Sweetman put out," Dr Vennell said in her office.

"What did you think?" Smith said.

"You weren't lying when you spoke about every serial killer cliché in the book. I was disappointed that she didn't tell us that he probably wet the bed when he was a child. Or perhaps he liked to torture animals."

"And he had a domineering mother," Smith added.

"Of course. That goes without saying."

"The public are lapping it up," Smith said. "And it's all bullshit. Help me."

"What is it you need my help with?"

"I want you to help me to get inside his head."

"You're convinced that it's a man?" Dr Vennell said. "Are you sure *The Optician* is male?"

"I'd prefer it if you didn't call him that," Smith said. "But yes, I think it's a man. I don't believe a woman is capable of such brutality."

"Drink your coffee. It's a new blend I'm trying out."

Smith obliged and took a sip. It really was good coffee.

"Talk to me about the brutality?" Dr Vennell said.

"We now know that he drugs them soon after they're abducted. He gives them some kind of muscle paralysing agent. Then, before he carries out the operations on their eyes, he doses them up with benzodiazepine."

"He displays a certain humility there."

"How did you come to that conclusion?" Smith asked.

"I don't know the details of the operations you've spoken about, but the fact that he administers a drug beforehand suggests that he wants to spare them the pain."

"He kills them afterwards," Smith said. "He's not sparing them anything."

"How does he kill them?" Dr Vennell said.

"With cyanide."

"It's a quick death if the dose is high enough."

"Are you suggesting he feels empathy?" Smith said. "Because that puts a whole new spin on the psychopath element."

Dr Vennell didn't offer an opinion on that.

"Tell me what he does to their eyes?" she asked instead.

"He removes the eyeballs," Smith said. "And he makes sure that the optic nerve and the retinal vessels are undamaged. Then he replaces the eyeballs, facing inwards."

"He wants them to be able to see."

"We've established that," Smith said. "It's what's known as a globe luxation. The eyeball is removed from the socket, but the eyesight isn't affected. What we haven't established is why? Why go to all the trouble of removing the eyeballs if you're going to replace them the wrong way round? The effort of the globe luxation is pointless if the parts of the eyes that do the seeing are facing inwards."

"Fascinating," Dr Vennell said.

"I'm glad you think so," Smith said. "Any thoughts?"

"I'll have to get back to you with that one."

"I don't have time to wait. I know for a fact that he's not finished."

"Tell me about the victims," Dr Vennell said. "Were they acquainted?"

"Not that we're aware of," Smith said. "Both of them were young women and both of them were extremely attractive. Model types."

"Is that the only connection between them?"

"It's the only one we've managed to establish."

"Then that's where we'll start. It's possible that their looks could be a coincidence. But I know that…"

"I don't believe in coincidences," Smith finished her sentence.

"Precisely. We have a killer who is targeting beautiful young women. Many serial killers have what's known as a *type* – you're very aware of that. Jeffrey Dahmer's targets were predominantly young Black men. Ted Bundy preyed on mostly college students, and John Wayne Gacy's preferred victims were young boys. Your optician chooses beautiful young women."

"The celebrity shrink seems to believe he was rejected by a beautiful woman somewhere down the line," Smith said. "Do you think there's any truth in that?"

"It's possible," Dr Vennell said. "But I think these murders are more deep-seated than that."

"So do I," Smith said. "There is more to it than a nutjob who likes to butcher pretty women."

"And you've hit the nail on the head beautifully there. He doesn't butcher them, does he?"

"No," Smith said. "In fact, there is no indication that he harms them apart from the obvious injuries to their eyes."

"He wants them dead, but he doesn't physically harm them. He lets the drugs do the work for him and that suggests the murders are born of necessity."

"Necessity?" Smith repeated.

"It's what he does to their eyes that's important to him. Unfortunately, their deaths are a by-product. He can't risk leaving them alive, so he kills them, albeit in a rather humane manner."

"I need to know why he does that to their eyes," Smith said. "We've been banging our heads together and nobody has been able to come up with a feasible reason for it. What is his fucking motivation?"

"Hold on to that frustration," Dr Vennell said.

"It's driving me nuts."

"You're in the right place then. I may have a theory for you to consider."

"I'm open to all suggestions," Smith said.

"He wants them to see."

"That part is obvious," Smith said. "But they can't see, can they? He's put their eyeballs in the wrong way round."

"Exactly. Perhaps that's the whole point. He wants them to see, but what he really wants them to observe is not what's on the outside."

"He wants them to look inwards," Smith said.

Dr Vennell nodded. "I think he does. He wants them to take a closer look inside themselves. He needs them to take a good look at what really lies beneath the beautiful exterior."

CHAPTER TWENTY THREE

"Who are you?" DI Smyth said. "And what have you done with DS Jason Smith?"

"It's still me, boss," Smith said.

"Do I need to be concerned?" DI Smyth said. "Because I could have sworn, I heard you agree to the Super's wishes without argument. Did I not make myself clear enough?"

"I heard you loud and clear, and I think it's just what we need right now."

DI Smyth had come to find Smith as soon as he got back from seeing Dr Vennell and he'd explained what Superintendent Smyth had in mind. The gormless public-school idiot had disregarded everything that was said in the meeting with Chief Constable Cartwright and contacted Dr Vanessa Sweetman directly. He'd outlined his idea for a new podcast and Dr Sweetman had agreed on one condition. The podcast would be recorded at the station as per Superintendent Smyth's wishes, but he wouldn't be in it. Dr Sweetman had insisted that she wanted Smith and only Smith.

"I thought you hated this kind of thing," DI Smyth said.

"I usually do," Smith said. "But I've just come from seeing a real shrink, and she gave me something to think about. I think I know why he does that to their eyes."

"Go on."

"The fact that he leaves their eyesight intact when he removes the eyeballs is important, and Dr Vennell believes he does that so they can look inside themselves."

"That's ridiculous."

"Is it though?" Smith said. "He wants them to see what's beneath the surface – what's underneath the superficial exterior, and that's why he replaces the eyeballs facing inwards."

"But they can't see inwards, can they?" DI Smyth said. "It's impossible to see anything after he's done that."

"I don't think that matters to him, boss. It's symbolic, nothing more."

"And are you planning on voicing these theories in the podcast with the pretty shrink?"

"I am," Smith confirmed. "There's a very strong possibility that he'll be watching. It's obvious that he wants his work seen, and I don't think he'll be able to resist an opportunity like this. He'll be watching, and he's going to see that we've figured out part of his motive."

"What exactly is that going to achieve?"

"It's going to rattle him," Smith said. "And we both know that a rattled serial killer often ends up making mistakes. We're going to catch this bastard, and the celebrity psychologist is going to help us without realising it."

"Be careful," DI Smyth said. "This could backfire."

"*Careful* is my middle name, boss," Smith said. "Have we had any more breakthroughs since this morning?"

"I believe we have. Come, walk with me – the rest of the team are waiting for us in the small conference room."

It was clear from the whiteboard at the back of the room that the team had been busy in Smith's absence. They now had the identity of the second victim and Casey Plant's name had been written below Gemma London's. Not only that, but there were also various new scrawls next to both names. Smith and DI Smyth took a seat at the table.

"Before I discuss what me and Dr Vennell spoke about," Smith said. "What have I missed?"

"Harry got a hit from the CCTV from the wine bar opposite *The French Connection*," Bridge said.

"She left in an Uber, Sarge," DC Moore said. "At seven minutes past ten on Wednesday night, a black car pulled up next to the pub. Gemma London emerged from the pub four minutes later and got into the car."

"Did we get a registration number?" Smith said.

"It was blank."

"Blank?" Smith repeated.

"The plates had been removed," DC Moore said. "Which makes me convinced that the driver of the Uber is *The Optician*."

"What have I told you…"

"Sorry, Sarge. I still think *The Optician* suits him."

"Surely there's some way we can check who the driver is," Smith said. "If he's a genuine Uber driver, I mean."

"I checked already," DC Moore said. "All Uber drivers have to be registered. They have to have a private hire license and that's issued by the council. Without a registration number, it was impossible to find the driver of the black car, but I got creative. All Uber pickups are logged in a central database. The drivers are not classed as sub-contractors, and their movements are regulated."

"He's not a genuine Uber driver, is he?" Smith said.

"He's not. There was an Uber sticker on the side of the vehicle, but anyone can get one of those made."

"I don't understand," Whitton said. "How did *The Optician* know that Gemma would be wanting an Uber?"

"I think I know how, Sarge," DC Moore said. "Gemma really did book a car, but it wasn't the car that picked her up. There was a booking at around that time from *The French Connection*. The driver was sent out, but he was stood up."

"Gemma had already left by the time he got there," Bridge said. "This is how he's abducting them."

"Casey Plant also booked an Uber," Smith said. "Her housemates told me and Kerry that she wasn't feeling well at the nightclub they were at, and she booked an Uber to take her home. They didn't see her leave, but I think we know what happened."

"Does the club have CCTV?" DC Moore said.

"Yes and no," Smith said. "They have cameras, but they were vandalised a few days ago."

"That's some coincidence," Bridge said.

"Shut up," Smith said.

"I was winding you up, mate."

"This is a breakthrough," DI Smyth said. "But how does he do it? How does he know when they order an Uber?"

"I did some research on that too, sir," DC Moore said. "It's actually a thing, these days. *Uber wars*, they call it. You get drivers poaching other drivers' fares. They're all logged onto the same system, and a driver can coast around and look for fares to steal. The passengers have no idea it's even happening. They just assume that the car they're getting into is the one they've booked."

"But when you book an Uber, the transaction goes through the app, doesn't it?" DC King said.

"Not in certain areas," DC Moore said. "London is cashless, but in most other cities, the drivers can take cash. That's how the *Uber wars* drivers are making their money."

"I thought you said this nutter isn't a genuine Uber driver," Bridge said.

"It doesn't matter," DC Moore said. "The security measures in place on the Uber system are laughable. I could pose as a driver if I wanted to. This is how he's abducting them."

"And this might be how we can stop him from taking another victim," DI Smyth said.

"We need to warn women about the dangers of getting into an Uber taxi alone," Whitton said.

"That might just work," Smith said. "And I happen to have the perfect platform to do it on."

"Is there something you're not telling us, Sarge?" DC King said.

"The Super is insisting on a podcast with the lovely Dr Sweetman," DI Smyth explained. "And the celebrity shrink wants Smith to join her."

"And you agreed to this?" Whitton said.

"I think it's a brilliant idea," Smith said.

"Are you ill?"

"I've never felt better," Smith said. "We're going to catch this bastard. He's not going to be able to resist watching that podcast and I'm going to tell the world how he takes his victims, and I'm also going to spill the beans about why he does what he does to their eyes. If that doesn't rattle him, I don't know what will."

CHAPTER TWENTY FOUR

Once again, Smith found himself in the office used by PC Neil Walker. He'd made an appointment with the press liaison officer to see if he had any pointers for him in the run-up to the podcast with Dr Vanessa Sweetman. PC Walker was more than happy to oblige.

"The first thing you need to realise about podcasts," he said. "Is they're not like press conferences. The feed does not go out live, and any questions that may be posed happen afterwards."

"That should make life easier," Smith decided.

"Yes and no. It's true that you won't be bombarded with questions for the duration, and a non-live recording means you don't need to be too worried about what you say. Anything that's said can be edited, but once it's posted live, that's it – there's no taking it back and it's there for anyone to see pretty much forever afterwards."

"I couldn't give a shit about that," Smith told him."

"I would advise you to give a shit, Sarge," PC Walker said.

"What do you know about Dr Sweetman?" Smith said.

"She's popular," PC Walker said. "The numbers don't lie, but numbers can be deceptive. I've seen a few of her posts and it's possible her popularity relies heavily on her looks. Your average podcast viewer is a simple animal – looks count more than anything else."

"She's a genuine doctor of Psychology," Smith reminded him. "Surely that ought to count for something."

"People aren't bothered about her qualifications. They barely see past the pretty face and firm legs. Have you run through the program with her?"

"Program?" Smith said.

"The items on the agenda as it were. It might be an idea to check what she's planning before you do the podcast. She hasn't attracted over half a million followers by playing safe."

"I thought you just said she got there with a pretty face and a hot body," Smith said.

"The content also has to be something people want to listen to – something controversial. When is this thing happening?"

"This evening," Smith said. "At eight."

"You don't have much time then. How are you planning on playing it? What's your agenda?"

"I'm going to tell the general public a lot more than I usually do," Smith said. "I've got a strong suspicion that the killer will be watching and I'm going to reveal information that's going to shake him up a bit. We now know how he abducts them – he poses as an Uber driver, and I'm going to warn women about getting lifts with Ubers alone."

"You're going to irritate a lot of Uber drivers if you do that."

"Tell someone who cares. If it can prevent more women from falling victim to this psychopath, then it's worth it. I'm also going to make him aware that we're onto his motive. We know why he does that to their eyes, and that should rattle him too."

"What are you hoping to achieve from that?" PC Walker said.

"I want to push him over the edge," Smith said. "Make him mad enough so he drops the ball. He's going to make a mistake after this, and I'll be there when he does."

"I hope you know what you're doing."

"So do I," Smith said. "Is there anything else you can tell me?"

"Just be yourself. Dr Sweetman obviously requested you for a reason, so just be yourself."

* * *

"Where am I?"

The three words were a real effort for Rachel Gold to get out. Her mouth felt like it wasn't hers and she thought that her tongue had swollen to twice its normal size. There was something covering her eyes and the skin around them was tingling.

Her question remained unanswered. Rachel tried to move her hand to scratch a new itch on her cheek, but something was preventing her. She had no idea where she was, and she couldn't recall anything after the brief conversation with the Uber driver. Her thoughts were hazy, and she felt sick. Something occurred to her, and it was a rather bizarre thought under the circumstances. She wondered if the modelling agency would give her another chance.

"Help me," she managed. "Please."

She was aware of the sound of heavy breathing close by. Someone was there with her.

"Who are you?"

There was another sound now. It was the rustling of something plastic. A quiet pop was followed by three taps in quick succession. Then Rachel felt fingers on her face. The touch was gentle, and it was disconcerting. There was a sharp pain on the side of her neck and Rachel flinched.

"You know why this is happening, don't you?"

The voice was vaguely familiar, and Rachel tried to recall where she'd heard it before. It was impossible – she felt like her memory bank had slammed its doors and no matter how hard she tried to focus, the doors remained shut.

"Soon, you will see for the first time."

The voice sounded different now. Rachel thought the owner of the voice was far away. She wasn't aware of the pressure on her eyeball. She couldn't feel the fingers prying and prodding and she didn't know that the eyeball wasn't where it was supposed to be. All feeling to her face had been shut off, and her brain wasn't registering anything from the various nerve endings there. She drifted off then. All sounds and smells gave way to a black nothing.

Rachel had no idea how long she slept the dreamless sleep, and when her senses returned, the first thing she registered was the tang of something chemical. She wanted answers but her voice refused her. There was also something covering her mouth.

"Soon, you will see."

It was the same voice as before.

The feeling was returning to her face, and Rachel had to fight the urge to vomit.

"All this." Gentle fingers touched Rachel's face. "Means nothing when you look at what's rotten inside. This is simply a mask. A mask that hides what's really there. You'll see soon – you'll see the vile, repulsive core of you and you'll recoil at the sight. You will thank me when you see it."

It was no use. Rachel felt the bile in her stomach rise and then her mouth filled with vomit. She gagged and swallowed, and the panic set in. Something was preventing her mouth from opening, and she was struggling to breathe. A chain reaction had been set in motion, and the gag reflex caused more vomit to fill her mouth.

"Take one final look. You'll die soon."

CHAPTER TWENTY FIVE

"Sergeant Plant reckons he knows what make of car Gemma London got into outside *The French Connection*," DC Moore said.

He'd come to Smith's office to share this information with him as soon as the duty sergeant identified the vehicle.

"It's a VW Passat," DC Moore added.

"How certain is he?" Smith said.

"Positive, Sarge. And he could be more specific. It's the SE Business model. The TDi sedan. He's got the same car, and he recognised the unique sloping wing mirrors and the distinctive upward curve of the louvre in the doors."

"Do we know how many of these cars there are in the city?"

"It'll be easy to check," DC Moore said. "I came straight here after Sergeant Plant confirmed the make of the vehicle."

"Good work," Smith said. "It gives me some more ammo for the podcast later. We can now warn women about getting into that particular make of Uber car. We're getting closer to this monster."

"The car that Gemma got into also has a scratch on the right rear fender," DC Moore said.

"We'll put the word out. Do you think the plates were only removed for the duration of the abduction of Gemma London?"

"Most likely. I doubt he'd be stupid enough to risk driving around with no plates. He could get picked up any time."

"I thought as much," Smith said.

"I'll get onto checking the list of cars," DC Moore said.

"There's something else I want you to take a look at," Smith said.

"Sarge?"

"You're quite an expert on CCTV cameras, aren't you?"

"I did an extensive course back in London," DC Moore said.

"Casey Plant's housemates mentioned something about the cameras at the nightclub in South Bank. The bartender told them that the CCTV had been vandalised recently."

"I see what you're getting at," DC Moore said. "It's possible the vandals were caught in the act. But why haven't the night club people already checked for that?"

"Perhaps they have," Smith said. "But they might have kept it to themselves. Find out, will you?"

"OK. But I've got a feeling that if the vandalism is the work of *The Optician*, we're not going to get anything useful."

"I get that feeling too," Smith said. "But it still needs to be checked out. What are the rest of the team up to?"

"The DI has got Kerry looking into companies that specialise in decals and stickers. It's a long shot, but someone might remember getting an order for a sticker for an Uber car. DS Whitton has gone back to speak to Casey Plant's parents. Their first meeting was rather eventful apparently."

"What happened?"

"Casey's dad is a bit of a pocket rocket by all accounts. He's about five foot tall but he's a proper angry little man. He threatened *The Optician* with lethal violence if he catches him, and DS Whitton thinks he was deadly serious. Hopefully, he'll have calmed down a bit by now."

"Don't bank on it, Harry," Smith said. "The father of a girl is a dangerous creature when that girl is hurt – you're looking at one. I can sympathise with the bloke. Where's Bridge?"

"The DI thought it was worth taking another look at the pub on Hull Road. Him and Bridge are there now."

"*The French Connection*," Smith said. "It's come up during the course of the investigation too many times for my liking. Both victims were at that pub the night they were abducted. It could just be coincidence, but you know how I feel about coincidence."

"I'll get to work."

Smith had three hours to kill before the podcast was due to be recorded, and he planned to use that time productively. He woke up his laptop and keyed Gemma London's name into the task bar. They'd spoken to the people who were acquainted with her, but experience had taught him that Google often gave them more info than the friends and family of the victims.

There wasn't much to look at. Gemma had a Facebook profile, and she was also active on Twitter and Instagram. Her Facebook security settings meant that Smith couldn't get any further than her profile picture and a few other basic pieces of information. He made a mental note to get assistance from someone in her friends list to rectify this. He needed to see what she'd posted on her Facebook.

She was last seen on Twitter three days ago, but Smith didn't think that the most recent post held any relevance to her murder. She'd made a comment about celebrities and their pets. There were very few re-Tweets.

Gemma's Instagram page looked more promising. As Smith clicked on the posts, he saw that they were mostly videos taken inside the gym where she worked. It was very clear that she wasn't shy to show off her body, and the poses she performed on the various pieces of gym equipment looked well-rehearsed. She looked comfortable in front of the camera and her Instagram consisted of very little else. Smith wondered if *The Optician* had seen her Instagram posts. It also occurred to him that social media made it extremely easy for murderers to monitor potential victims. People like Gemma London thought nothing of advertising every aspect of their lives, leaving them extremely vulnerable to predators.

He added Casey Plant's name to the search, but nothing cropped up. It didn't look like Gemma and Casey had ever crossed paths, even online, and

Smith was disappointed. He wondered if the killer had really selected his victims randomly – their looks being the deciding factor. It didn't feel right. He was convinced that the two victims shared more in common than their physical appearance, but there was nothing on the Internet to substantiate this.

Smith rubbed his eyes, and his vision blurred for a second. He waited for it to clear and began a new search. Something about James Norton was bothering him, and Smith wanted to find out more about the man. The first thing that struck Smith as odd when he clicked on the first post was the fact that James really was an American. His accent wasn't as fake as it sounded. He'd arrived in England in the late nineties, and he'd built up an empire of sorts in Yorkshire. Apart from the gym and the pub, James owned two supermarkets and there were talks of him investing in a nightclub.

Smith was surprised to see that James's Facebook was open for anybody to look at. The most recent posts were all related to the opening of *The French Connection*. There was a lengthy post outlining the history behind the decision to open a pub with a 70s film theme and Smith didn't bother reading any more when he realised it was basically a synopsis of the movie.

Instead, he scrolled down James's list of friends. The majority were women, and Gemma London was one of them. Smith realised that James had liked every single thing she'd posted on Facebook. He carried on looking at the names on the list and he stopped when his eyes fell on another familiar name. James Norton was also friends with Casey Plant.

The rest of the names on the list were unfamiliar ones, but there was a name here that was going to come to Smith's attention very soon. The woman was called Rachel Gold – she was twenty-one years' old, and she'd always dreamed of becoming a successful model. Unfortunately, that bird had now flown – Rachel had recently choked on her own vomit in the basement of a house in Heworth.

CHAPTER TWENTY SIX

The first thing that struck Smith when he came face to face with Dr Vanessa Sweetman was she didn't look real. It was the only way he could describe her. She was dressed in a smart suit that he assumed was supposed to lend her a professional appearance, but it was her face that he was drawn to, and he found himself staring at it for much longer than he would like.

He'd seen her on the screen of his tablet, but close up, she was even more perfect. There was a symmetry to her face that didn't seem natural. This was a face that an artist might paint in a quest to create the epitome of a beautiful woman. Her skin was flawless and there were no telltale signs of age. Her deep brown eyes were the only part of her face that seemed human. There was a warmth to them that was at odds with the rest of her face. Smith had never met anyone like her before.

"It really is a pleasure to meet you."

Her voice sounded different to the voice Smith remembered from the podcast. She was local – that was clear, but her accent had been diluted somewhat. She held out her hand.

Smith took it. "Likewise. I wasn't sure if you really looked like that."

Dr Sweetman laughed. "I'd heard that you were brutally honest."

"My wife reckons there's a loose connection between my brain and my mouth," Smith said. "I've learned to not give a shit anymore. Can I get you some coffee?"

"I never touch the stuff. Is there somewhere we can talk in private? I can feel eyes on me."

It was true. The PCs Griffin and Miller weren't even trying to hide it. The two uniformed officers were whispering by the front desk like a pair of teenagers.

"What is it you need to talk about?" Smith asked.

"I'd like to run through your feelings about the podcast before we start recording."

"As long as you don't try to psychoanalyse me," Smith said. "We can talk in my office. I just need to grab a cup of coffee from the canteen first."

"I watched your first podcast," Smith said inside the office.

"What did you think?" Dr Sweetman said.

"Honestly?"

"I'd appreciate it if you could be as honest as possible."

"I thought it was sensationalist drivel," Smith said.

He didn't expect her to take this well, but the smile on her face was genuine.

"No offence," he added.

"None taken," Dr Sweetman said. "I've grown a thick skin over the years. You don't attract half a million followers and expect to please all of them. Go on."

"I didn't appreciate the way you claimed to be qualified to offer your subscribers a profile of this man when it's clear you know nothing about him. All you came up with was the bog-standard serial killer crap."

"Who do you think he is?"

"Not some stereotypical psychopath," Smith said. "There's no such thing. This is not a Hollywood movie."

"You've had a lot of experience with serial killers, haven't you?"

"More than most," Smith said. "And none of the ones I've seen wet their beds when they were kids. None of them liked to torture animals, and apart from the sickos who had a thing for setting stuff on fire, there was no pyromaniac tendencies in them."

"You're not familiar with the concept of a podcast, are you?" Dr Sweetman asked.

"I know the basics," Smith admitted. "It's not posted live until you're sure that it's polished enough, and the comments are only turned on then."

"Think of it like a TV series. The most successful podcasts are broadcast in episodes. You need to keep the viewers hooked, and you don't give them all the information at once. It's not unlike a crime thriller where the writer holds the readers' attention by keeping them guessing."

"This is real life, Dr Sweetman," Smith said.

"Please, call me Vanessa."

"I prefer Dr Sweetman. It's clear that we have very different agendas here. I'm not interested in ratings and entertainment value – my goal is to use this to inform this sick fuck that we're onto him. We know how he abducts them, and we know why he's doing it."

Dr Sweetman nodded.

"And I'm not planning on making the public wait to hear this," Smith said.

"I understand that absolutely."

"There's a strong possibility that the psycho the city has dubbed *The Optician* will subscribe to the podcast," Smith said.

"I'm hoping that he will."

"And he'll be waiting to see the reaction to his actions," Smith said. "I get the impression that he wants his work seen. He needs it to be acknowledged and that's precisely what I'm hoping to do tonight."

"Be very careful."

"Why would you say that?"

"I'm not just a podcast queen," Dr Sweetman said. "I also happen to be a psychologist, and it's possible you'll trigger him, and that could have devastating consequences."

"He's going to kill again. Of that there is little doubt. Time is running out, and I'm only here because I know he'll want to hear what we have to say about him."

"OK," Dr Sweetman said. "Let's agree on a compromise. You do your thing and let me do mine."

"I don't even know what that means," Smith said.

Doubts were starting to creep in, and he wondered if this was the right thing to do. He wasn't sure if Dr Sweetman's podcast was the way forward and he told her as much.

"This can benefit us both," she said. "I get some sensational content, and you get to say your thing."

"No," Smith said. "This isn't going to work."

Dr Sweetman fixed her eyes on him and Smith detected a flicker of anger in them.

"The podcast is going ahead, regardless of what you think, Detective Sergeant."

"Well, I won't be in it," Smith told her.

"That's unfortunate."

"I'm sorry you've had a wasted trip," Smith said.

"Wasted trip?"

"Do you need a lift somewhere?"

"I'm not going anywhere," Dr Sweetman said. "I've been personally invited here tonight by your boss."

"Superintendent Smyth?"

"That's the one."

"That public-school amoeba isn't a boss's arse," Smith said.

"I got that impression too," Dr Sweetman said. "But, as I said the podcast is happening, and if you won't be a part of it, I know a public-school amoeba who will be more than happy to fill your shoes."

CHAPTER TWENTY SEVEN

Smith wasn't happy. He felt like he'd been tricked. Dr Sweetman had put him in an impossible position and the ultimatum she'd issued wasn't a pleasant one. He had a choice: Either he joins the beautiful celebrity psychologist in front of the camera or Superintendent Smyth does, and the latter option wasn't worth thinking about.

He had twenty minutes to prepare himself and he was outside in the car park smoking his third cigarette in the space of fifteen minutes. He'd received seven phone calls in that time, and he'd ignored six of them. They were numbers not stored in his contacts' list and he assumed they were journalists. The other call had come from Whitton, wishing him luck. She'd also informed him that she wouldn't be watching. Her dad had taken another turn for the worse and she'd gone round to see him.

Smith wondered how long it would be before he would have no choice but to get proper care. Harold had made it known that he wasn't going to die in a hospital room, but it was becoming increasingly clear that it was the only option. He was in permanent pain, and he needed to be in a hospital. Palliative care, Smith recalled that's what it was called and the concept made him shiver.

"They're almost ready for you, Sarge."
DC King's voice sliced the unpleasant thoughts in two.
"I'll just finish this cigarette," Smith told her.
"Dr Sweetman wanted me to ask you if you'd like her makeup guy to have a go at you beforehand."
Smith raised an eyebrow. "What do you reckon?"
"I don't think there's enough time," DC King dared. "You've only got five minutes."
Smith started to laugh. "You're dead right there, Kerry."

He finished the cigarette and went back inside the station.

The small conference room had been transformed. The table where they'd spent hours discussing the ins and outs of countless murder investigations had been pushed against one of the walls and it made the room seem much bigger than it was. Smith glanced at the whiteboard at the back, and he was relieved to see that someone had covered it with a dirty sheet. The information written on it wasn't something Smith wanted broadcast far and wide.

Dr Sweetman was seated in the corner of the room opposite the whiteboard. Smith assumed the empty chair next to her was where he was going to sit. A huge man with a tattooed scalp was applying the final touches of makeup to the celebrity psychologist's face, and the woman in charge of the camera looked like she was running though some final quality checks. Smith took a deep breath and walked over to them.

"Is there any way to dim the lights a bit?" the camera operator asked.
"God knows," Smith said. "I only work here."
The makeup artist turned around and looked up at the ceiling. The room was lit by a number of fluorescent lights in a row. The tattooed man picked up a chair and positioned it underneath the closest light to the makeshift stage that had been set up. Smith watched as he stood on the chair, removed the outer cover and unscrewed something on the side of the light fitting. The lighting in the room changed immediately.

"That's better," the camera operator said.
Her voice was deeper than Smith's, and he was sure there was a growth of beard on her chin.
"Don't panic," the makeup man said. "I just removed the starter. I'll put it back when we're finished. That glare was oppressive. You could do with a bit of slap before we're ready to roll."
"Are you talking to me?" Smith said.

"I can apply some subtle concealer. It'll do wonders for the bags under your eyes."

"I'm good thanks," Smith said. "Can we get started?"

The camera operator explained that she wanted to check the sound levels from the two microphones. She asked Smith to say anything that came into his head. He sat down and leaned closer to the microphone.

"Rock 'n roll ain't noise pollution."

He didn't know why the classic ACDC track had come to him.

"You don't need to be so close to the mic," the camera woman told him. "They're sensitive."

Smith moved back and repeated the words.

"Better."

The camera operator nodded and informed them that she would start filming in five seconds. Dr Sweetman donned a pair of glasses and brushed a loose strand of hair from her face. The countdown began and Smith focused on the lens of the camera. The light below it changed from red to green and Dr Sweetman began with a brief introduction.

"Tonight, we have a special treat," she said afterwards. "None other than Detective Sergeant Jason Smith has agreed to join me. Unless you've been in outer space for the past decade, you'll probably know who he is. DS Smith, how many murderers have you caught?"

Smith hadn't anticipated this question.

"My team has a good track record," he said.

"Is it not true that you have a hundred percent clear up rate?"

"Something like that," Smith said.

"Are you confident you'll keep that track record going with the man everyone is talking about?"

She didn't wait for Smith to reply.

"*The Optician* has captured the imagination of the entire city," Dr Sweetman said. "Why do you think that is?"

"People have always been fascinated by the macabre," Smith said.

"Interesting answer, but I agree. We as a species love a good dose of evil as much as we like a feelgood story. Life loves a tragedy, as it were."

"To answer your first question," Smith said. "Yes, I believe we will catch this sick individual. He's no different to any other twisted killer, and he will make a mistake that will cost him. They all do."

"Any comments on that are most welcome," Dr Sweetman said to the camera. "What do you think, people? Is *The Optician* just any old serial killer, or is there something special about him?"

"He's not special," Smith said. "He's a killer who preys on women. If you're watching out there, I hate to inform you that it's all been done before. There is nothing original about you."

"The majority of comments from the initial podcast suggests otherwise."

"The people who made those comments have been given bum information," Smith said.

"Would you care you give them something more then?" Dr Sweetman said. "Something straight from the horse's mouth as it were."

Smith turned his head slightly, so he was looking straight at the camera. His eyes were burning for some reason, and he had a sudden urge to close them. He blinked a few times and refocused on the eye of the lens.

"The killer the people of this city are calling *The Optician* is not a sad, lonely loser. He may or may not live alone, and he is by no means someone of below average intelligence. He's driven and he's focused and everything he's done so far suggests a highly organised individual."

"A moment ago, you commented on his lack of originality," Dr Sweetman pointed out.

"And I meant it. He's nothing special. He watches women for a long time – beautiful women, and he waits until the perfect time before he moves in."

"I believe you have a theory about how he abducts his victims," Dr Sweetman said.

"It's more than a theory," Smith said. "We know how he does it. He monitors the Uber database. It's likely he's seen his victims using Ubers in the past, and he waits for them to book a car. He poses as an Uber driver, and the women don't suspect a thing. And I'm advising women not to travel in Uber cars alone. Make life difficult for him."

"Do you believe that this will stop him?" Dr Sweetman asked.

"No," Smith said without thinking. "I don't think it will stop him, but it will cause him to take a step back to consider his options. That will take time."

"If he's out there somewhere, watching this, is there anything you'd like to say to him?"

"I'll tell him face to face," Smith said. "I'll tell him everything I need to tell him when he's in handcuffs."

Dr Sweetman smiled.

"That feels like an opportune time to wrap this podcast up," she said. "DS Smith and I will be back the same time tomorrow with more."

"That wasn't what we discussed," Smith said.

"Detective Sergeant Smith believes he knows the story behind the mutilation of their eyes," Dr Sweetman said. "Until next time. Stay warm and stay safe. To the women out there - travel in packs and stay away from Uber taxis."

CHAPTER TWENTY EIGHT

"What the fuck are you playing at?" Smith asked when the camera was switched off.

"He's a lively one, isn't he?" It was the makeup artist. "I like him."

"He's a natural," the camera operator added. "He was born to be clickbait."

"What's your game?" Smith said to Dr Sweetman. "I told you this was a one-off thing. There is no way in hell I'm doing this again tomorrow."

"Take a chill pill, Sherlock," the tattooed makeup man said. "We're just taking a break."

"Dr Sweetman told the viewers that the next one would be out tomorrow."

"That's true," Dr Sweetman said. "This one will be aired shortly, and the next instalment will be the same time tomorrow, but we'll record it after a short break tonight. Go and smoke a cigarette. You look like you need one."

Smith didn't need to be asked twice. He was out of the room and down the corridor in a flash. DC King had to run to catch up with him.

"Was it that bad?" she said.

"She thinks this is some kind of reality TV, Kerry," Smith said. "She's turning it into entertainment for fuck's sake."

"It's what people want to watch these days. It's sad but it's true."

"This world just gets sicker and sicker."

"Was it really that bad?"

"I don't appreciate being kept in the dark," Smith said. "And her entourage look like they've been allowed out on day release from the circus. I really need a smoke."

It was bitterly cold when he went outside but he was glad. His face felt flushed, and his eyes were still burning. He dreaded to think how he'd looked on the podcast.

"Did you get to talk about the Uber thing and why he does that to their eyes?" DC King said.

"I warned women about getting in an Uber alone," Smith said. "But apparently the violation of the eyes is scheduled for part two. Can you believe she's serialising the fucking thing? Keeping her audience guessing."

"Don't take it too personally, Sarge," DC King said. "It's what she does – it's her job, and she has a huge enough following to be able to get away with it."

Something suddenly occurred to Smith. In the heat of the moment, in front of the camera he'd neglected to mention the make and model of the vehicle that Gemma London got into outside *The French Connection*. He wasn't a big car enthusiast, and the name of the vehicle eluded him now.

"Kerry," he said. "Could you get hold of Harry and ask him about the car that drove away with Gemma London in it on Wednesday night?"

"Will do, Sarge," DC King said and took out her phone.

* * *

"I need you to record an addendum of sorts for the podcast we just did," Smith told Dr Sweetman back in the small conference room.

"It's too late for that," she informed him. "It's already been edited and put out there for the world to see."

"Can't you add to it?"

"Where's the fun in that?" Dr Sweetman said.

"I forgot to mention something important," Smith told her. "And this is not supposed to be fun. The lives of the women in this city are at risk. This isn't some kind of reality TV show. We know the make, model and colour of the car that one of the victims was taken away in, and I need to advertise the fact. This is not a fucking joke – more women are going to die."

"Calm down. Give Graham the details."

"Who's Graham?"

"He's my tech guru."

A man sitting in front of a laptop raised his hand. Smith hadn't noticed him before.

Smith gave him the details of the vehicle, and his response surprised him. It took no longer than three minutes to find a photograph of a similar vehicle and post it online, directly linked to the podcast. Smith thanked him and returned to the chair next to Dr Sweetman. Her makeup artist was applying some fresh war paint.

"Happy now?" Dr Sweetman said.

"I'll be happy when this nutjob is caught," Smith said.

"Are you ready for round two?"

"I don't suppose you'll change your mind and air this immediately after filming?"

"No chance," Dr Sweetman said. "You make your living out of catching psychopaths – I make mine doing things like this. It'll be broadcast at the same time tomorrow. The first podcast attracted over a hundred thousand views, and the one we filmed this evening has topped that in less than an hour. This thing is huge."

"I'm glad you see it like that," Smith said. "Can we get this over and done with?"

Dr Sweetman began with a similar introduction to the one before, and the first topic she brought up dealt with the details of what had been done to the victims' eyes.

"Why does he do that?" she asked Smith.

"I'm not going to discuss the gruesome details," he said. "I'll focus on the reasoning behind it. We believe that he wants them to see. He wants them to look deep inside themselves."

"He removes their eyes, and he replaces them, doesn't he?"

Smith glared at Dr Sweetman. He'd purposefully omitted this bit.

"He does," he admitted.

"He replaces their eyes so they're facing inwards," Dr Sweetman said. "And you believe the purpose of this is to enable them to see inside themselves. Interesting theory. Could you elaborate?"

"There isn't much more to say on the subject," Smith said. "He wants them to see themselves from the inside out, and not the other way round. He's sending out a message."

"What's the tone of that message?"

"Appearances are superficial."

"That's very deep."

"What he does is symbolic," Smith carried on. "They're not able to see, literally, but this is the reason he does it."

"In a nutshell then," Dr Sweetman said. "It's a variation on the old adage – beauty is only skin deep."

"That's a crude comparison," Smith said. "But yes, that's the message he's trying to get across."

Dr Sweetman turned to face the camera again. "I'll look forward to your comments on this."

"I think I've said everything I wanted to say," Smith said.

In truth, he couldn't wait to get out of there. He was planning on getting a bit drunk when he got home. If there was ever a time that he needed a drink, that time was now.

"Just one more thing," Dr Sweetman said.

"That's my line," Smith told her.

"It's actually Columbo's line."

"I've been working on a new one," Smith said.

"You've touched on the reasoning behind his actions, but we've yet to discuss his motivation. Surely, he doesn't violate their eyes simply to show them that their beauty is superficial. There must be more to it than that. What's his motive?"

Smith didn't reply straight away. He knew that Dr Sweetman was right – there was a lot more to the actions of *The Optician* than they knew about, but right now the motive was proving to be elusive.
He looked at the camera. "We're going to find out. It's only a matter of time before we figure out his motive, and when we do, it's going to lead us straight to him."
"Those are brave words," Dr Sweetman said.
"It's the truth," Smith said. "We're going to catch *The Optician* – that's a promise."

The podcast was wrapped up five minutes later. Smith had never felt so relieved in his life. Dr Sweetman didn't linger. She explained that she still had a lot of work ahead of her, and she would prefer to do that work in the comfort of her own house.

"Thank you for agreeing to this," she said by the front desk.
"You didn't give me much choice," Smith said. "It was either me or the Super, and that would have been disastrous."
"You did OK in there," Dr Sweetman said. "You really are a natural."
"I'd rather not be."

Dr Sweetman's phone beeped.
"That will be my ride," she said without bothering to read the message. "I'd like it very much if we crossed paths again."
"You never know," Smith said. "I'm heading home myself."
He opened the door for her and a blast of icy air blew in. A black car was parked right outside the entrance. Smith watched as Dr Sweetman got in the passenger side. She closed the door and the car drove off. If Smith knew anything about vehicles, he would see that the car was a VW Passat. It was

the Business model TDi, and there was a scratch on the rear right-side fender.

CHAPTER TWENTY NINE

Whitton was still not home when Smith got back. He made a beeline straight for the kitchen and took two beers out of the fridge. He drained one of the bottles in one go and opened the second one. He sat down at the kitchen table and ran his hands through his hair.

"You were great tonight."
It was Lucy. Smith didn't even realise she was there.
"What are you doing here?"
"Mum had to go to her parents'. You really were good in that podcast."
Smith took a sip of beer. "I don't know about that. Dr Sweetman didn't take it seriously at all. She's supposed to be a medical professional, but she came across as more of a reality TV host. The world's gone mad."
"It certainly has," Lucy said.
"How did you even watch it? I thought you had to subscribe."
"I have a YouTube account."
"How does she make any money out of it?"
"Plenty of ways," Lucy said. "There are ads every thirty seconds, and the next instalment is a pay per view only thing."
"I wouldn't bother," Smith said. "I can give you the gist of it in two minutes, without annoying advert interruptions."

"Mum has been gone for ages," Lucy said. "Do you think her dad is OK?"
Smith sighed. "He's going downhill fast. I don't think he has long left."
"Laura is taking it badly. I found her in her room earlier, crying her eyes out."
"Laura hardly ever cries," Smith said.

"I know, and when I asked her what was wrong, she told me to leave her alone. She's close to Harold, isn't she?"

"They have a special bond. She's his first grandchild, and he adores her. The feeling's mutual. Where is she now?"

"She said she was going to bed, but I keep hearing her up there."

"I'll go and speak to her," Smith said. "Thanks for looking after the girls."

"They're my little sisters," Lucy said. "I'm here anytime for them."

She wrapped her arms around him, and it took him by surprise. She broke the embrace and took a step back.

"What was that for?" he said.

"You looked like you needed it," Lucy said.

"Thank you."

"I'll see you tomorrow," Lucy said.

After she was gone, Smith got another beer from the fridge and went outside to smoke a cigarette. He wondered what time Whitton would be home. She hadn't let him know how things were going, and he knew that it meant things weren't going well. Harold's fate was already sealed, and even though they'd known for some time that he didn't have long left, his death was going to leave a gaping hole in their lives. Whitton was an only child, and she'd always been close to her mum and dad, and Smith wasn't sure what it was going to be like without Harold around.

His thoughts turned to the podcast. It had been unpleasant, and Smith had hated every minute of it, and he hoped that some good would come of it. He knew that *The Optician* would watch the Podcast – he wouldn't be able to help himself, but Smith didn't know what his reaction would be. Would he retaliate by taking another victim soon? Smith didn't think so. *The Optician* was working to a carefully thought-out plan – his victims had already been chosen, and Smith didn't believe he would deviate from that plan because of a sensationalist Podcast.

He finished the cigarette and went upstairs. He paused for a moment outside Laura's room and opened the door. The light was on inside, and Laura was on her bed, facing the wall.

"Sweetheart," Smith said. "Are you awake?"

Laura didn't reply.

"Are you sleeping?"

Laura turned to face him. Her eyes were red and puffy, and her cheeks were smudged with dry tears.

"That's a silly question."

"I'm full of them," Smith said.

"There's only one possible answer," Laura said.

"And what would that be?"

"No," Laura replied. "Obviously. Because how can someone reply *yes*? It would be a lie, because you can't have a conversation if you're sleeping, can you?"

"You're a lot smarter than me," Smith said. "Are you OK?"

Laura turned back to face the wall.

Smith got on the bed next to her. "Shift up."

Laura obliged by shuffling over a few inches.

"The front of your head is much easier to talk to than the back," Smith told her.

Laura compromised by turning her head ninety degrees, so she was facing the ceiling.

"You're sad about Granddad," Smith said.

He got a nod in reply.

"It's OK to be sad," Smith said. "It's going to be strange without him around."

A tear formed in the corner of Laura's eye. "I don't want him to die."

"Me neither," Smith said. "He's a special man. And we're all going to miss him."

"Mum wouldn't let me go with her. There's no school tomorrow, so why couldn't I go with her?"

"He's your Granddad," Smith explained. "But he's Mum's dad. And she's very sad."

"I'm sad too."

"I know you are," Smith said. "Mum knows that too, but she needs some time alone with Harold right now."

"Can I go and see him tomorrow?"

"I'm sure we can sort something out," Smith said. "He might have to go to hospital for a bit."

"He doesn't want to."

"Did he tell you that?"

Laura nodded. "He tells me all sorts of stuff. He let me have some of his beer too."

"Did he now?" Smith said.

"It tasted yuck."

"It's an acquired taste."

"Why do people have to die?" Laura said.

Smith had no idea how to answer that.

"Fran's real mum died," Laura said. "Lucy's real mum and dad are dead. Why can't people live forever?"

"That's how life works, sweetheart. It's sad but that's just how it is. And think how many people there would be in the world if nobody died. We wouldn't be able to move for people."

"It would be OK if all the bad people died, but the good ones should be able to live forever."

Smith couldn't argue with that.

"We'll be right," he said. "It's terribly sad that Granddad has to die, but you have to hold onto the good times you had with him. And Nanna is going to need more hugs than normal."

"Can I go and live with Nanna?"

"You can stay over sometimes," Smith said. "How about that?"

"That's what's called a compromise," Laura told him. "We learned about it at school."

"You get some sleep now. And have lots of sweet dreams."

"I'm going to dream about Granddad," Laura said.

"Don't you be drinking beer in that dream."

"Why would I do that? It's yucky."

"Fair enough," Smith said. "Night night."

CHAPTER THIRTY

When Smith woke up the next morning, Whitton's side of the bed was cold, and it was clear that it hadn't been slept in. Smith got up, dressed and did what he needed to do in the bathroom. The doors to Laura's and Fran's rooms were closed and the house was silent. Smith decided to let the girls sleep a bit longer.

The explanation for Whitton's absence was in a lengthy message on his phone that Smith hadn't seen the night before. She told him she was spending the night at her parents' place. Her dad was refusing to budge, and her mum was distraught. Harold was in a lot of pain, but he was sticking to his guns. He was not going to live out his final days in a hospital bed.

Smith smiled. This was typical of Harold, and he wondered whether his mind could be changed. He made some coffee and brought up the number for DI Smyth. The boss answered straight away, and Smith explained Whitton's situation. He didn't have to ask if she could have some time off – DI Smyth gave it to her without hesitation.

The next call was to Whitton. Smith thought she sounded tired when she answered the phone.

"Are you alright?" he asked.

"I didn't sleep much," she said. "Neither did Mum. We did shifts by Dad's bedside. He's going downhill fast."

"I'm sorry," Smith said. "He needs to be in hospital, and I never thought I'd ever say that."

"We all know that but try convincing a stubborn Yorkshireman. He's behaving like a toddler, and I don't know what to do."

"The boss is aware of what's happening," Smith said. "And he said you can take as much time off as you need."

"What about the investigation?"

"This is more important. I'm sorry I can't be there with you."

"You're better off at work," Whitton said. "Catch this bastard."

"I'm planning to," Smith said. "I'd better go. I love you."

"I love you too."

Laura made an appearance ten minutes later. Her pyjama top was on back to front, and Smith took this as a good sign.

"Do you want some breakfast?" he asked.

"Where's Mum?" Laura said.

"She's at Nanna and Granddad's."

"Can I go and see him?"

"I don't see why not," Smith said. "He's very sick, so he needs to rest a lot more than he used to but I'm sure he'll be happy to see you."

"I made him a card."

"He'll love that. I tell you what – if you and Fran can be ready in ten minutes, I'll drop you off there on my way to work."

Smith had never seen Laura move so quickly. He could hear her footsteps as she raced upstairs and soon afterwards, he heard her yelling at Fran to get up.

* * *

He knew that something had happened as soon as he set foot inside the station. There was something in the atmosphere in there – something electric. Baldwin was manning the front desk. She was talking to someone on the phone. She ended the call, but the phone started to ring immediately afterwards. Smith thought she seemed stressed. She held up her hand to indicate that she wanted to talk to him and he waited as she told the person on the other end of the line that she didn't have any information at this time. She ended the call and left the phone off the hook.

"I know I shouldn't really do that, but I need a bloody break. That thing hasn't stopped ringing since I arrived."

"What's happened?" Smith said.

"Where do I begin?" Baldwin said. "A young woman has been reported missing by her boyfriend. She left for an appointment at a modelling agency yesterday afternoon, and she didn't come home."

"Do you think there's anything to it?" Smith asked.

"I get the feeling that there is. She's a model and she booked an Uber to take her to the agency."

"Fuck it," Smith said.

"That's not the worst thing, Sarge," Baldwin said. "She's not the only one who's been reported missing. Another woman has disappeared into thin air, and you're not going to like this."

"I don't like it already," Smith said.

"It's your celebrity shrink, Sarge. Dr Vanessa Sweetman has gone missing. That's what all the phone calls have been about."

"You can't be serious?"

"I'm afraid I am. This is bad."

"You can say that again. Is the boss in yet?"

"He was here first thing," Baldwin said.

"I'd better go and see him then," Smith said. "It's going to be a long, shitty day – I can feel it."

DI Smyth was in the small conference room with DC Moore. The room had been put back to normal after the podcast and the first thing Smith noticed was the two new names on the whiteboard.

"Morning," he said. "How sure are we about those two?"

He pointed to the board.

"The boyfriend of Rachel Gold is pretty cut up, Sarge," DC Moore said. "He said that she would have told him if something had come up, and she wasn't able to come home."

"Rachel Gold," Smith repeated. "Why does that name ring a bell?"

"We've got a few decent photographs of her," DI Smyth said. "Another supermodel type, and the fact that she booked an Uber to take her to the modelling agency means we have to take it seriously."

"I agree," Smith said. "Where have I seen her name before?"

"It'll come to you," DI Smyth said. "And then we have the headache that is Dr Sweetman. Somehow, the press has got wind of the fact that the celebrity psychologist was last seen right here in this room."

"I couldn't give a fuck about the press, boss."

"You should," DI Smyth said. "Because this is not good. It's possible that you were the last person to speak to her. Talk me through what happened last night."

"It was a circus," Smith said. "That's what happened. Dr Sweetman is nothing more than a glorified reality show host. She cares about ratings and nothing else. I wouldn't be surprised if this is just another publicity stunt of hers."

"We need to take it seriously."

"I'm going to focus on the other one if that's alright with you."

"It's not alright with me. Dr Sweetman has gone missing and it's our job to investigate it."

"You came across as a bit macho in the podcast, Sarge," DC Moore said out of the blue.

"What?" Smith said.

"All that big talk about bringing *The Optician* down. It was a bit over the top."

"Bullshit. I spoke my mind."

"Have you read the comments?" DC Moore said.

"Why would I want to do that?"

"I suggest you take a look. You're not the most popular bloke right now."

"I didn't realise that I'd entered a popularity contest."

"You're getting a lot of stick, Sarge," DC Moore said.

"Tell someone who cares."

"A lot of the comments are hinting that you're partly to blame for Dr Sweetman's abduction."

"We don't even know if she's been abducted."

"Come on, Sarge," DC Moore said. "She disappeared right after the podcast with you. The general consensus is that you all but dared *The Optician* to take her. I'd watch your back if I were you."

"Fuck that," Smith said. "I'm going to look at Rachel Gold's disappearance. Someone else can deal with the celebrity shrink. I promise you – she's set this up herself to boost her ratings."

CHAPTER THIRTY ONE

"Look at me."
The woman strapped to the bed wasn't looking at anything. Her deep brown eyes were open but the expression in them was blank.
"You don't remember me, do you?"
There was a flicker of something in the eyes now, and the woman managed to blink.

"Soon, you'll understand. And because you're the one most responsible for making me what I am today, I'm not going to give you the anaesthetic. You're going to experience pain like you could never imagine. It will hurt – it will hurt a lot."
"I..." That was as far as she got.

She gasped as fingers surrounded her left eyeball. Something was stuffed inside her mouth and the scream that she let out when the eyeball was popped out of its socket was muffled. The process was repeated with the right eye, and the woman felt an intense burn inside her eye sockets.

She was still able to see, and the sensation was disturbing. She could see blurred closeups of the fingers of her abductor as they played with and prodded her eyeballs. A hard flick caused her to stop breathing for a few seconds.

"Do you remember yet?"
The woman managed a shake of her head.
"Le Havre 2015. What about now?"

The woman trawled her memory bank, but she could find nothing to explain this.

"Gemma." The voice had changed. It was deeper somehow.
"Casey, Rachel and you. What about now?"
The woman froze.

"Now, the real pain starts. I'm going to enjoy this a lot more than you are."

The woman was dead less than an hour later, but before her heart stopped beating, she experienced unbelievable pain. For forty-five minutes she was taken to hell, and she stayed there. There was burning, stinging and an intense ache that throbbed and shook her entire being. She'd never wanted to die but she wished for death now. The end couldn't come quickly enough.

Shortly before it did the woman was aware of three words – three words that she would take with her on her final journey.

"Do you see?"

* * *

Smith was racking his brain trying to figure out why Rachel Gold's name seemed familiar. He was sure that he'd heard it during the course of the investigation, but he couldn't recall when that was. He was on his way to the house Rachel shared with her boyfriend and he hoped that Wayne Lively would be able to shed some light on things.

"Do you think Dr Sweetman has really staged her own abduction?" DC King asked.

They were two miles away from Bootham.

"I wouldn't put it past her," Smith said. "A publicity stunt like that is right up her alley. I imagine her ratings will be going through the roof right now."

"It doesn't make sense though," DC King said. "It was her boyfriend that raised the alarm, and that means he's either been kept in the dark about her plan or they're in it together."

"She's a cold-hearted woman, and I wouldn't put anything past her."

"Do you think this one's genuine?" DC King said. "Rachel Gold, I mean?"

"I've got a terrible feeling that she's dead," Smith said. "She's a model and she was picked up in an Uber. It's not looking good for Rachel. Shit."

"What is it?"

"Get hold of Harry now," Smith said.

"What's wrong?"

"Get hold of Harry and tell him to look at the CCTV footage from the camera over the front entrance of the station. We finished filming the podcasts at just after eight, so tell him to check the footage after that. Dr Sweetman was picked up in a black car. I can't remember what kind of car it was, but we need to see if it was an Uber."

DC King called DC Moore and relayed the message.

"If it was *The Optician* who picked her up," she said afterwards. "It's a bit brazen, isn't it – abducting a victim outside a police station?"

"He's not subtle, Kerry," Smith said. "Nothing he's done so far has displayed one ounce of subtlety."

"If it does turn out that she was abducted outside the station, things are going to get even worse for you."

"Don't I know it. People already think I'm responsible for the abduction, and this is going to make things ten times worse. I watched that car drive away with Dr Sweetman in it."

"Perhaps we should keep that bit quiet, Sarge."

"It might be a good idea," Smith agreed. "What's the address again?"

Wayne Lively wasn't what Smith was expecting. He'd imagined the boyfriend of a model to be model material too, but the man who opened the door of the house in Bootham looked more like a computer geek. His hair looked like it had never been brushed, and he was wearing glasses with thick black frames. Smith explained who they were, and they were invited in.

"Do you have any news about Rachel?" he asked in the living room.

"Not yet," Smith said. "Can you go through Rachel's movements yesterday. What time was her appointment with the modelling agency?"

"Half-two," Wayne said.

"Do you know when the appointment was made?" DC King asked.

"Last week sometime."

"What's the name of the agency?" Smith said.

"Something to do with a face," Wayne said. "*Face of the Future*, that's it."

"Do you know if she made the appointment herself?" DC King said.

"I haven't checked."

"That's fine," Smith said. "We can do that. *Face of the Future*, you say?"

Wayne nodded. "It's a pretty crap name for a modelling agency."

"Is it possible that Rachel hooked up with some friends?" Smith said. "Perhaps she got the gig at the agency and went out to celebrate."

"She would have told me," Wayne said. "Although..."

"What?" Smith said.

"We didn't exactly part company on good terms. I said some things I'm going to regret if something's happened to her."

"We don't know that anything has happened," DC King said.

"In the majority of cases like this," Smith said. "The person reported missing shows up soon after the report has been made. There's usually a perfectly reasonable explanation for their disappearance. Have you contacted Rachel's family and friends?"

"I called a few of her friends," Wayne said. "I didn't want to worry her family yet, especially with all the talk of *The Optician*. He's taken her, hasn't he?"

"It's too early to jump to conclusions," DC King said.

"When did Rachel book the Uber?" Smith asked.

"Two days ago," Wayne said.

"Two days ago?" Smith said.

"I know – it's a bit weird, but she wanted to make sure she didn't miss the appointment. This is important to her."

"Do you know if Rachel knew Gemma London or Casey Plant?" Smith asked.

"I don't recognise the names."

"Does she have a Facebook profile?"

"Of course."

"I assume you and Rachel are friends on Facebook," Smith said.

"We are, yes."

"Could you log in now please."

"What for?"

"Please," Smith said. "Humour me – there's something I need to check."

It came back to him now. He remembered where he'd seen Rachel Gold's name. It was on the list of James Norton's friends on Facebook. And he also knew that if this was confirmed, and Rachel Gold did turn up dead somewhere, the owner of *The French Connection* was friends with all three victims of *The Optician* and that was something that couldn't be ignored.

CHAPTER THIRTY TWO

"James Norton is being picked up as we speak."
DI Smyth looked exhausted. It was clear that he hadn't had much sleep in the past few days. Smith knew that he was getting heat from above and he didn't envy him. Top brass were putting pressure on him and it was taking its toll. The disappearance of Dr Sweetman hadn't helped matters. If Smith were to check the comments on the podcast, he would see that he was officially public enemy number one in the city.

"Will he be arrested?" DC Moore asked.
"No," DI Smyth said. "He's being brought in for questioning. Mr Norton was acquainted with all three victims and that's suspicious."
Smith raised his hand. "Rachel Gold isn't officially a victim, boss. She's disappeared, but until we find her dead body, we can't afford to label her one of *The Optician's* victims."
"Since when did you raise your hand to offer your opinion?" DI Smyth said.
"I thought it was only polite."
"Do you believe that Rachel is still alive?"
"Nope. She's dead."
"What was the point of the comment then?" Bridge wondered.
"I was just thinking out loud again," Smith said.
"There is something seriously wrong with your brain."
"Thank you. Carry on."

DI Smyth let out a long sigh. "Harry. Could you give us a rundown of the CCTV footage from the camera over the entrance to the station."
"It's bad news, sir," DC Moore said. "Very bad news. I can confirm that the vehicle that picked Dr Sweetman up last night was a black VW Passat SE. It's the business model TDi and it's identical to the one that Gemma London got into outside *The French Connection*. This is not good."

"Was it posing as an Uber?" Smith asked.

"There was nothing advertising the fact on the vehicle, Sarge."

"Shit," Smith said. "I warned women not to get into Uber cars, and the bastard was watching. He removed the stickers."

"This sheds some doubt on your staged abduction theory, doesn't it?" DC King said.

"What did Dr Sweetman's boyfriend have to say?" Smith said.

"He seemed genuinely concerned," DC Moore said. "I didn't get the impression that he was party to the staging of a cover up."

"Was he aware of her schedule?" Smith said. "Did he know that she would be getting picked up?"

"We only had a brief chat," DC Moore said.

"That will be a question we'll put to him when we speak to him again," DI Smyth said. "Among others. Did Dr Sweetman mention anything to you about how she was getting home?"

"Her phone beeped," Smith said. "And she said it was her lift without bothering to check. That strikes me as a bit weird."

"It is a bit strange," DI Smyth agreed.

"Is there any way we can check her phone log?" DC King said.

"That will take time," Smith said. "And we don't have time. If she has been taken by *The Optician,* we're already too late, but something about her abduction is bugging me."

"Here we go," Bridge said.

"If we're assuming that Rachel Gold is the third victim of *The Optician*, then she has something in common with the first two. Rachel is twenty-one. Gemma London was also twenty-one and Casey Plant was about to turn twenty-one. They were all roughly the same age, but Dr Sweetman is almost ten years older than them. She doesn't fit the profile of the victims."

"Perhaps the age isn't important," DC Moore said.

"I think it is. We've got three women. All of them were incredibly beautiful, and all of them were the same age. We can't ignore that fact."

"Nothing we've found so far suggests they were acquainted," DI Smyth pointed out.

"I'm aware of that, boss," Smith said. "But it's bothering me."

"Right," DI Smyth said. "This is the plan of action for today. Smith, I assume you'll want to interview James Norton?"

"Does the Pope shit in the woods?" Smith said.

DC Moore stared at him. "That's just wrong, Sarge."

Smith shrugged his shoulders.

"You and Kerry can tackle that then," DI Smyth said to him. "Bridge, I want you and Harry to see if you can retrace Rachel Gold's movements. We know that she left for the modelling agency at around two yesterday afternoon. Find out if she made the appointment."

"*Face of the Future*," Smith said. "That's the name of the agency."

"Got it," Bridge said.

"I've got the pleasure of a meeting with the important people in the building," DI Smyth said.

"Important people, my arse," Smith said. "If they were so important, they wouldn't insist on wasting our time with pointless meetings."

"It is what it is. See what James Norton has to say for himself, and then I want you to pay a visit to Dr Sweetman's boyfriend."

"With pleasure, boss," Smith said. "There's something dodgy about the celebrity shrink's disappearance. It all feels a bit convenient to me."

"We can't ignore the car she was taken away in."

"I appreciate that."

"We also need to question the other people involved in the podcasts," DI Smyth said.

"A bunch of circus freaks," Smith said. "A giant tattooed makeup artist, a bearded woman behind the camera and a geek called Graham who deals with the tech stuff, and who also has the ability to make himself invisible."

"They sound lovely," Bridge said. "Me and Harry will talk to them when we're finished at the modelling agency. I wonder if they're hiring."

"It's called *Face of the Future*, mate," Smith reminded him. "That face of yours is at least a decade and a half too late."

"Jealousy doesn't suit you."

"I'm just saying how it is."

"I'm not the one knocking on for forty," Bridge said.

"That's enough," DI Smyth said. "There's work to be done."

CHAPTER THIRTY THREE

James Norton arrived with his lawyer in tow and Smith had anticipated it. James's legal representation was a middle-aged man with peculiar eyes. His left eye didn't move. It stared straight ahead and there was no sign of life in it. Smith wondered if it was made out of glass. The right eye wasn't much more active, and the overall effect was somewhat disconcerting. Within two minutes of being introduced, Smith couldn't bring himself to look into the eyes of Daniel Peters.

After going through the motions for the tape Smith asked James Norton if he understood why he was there.
"I've advised my client to answer all questions as best as he can," Daniel said.
"Could you let him do that please?" Smith said. "We don't have time to mess around."
"What was the question again?" James asked.
"Do you understand why you're here?" Smith said.
"You think I had something to do with the murder of Gemma," James said.
"Considering the fact that you've just referred to her by her first name only, and you earlier didn't think it was important to mention that she worked for you, I reckon we have reasonable grounds for suspicion, don't you agree?"
"I told you," James said. "A lot of people work for me. I own a lot of businesses in the city."
"Is it usual for you not to know who works for you?" DC King asked.
"Is this line of questioning relevant?" Daniel Peters said.
"It's extremely relevant," Smith said. "We don't waste time on irrelevant questions. Mr Norton, do you have a Facebook account?"
"It's not illegal, is it?" James said.
"Please answer the question," DC King said.

"I have a Facebook account. It's a useful forum for advertising purposes."

"And is that what you use it for?" Smith said.

"Mostly."

"Do you have many friends?"

"Where is this going?" Daniel said.

"James," Smith said. "Do you have a lot of friends on Facebook?"

"A few," James said.

"How are you acquainted with Casey Plant?"

"I don't think I am."

"You're friends with her on Facebook," DC King said.

"Is that what this is all about?" James said. "I heard about what happened to her, but I had nothing to do with it. And before you say anything, I *am* friends with Casey on Facebook, but we've never met. It's not uncommon to have friends on social media without ever meeting them face to face. You must know that."

Smith didn't really understand this. He had a Facebook account, but he rarely logged on, and when he thought about it, he realised that he had very few friends on there and most of them were now deceased.

"Why did you befriend Casey?" he asked. "If you've never met."

"She asked me, if I recall correctly," James said. "It probably had something to do with one of my businesses."

"Does that happen a lot?" DC King said.

"I get a lot of friend requests from people wanting freebies and special treatment at the bars and clubs I'm involved in. I also get requests from people looking for work. I own a lot of other businesses too. Look, I didn't touch either of those women."

"Do you own a vehicle?" Smith said.

"What?"

"Do you own a car?"

"Of course, I do. Who doesn't?"

"What kind of car is it?" DC King said.

"I have a Mercedes C Class," James said. "And a little runaround – a Hyundai."

"We're going to need to check that," Smith said.

"Feel free."

"Where were you yesterday afternoon?" Smith said. "Between two and three?"

"I was at the pub," James said.

"*The French Connection*?" DC King said.

"It's the only pub I own."

"You just mentioned bars," Smith said. "As in plural."

"I'm part owner of a couple of others," James said. "But I don't play much of an active role in them anymore."

"What about the nightclubs?" DC King said.

"Same story."

"Which nightclubs are you invested in?" Smith said.

"I own half of *The Parker* in Holgate and I'm also a shareholder in *Blast* in South Bank."

"Interesting," Smith said.

"It's not as glamorous as you think."

"That's not what I meant. Casey Plant was last seen at *Blast*. I've been doing this for a long time and I'm sensing something a bit off about you, Mr Norton. There are far too many connections to you and the dead women for my liking. Does the name Rachel Gold ring any bells?"

"It sounds familiar."

"Could you think hard," DC King said. "Rachel Gold. We know that you and Rachel are friends on Facebook."

"She's a model," Smith said.

"There you go then," James said. "That's probably where I know her from."

"I'm not following you," Smith said.

"I told you I have a lot of business interests in the city. If Rachel is a model, she probably sent me a friend request as something to do with the modelling agency I set up."

Smith didn't think this could get any more bizarre. He really didn't want to hear the answer to his next question, but he knew he had to ask it, nevertheless.

"What's the name of the modelling agency?"

"*En Vogue*," James said.

CHAPTER THIRTY FOUR

"You really thought he was going to say *Face of the Future*, didn't you?" DC King asked afterwards.

"Didn't you?" Smith said.

"I suppose I did, but surely, he can't be involved in every aspect of the dead women's lives. That would be too much to ask for."

"Do you think he's *The Optician*?"

"I really don't know. What about you? Is James Norton *The Optician*?"

"No," Smith said without thinking. "He doesn't fit the profile."

"Do we even have a profile of him?"

"It's a hypothetical one," Smith explained. "And James Norton doesn't tick any of the boxes. We're dealing with a highly intelligent, driven individual who works to a specific agenda. He's abducted and killed two women, probably three, and he hasn't made a single mistake."

"James Norton is a successful businessman, Sarge," DC King said. "He's obviously not stupid."

"He's not a serial killer, Kerry. I don't claim to be able to spot one a mile away, but I know for sure that James Norton isn't one."

Smith flicked on the indicator and pulled away from the kerb.

"Where are we going?" DC King said.

"Something connects those women," Smith said. "I don't know what it is, but I'm going to find out."

"Nothing we've learned about them so far suggests that they're connected."

"We haven't been looking in the right places," Smith said. "Those women were not selected at random – there is something that ties them together and when we discover what that is, it's going to lead us straight to *The Optician*."

The doors to *The French Connection* were open when they got there. It was early afternoon, and music could be heard from within.

"DS Bridge and the DI were just here," DC King reminded Smith.

"It can't hurt to ask a few more questions."

"Do you think James Norton will be here?" DC King said.

"I couldn't care less if he is," Smith said. "There is something about this place – something we've failed to notice, and I want to see if anything comes to me now. Is it too early for a beer?"

"We're on duty, Sarge."

"I was pulling your leg, Kerry."

Smith realised what the music was when they went inside. It was an old Led Zeppelin song, and he wondered why a pub with a French Connection theme would be playing it. There were a few people gathered around the bar but very few of the tables were occupied. The woman they'd spoken to on Thursday was behind the bar. Smith walked over and got her attention. Once again, her face was plastered with makeup. Smith wondered why she needed to slap it on so thick.

"What can I get you?" she asked.

Smith took out his ID.

"I was kidding," the woman said. "I remember you. I spoke to a couple of detectives not long ago."

"We just have a few more questions," DC King said.

"Could we have a word?" Smith said. "It's Hailey, isn't it?"

"Close. Holly."

"Could we have a word, Holly?"

"Sure. I was just about to take a break anyway. We can talk in the back. I'll just get Paul to cover the bar."

"Is Mr Norton here?" Smith asked in the room at the back of the bar.

"I thought he was with you lot," Holly said.

"He told you about that?" DC King said.

"He said he'd been asked to come in for questioning."

"Did he tell you why that was?" Smith said.

Holly shook her head. "I imagine it's something to do with *The Optician*."

"Why would you think that?" Smith said.

"Because I've been following the news on social media. Both women were in here shortly before they were taken."

"You got that information from social media?" Smith said.

"I think it was on some Twitter posts. Do you think Mr Norton had something to do with their murders?"

"We can't go into that," Smith said. "When we spoke to you briefly on Thursday you told us that you remembered Gemma London because she was hard to forget."

"You know the type," Holly said. "Gorgeous and fully aware of it. I suppose you can't blame her – if you've got it, flaunt it, and the blokes were lapping it up."

"You also said that she didn't appear to hook up with anyone in particular."

"Oh, she had a lot of takers," Holly said. "There was drool all over the floor by the time she left, but I don't think she left with any of her admirers."

"How long have you worked here?" Smith asked.

"Since the place opened," Holly said. "Which was precisely three days ago."

"Where did you work before?" DC King said.

"I was the assistant bar manager at another one of Mr Norton's pubs. The one in Rowntree Park."

"Have you worked for Mr Norton long?" Smith asked.

"About a year. I worked at *The Norton* part time. That's the pub in Rowntree Park. I finished the third year of my degree last year, and I'm taking a year out to save some money before I resume my studies."

"What are you studying?"

"Dentistry. I was allowed to defer."

"You're the bar manager here?" Smith said.

"It makes me sound more important than I am. Mr Norton trusts me, and he was impressed with my work ethic at *The Norton*. He's aware that I'll be resuming my studies in September."

Smith decided to take a wild stab in the dark.

"Do you know a woman called Rachel Gold?"

"I don't think so," Holly said.

"Mr Norton is friends with her on Facebook," DC King said.

"Mr Norton is friends with a lot of young women on Facebook. He runs a modelling agency."

"I didn't say that she was young," Smith said.

"Is she dead?"

"Why would you think that?" Smith said.

"You're a detective sergeant," Holly said. "You're here because you're investigating the murders of two young woman. I suppose I just assumed."

"Have you sorted the CCTV cameras out yet?" Smith said.

"That's not my department," Holly said. "Mr Norton has a guy who deals with that kind of thing."

"I think we've covered everything," Smith said. "I like the music you play in here."

Another Led Zeppelin song was playing. It was one of Smith's favourites.

"No Quarter," Holly said. "You've got good taste in music."

"It doesn't really go with the theme of the pub though."

"I get to play what I like when Mr Norton isn't here," Holly said. "And the customers seem to dig it."

"What does Mr Norton play?" DC King said.

"Mostly morbid old French crap," Holly said.

"Sounds lovely," Smith said.

"Hardly. I don't think anything lovely has ever come out of France. I have to get back. I hope you catch him. I hope you catch *The Optician*."

"We will," Smith said. "It may take a bit of time, but we will catch him."

CHAPTER THIRTY FIVE

Bridge was feeling a bit depressed. It only took a quick glance at the photographs on the wall in the reception area of *Face of the Future* to come to the miserable conclusion that Smith had been right. He was at least a decade older than most of the faces on display here. He'd always considered himself a decent looking bloke, but that was as far as it went. He was never going to get paid for his looks. The fresh smiles and flawless skin in the photographs made that abundantly clear.

"Can I help you?" a woman who looked to be in her mid-twenties enquired.

Bridge took out his ID and explained the nature of the visit.

"We're all still in shock about Rachel."

The woman introduced herself as Belinda. She didn't offer a surname.

"I'm the primary agent here," she added. "We were all so excited about Rachel. Her portfolio showed real promise."

"Is there somewhere we can talk in private?" Bridge said.

"Come through to my office," Belinda said.

"We'll try not to take up too much of your time," DC Moore said.

"I can spare an hour."

"We'll be out of your hair before then," Bridge promised.

There were more photographs on the walls inside the small office. Belinda offered them something to drink.

"Coffee, if it's not too much trouble," Bridge said.

"No trouble at all." Belinda studied his face. "You have an interesting bone structure."

Bridge didn't know what to make of this.

Belinda made the coffee and sat down opposite them at the desk.

"What did you mean when you said you're still in shock about Rachel?" Bridge said.

"I saw something on Facebook – something about her disappearance," Belinda said. "And when you phoned earlier, I put two and two together."

"We still don't know what's happened to her," Bridge said. "It's possible there's a perfectly reasonable explanation for her disappearance."

"You don't really believe that do you? I know very little about police procedure when people are reported missing, but I do know that you don't put in so much effort after such a short time has passed. And the whole city is talking about *The Optician*."

"Do you know Rachel?"

Bridge opted to talk about her in the present tense for the time being, for what it was worth.

"I never met her in person," Belinda said. "Only via email. Like I said, we were very excited about her."

"Forgive me my ignorance," Bridge said. "But how exactly do modelling agencies work? Do you have talent scouts who go out looking for future supermodels?"

Belinda laughed. "That's a fallacy. Something dreamed up in Hollywood. In reality, fewer than one percent of one percent of models are discovered." She emphasised the last word by making some imaginary speech marks with her fingers.

"We have a list of clients," she continued. "We deal with fashion brands, photographers, record companies and basically anyone who is on the lookout for a face to fit their brand."

"What does the agency do for the model?" DC Moore asked.

"We aim to fit the model to the client. We negotiate the terms of the contracts, and we manage the bookings and the test shoots. It's an intensive procedure."

"And you take a cut?" DC Moore said.

"Nobody works for free," Belinda said.

"I believe there's another modelling agency in the city." Bridge said.

"There are a few," Belinda said.

"*En Vogue*," Bridge said. "It's owned by James Norton."

"I know it well. In fact, I worked there for a short while."

"Why did you leave?" DC Moore asked.

"I wasn't happy there."

"What did you think of Mr Norton?" Bridge said.

"Mr Norton had very little to do with the day-to-day operations," Belinda said. "Which is probably for the best."

"Can you elaborate on that?"

"I'm not one to speak out of turn, and I'd appreciate it if this went no further."

"You have my word," Bridge said.

"I get the impression that Mr Norton has fashioned himself on some kind of Godfather of glamour. He sees himself as a variation on the Stringfellow image, but those days are long gone. Women are infinitely more empowered these days."

"You're not a big fan of James Norton then?" DC Moore said.

"To be honest, I feel sorry for him. Money does not make you a man."

"I couldn't agree more," Bridge said. "How did Rachel hear about the agency?"

"It could have been through one of the advertising platforms, or it might have been word of mouth. Do you think she's dead?"

Bridge didn't reply to this.

"How many models do you have on your books?" he asked instead.

"Around fifty," Belinda said. "Our clients are diverse, and we aim to offer them plenty of options."

"I'm not following you."

"Modelling comes in many shapes and sizes. One day we might be involved in a shoot that requires a particular pair of eyes, and then we may have a client who needs a model with horse riding experience."

"I didn't realise how much was involved," Bridge said. "I thought it was just a matter of sticking a pretty face in front of a camera."

"Have you heard of Irving Penn?"

"I can't say I have," Bridge said.

"He was a fashion photographer who rose to fame in the 1950s. He was renowned for his minimalistic studio approach, but often he would spend hours getting the optimal shot."

"He sounds a bit anal," DC Moore offered.

"He was a perfectionist," Belinda said. "And he was in high demand. Modelling is not for the faint hearted, and it's probably the only profession where there is a gender gap leaning towards the woman. On average, women earn fifty percent more than men."

"I have no problem with that," Bridge said.

"You're a modern man, I see."

"Not at all," Bridge said. "I'm a Yorkshireman, through and through, but I'd much rather look at the pretty face of a woman in a magazine than the mug of some bloke."

This earned him a smile.

"Did you ever cross paths with Gemma London and Casey Plant?" he asked.

"The first two victims of *The Optician*?" Belinda said.

"They were beautiful young women," Bridge said. "Did they ever come to the agency?"

"No. I never met them. He's going to carry on, isn't he? He's going to keep on killing beautiful women?"

"We can't comment on that."

"Beauty is not skin deep. You do understand that."

"I've never really thought about it," Bridge said.

"Think about it now," Belinda said. "Everything I've seen so far about this Optician has painted a very ugly picture of beauty. People are making out as though it is something only shallow, vain women are gifted with. That's simply not true."

"I think we've taken up enough of your time," DC Moore said.

"*The Optician* is greatly misinformed," Belinda said. "I deal with beauty on a daily basis, and I can tell you with absolute honesty that he's wrong. People are people, whatever they look like on the outside. Plain people can be vile – fat people can be vindictive; there isn't one size fits all where appearance and personality are concerned."

Bridge didn't feel like getting involved in this kind of debate.

He got to his feet to indicate that the discussion was over.

"Thank you for your time."

Belinda stood up too. "I'm sorry. I'm rather emotional right now. Social media is crucifying this industry and the people in it. We are not bad people."

"I'm sure you aren't."

"You're not listening," Belinda said. "You don't realise how much damage this is doing, and all of it is based on misinformation. They're all wrong - every single one of them."

CHAPTER THIRTY SIX

"She was a few cans short of a six-pack, wasn't she?" DC Moore commented as they drove away from the modelling agency.

"She was definitely passionate about the modelling industry," Bridge said.

"All that talk about beauty not being just skin deep. Who does she think she's kidding?"

"She was right about one thing though," Bridge said. "The general consensus on social media is that beautiful women get more attention than ugly ones, and they're right. As soon as Gemma London's and Casey Plant's photos were out there, emotions started to run high. I don't like it."

"I thought you were a big fan of pretty women, Sarge."

"That's not what I meant. All this debate about the value we put in appearances is not doing us any favours – it's muddying the investigation, and it's pissing me off."

"Where to now?"

"If the trolls on social media are to be believed," Bridge said. "We're going to speak to some more superficial human beings."

"Dr Sweetman's entourage?" DC Moore guessed.

"Got it in one."

They were less than halfway to their destination when Bridge's phone started to ring.

"It's Smith," DC Moore informed him.

"Answer it then," Bridge said. "Stick it on speaker."

DC Moore obliged.

"Where are you?" Smith said.

"En route to the celebrity shrink's team," Bridge said. "Something's happened, hasn't it?"

"Rachel Gold has been found."

Bridge sighed. "She's dead, isn't she?"

Smith replied in the affirmative and gave them the location.

"Damn it," Bridge said.

"We expected it, didn't we?" DC Moore said.

"He's like a bloody machine," Bridge said.

He turned right onto Tang Hall Lane.

"He abducts them, carries out the operations on their eyes, kills them and dumps them. All in the space of twenty-four-hours."

"He's planned it carefully."

"That's obvious. How the hell does he do it though?"

"The podcast is going to make life hard for him," DC Moore said. "Women have been warned about Ubers."

"That didn't help Dr Sweetman, did it? The celebrity shrink was taken right outside the bloody station."

The rest of the drive to Heworth passed in silence. Bridge was visibly upset, and DC Moore knew better than to make small talk. Smith had told them that Rachel Gold's body had been found by a family out for a walk in the woods adjacent to Heworth Community Park. It took no time at all to determine that the woman was definitely Rachel. Her name was written on every single one of the photographs that had been found around her body. The photos were from her portfolio – and it confirmed that she'd been on her way to the modelling agency when she was abducted.

Bridge parked next to Smith's Sierra, and he and DC Moore got out of the car and made their way towards the crowd of people gathered behind the goalposts at the far end of the football field. Smith approached them before they got there.

"Is it definitely her?" Bridge asked.

"No doubt about it," Smith said. "We might get lucky with the photos. They weren't just thrown on top of her – he pinned them to the ground around her body, and it's possible he's left prints."

"Why would he do that?" DC Moore said.

"It could be he didn't want the wind to blow them away," Smith said. "He wanted us to see his display – some kind of before and after effect."

"Who is this sick bastard?" Bridge said.

"He's no sicker than any other serial killer," Smith said. "Keep remembering that. He's no different to any of the ones we've caught before."

DC King walked over to them.

"Webber wants you to come and have a look at something, Sarge," she said to Smith.

"Why couldn't he have told me that before?" Smith said. "I've just taken off the SOC suit, and I can't get rid of the itch. It feels like I've been rolling in a bunch of bluebottle jellyfish on the beach."

"Do you want me to piss on you?" Bridge said. "I've heard that works."

"You'd love that, wouldn't you? And that only works for stonefish, you wombat."

"You two are seriously weird," DC Moore said.

"Come on," Bridge said. "Let's go and talk to the family who found her."

Smith squeezed himself into another SOC suit and went to see what Webber had found. The Head of Forensics was standing next to a row of trees ten metres away from the woman on the ground. Smith avoided looking at her. He would do that later.

"What is it?" he asked Webber.

"What do you make of this?" Webber nodded to something attached to one of the lower branches of the tree.

"It looks like a bit of cloth," Smith said.

The fabric was bright red, and it was difficult to miss.

"It could have come from anywhere," Smith said.

"I don't think it did," Webber said.

"People come and go in here all the time. The park is open to the public. Someone could have brushed up against the tree and tore a piece of clothing on it."

"I tried to do precisely that," Webber said. "These are beech trees. The bark is as smooth as a baby's bottom, and there is no way a piece of cloth that thick could get snagged on that branch without some help. And look at the shape of the fabric."

Smith humoured him. Webber was right – the branch was not only smooth, but it also looked like someone had sharpened the end of it to a point. The piece of red cloth had been skewered dead centre.

"I see what you mean about how the cloth has been pierced," he said. "But I have no idea about the shape of it."

"Someone has cut it to that shape," Webber said. "It's a perfect reproduction of the outline of the map of France."

CHAPTER THIRTY SEVEN

"Do you think *The Optician* could be French?" DC Moore was the first to speak at the afternoon briefing.
"How sure is Webber that the piece of material was left there recently?" DI Smyth said.
"He's sure," Smith said. "It rained last night, and the fabric was bone dry. The bark on the beech trees was still damp. When Webber gets a feeling about something it's important to listen to him."
"I agree," Bridge said. "But what are we going to get from a piece of fabric cut into the shape of the map of France? How is this connected to any of the victims?"
"You've just said it," Smith said.
"The French Connection," DC King said.
"You can't be serious?" It was DC Moore.
"It's worth looking into," Smith said.
"That is the most ridiculous connection I've ever heard of. You're clutching at straws."

"Let's say, for argument's sake that there is something to the map of France," DI Smyth said. "What purpose does it serve? Is *The Optician* giving us a clue? Is he giving us a helping hand here?"
"It's not unheard of, boss," Smith said. "Many serial killers have been known to become frustrated with the progress law enforcement are making. Perhaps he's pissed off that the real reason for the murders of the women hasn't been touched on yet – he's not getting the notoriety he seeks, and he's doing something about that. Maybe we're not working quickly enough for his liking. That French map is significant. Webber believes so, and therefore, so do I. Hold on..."
"I wish you wouldn't keep doing that," Bridge said.

Without offering any explanation, Smith took out his phone and tapped out a quick message. He put the phone on the table and remained silent.

"What was that about?" DI Smyth said.

"Gemma London was wearing a bright red shirt when she was abducted, boss," Smith said. "I'm sure it's the same material as the fabric found on the tree close to where Rachel Gold was found."

"Webber would have picked up on it if it was," Bridge said.

"Not necessarily."

Smith's phone beeped and he snatched it up. The message he'd sent was to Dr Bean. Smith had asked the Head of Pathology if he'd noticed anything odd about Gemma's shirt and the peculiar pathologist had replied in the affirmative. A section of Gemma's shirt had been cut out. There was little doubt now that Rachel Gold was the third victim of *The Optician*. Smith told the team as much.

"He left that fabric there for a reason," he said. "He used some material from Gemma London's shirt to send out a message about France."

"What is the message though?" Bridge said.

"Beats me, but there is something there."

"We'll come back to that," DI Smyth said. "We have a number of other matters to discuss. There are only six black VW Passat SEs registered in the city. Of course, it is possible that the vehicle that *The Optician* was driving is from further afield, but we'll focus on the local cars first. I've tasked a team of uniforms with that job, and we should have something before the end of the day."

"I think he'll have parted company with that car as soon as the podcast was aired," Smith said.

"After he abducted the pretty celebrity shrink in it right outside the station, you mean?" DC Moore said.

"Are you deliberately trying to wind me up, Harry?"

"I was just making an observation, Sarge."

"Lose the sarcasm next time," Smith said. "Southerners aren't very good at it."

"I was just…"

"Enough," DI Smyth said. "Moving on."

"We didn't get much from the modelling agency," Bridge said. "Apart from an education in how the industry works and a social commentary from the head agent, we came away with nothing useful."

"Social commentary?" Smith said.

"You should have heard her, mate," Bridge said. "She reckons the uproar on social media about *The Optician* is damaging the modelling industry. She tried to convince us that models can be good people too, and she thinks I've got an interesting bone structure."

"It sounds like her eyesight is even worse than mine. And how can a series of brutal murders possibly damage the modelling industry? I'd say the opposite is the case. It's a notoriously fickle business, and publicity is king. They're getting plenty of that, aren't they?"

"Speaking of which," DI Smyth said. "There is still no sign of Dr Sweetman. The celebrity psychologist is proving to be elusive. There has been no communication on her mobile phone, and nothing on her social media. It doesn't look promising."

"If she is dead," Smith said. "If she is the fourth victim of *The Optician* her body will be found tomorrow."

"He works quickly, doesn't he?" DC King said.

"Like clockwork, Kerry. He abducts them, does his thing with their eyes, kills them and dumps them, all in the space of twenty-four hours. And that makes me wonder about Dr Sweetman. There's something wrong with the timing."

"Not this again," Bridge said.

"If we analyse that timeline," Smith carried on, nevertheless. "We know that Rachel Gold was intercepted outside her house. She got into an Uber just after two yesterday afternoon and that was the last time she was seen. She was discovered less than a day later, which means she was mutilated and killed sometime yesterday or in the early hours of this morning. Dr Sweetman got into an Uber at just after eight last night. If she is one of his victims, it means there's a timeline overlap."

"What's your point, Sarge?" DC Moore said.

"My point is this," Smith said. "I think he's feeling the heat. He's deviating from his original plan and that might help us."

"If he's feeling pressured, there's more chance of him making a mistake," DC King said.

"Right. And he took a big chance in taking Dr Sweetman before he was finished with Rachel Gold."

"Where does he take them?" Bridge wondered. "Is it worth working on a geographical profile?"

"It's worth a shot," Smith said. "We know where the victims were abducted and we know where they ended up, and it's possible that the place where he operates on them is somewhere in between, but I doubt it's that simple. So far, the final resting places of his victims have appeared to be random. There's no logic to them, from a symbolism perspective. A sports village, an abandoned golf club and a community park. I can't see any connection there, and I can also think of plenty of better places to dump a few bodies in the city."

"He seems to know how we operate," DI Smyth said.

"Don't they all?" Bridge said. "Detective thrillers are a bloody curse. Anyone who subscribes to Netflix can get a detailed lesson in what not to do at a crime scene if you want to get away with murder."

Smith walked up to the whiteboard at the back of the room. He rubbed his chin as he looked at the names of three of the four women listed on the lefthand side. These women were alive last week – their hearts beat as they always had, and none of them were aware that in the space of a few days, they would cease to exist. Smith's eyes fell on the fourth name on the list. Dr Vanessa Sweetman. Where did she fit into this elaborate puzzle?

Then he looked back at his colleagues.

"What if?" he said.

"What if what?" DC Moore said.

"I think we've been looking at this all wrong," Smith said. "What if the answer we've been looking for has been staring us in the face the entire time?"

"I can't see anything staring me in the face, Sarge," DC Moore said.

"What if." Smith tapped his finger on the fourth name on the list. "What if Dr Sweetman is *The Optician*?"

CHAPTER THIRTY EIGHT

"I've heard some fanciful ideas come out of that gob of yours over the years," Bridge said to Smith. "But this one has to take first prize. Did you not sleep last night?"
"I slept perfectly well," Smith said. "Think about it and keep an open mind. What does the celebrity shrink desire more than anything else in the world? Fame and attention. She just happened to appear on the scene when all of this shit started to happen."
"It was the Super who invited her to the party," Bridge reminded him.
"Was it though? What if she contacted *him*?"
"You need to stop with your *what ifs*. It's not helping."
"Get hold of the boss," Smith said. "Find out exactly how Dr Sweetman ended up filming her Podcast at the station."
"I'm going to sound like a prat," Bridge said. "You call him."
"I'm the one that's driving."
"There is such a thing as hand's free."
"Phone the DI and find out," Smith said. "Please."

They were halfway to the address they'd been given for Ronnie Higgins. Ronnie was the tattooed makeup artist Smith had met shortly before the Podcast. DI Smyth had wanted Bridge and DC Moore to speak to the owners of the VW Passats, but Smith had insisted that Bridge go with him to the makeup artist's house, and he hadn't taken no for an answer.

"The DI said he'll find out," Bridge said. "You're wrong about this, you know."
"Where is she?" Smith said. "Where has the celebrity shrink disappeared to?"

"I thought we were presuming she's the fourth victim of *The Optician*," Bridge said. "She was last seen getting into a black VW Passat. What more do you need?"

"What if the car was the same one that Gemma London was picked up by?" Smith said. "But what if it's actually Dr Sweetman's car?"

"You're doing it again with your *what ifs*. We have the list of the Passat owners, and Dr Sweetman's name isn't on it."

"I want this bastard," Smith said. "I really want to nail this fucker."

"We all do," Bridge said. "And we will catch him. This is like old times, isn't it?"

Smith didn't comment. His eyes were focused on the road ahead, but his mind was miles away.

Ronnie Higgins lived in a terraced house two streets away from the old football ground. Smith was forced to park fifty metres down the road.

"Parking in this city is a nightmare," Bridge said. "There are far too many cars on the road these days."

They got out of the car.

"How are we going to play this?" Bridge asked.

"We'll have Ronnie think we're working on the assumption that Dr Sweetman has been abducted by *The Optician*," Smith said. "See if he lets anything slip."

"Do you think he could be in on the fake disappearance?"

"It's possible. She went missing straight after the podcast, and I don't think she will have been able to pull that off without a bit of help."

Ronnie Higgins opened the door wearing a pink dressing gown, and Bridge took a step back.

"Boo!" Ronnie said.

"Mr Higgins," Smith said. "Can we have a word?"

"Call me Ronnie."

"We're not interrupting anything, are we?" Smith said.

"I was just making some breakfast."

"At two in the afternoon?" Bridge said.

"I had a late night," Ronnie said. "You'd better come in."

The smell of bacon filled the house, and it reminded Smith that he hadn't eaten anything all day.

"Do you want some?" Ronnie asked.

"No thanks," Smith said, even though he was starving.

"Give me a sec. Take a seat in the living room. Excuse the mess."

"I wouldn't like to bump into him in a dark alley," Bridge whispered. "You wouldn't think he was a makeup artist. He looks more like a nightclub bouncer, apart from the pink dressing gown that is."

"You shouldn't judge a book by its cover," Smith said.

"He doesn't seem too bothered by us being here."

"Let's see what he can tell us," Smith said.

Ronnie appeared a few minutes later.

"Sorry about that. I was starving. What can I do for you?"

"How long have you known Dr Sweetman?" Smith asked.

"A couple of years," Ronnie said. "I met her shortly after I got out."

"Got out?" Bridge repeated.

"Prison. Vanessa was one of the few people who gave me a chance. It's not easy to find work with a record. Vanessa isn't like most people – she sees what's inside a person, not what's on file about them."

"What were you inside for?" Smith said.

"Manslaughter," Ronnie said. "Although you'll already know about that, won't you?"

Smith wasn't aware of it, and he should have been. He cursed himself for not knowing about the tattooed makeup artist's criminal record.

"I killed a bloke who was attacking a woman in a club. The bastard was strangling her, and I figured it was either her or him."

"That's rough," Smith said.

"Surely they should have looked at the circumstances," Bridge said.

"I had a lawyer who'd never heard of mitigating circumstances," Ronnie said. "And fair play, I should have stopped smacking the bloke with the wine bottle when he was out cold on the floor, but I didn't. It's all in the past now – I did my nine years, and I've got my life back. And I didn't waste my time inside. Where do you think I learned my craft?"

"You learned about makeup in prison?" Bridge said.

"Don't sound so surprised. You won't believe how many blokes like to slap on a bit of warpaint to brighten up the days inside."

"What do you think has happened to Dr Sweetman?" Smith wasn't interested in correctional services cosmetics courses.

"You tell me," Ronnie said. "She's not answering her phone, and she hasn't posted anything online since the podcast went live last night and that is not like her. Vanessa cannot go more than ten minutes without going online – we often joke about it."

"You joke about it?" Bridge said.

"I told her it's bordering on addiction," Ronnie said. "I said she should maybe psychoanalyse herself to see if she can get to the bottom of it."

"What car does Dr Sweetman drive?" Smith asked.

"She doesn't," Ronnie said. "She doesn't have a license."

"How does she get around?" Bridge said.

"Taxis, mostly. Or she might get a lift with a friend."

"What about you?" Smith said. "Do you have a car?"

"I do. I've got a beat-up old Beetle. She's not pretty but she runs like a dream. Why are you asking about cars?"

"We're just ticking things off a list," Smith said. "We need to ask these questions in missing persons cases."

"Are you treating her as a missing person?"

"A report hasn't been filed," Smith said. "But the fact that she hasn't been in contact with anyone since the podcast last night is concerning. Do you know her boyfriend?"

"Steve? I've met him a few times."

"Do you know what car Steve drives?" Smith said.

"I don't. It's black – that's all I can tell you. I'm not too clued up about cars."

"Can you think of anywhere Dr Sweetman might have gone?" Smith said. "Does she have somewhere she likes to go when she wants some peace and quiet?"

"Vanessa doesn't do peace and quiet," Ronnie said. "She likes chaos and noise. He's taken her, hasn't he? The psycho everyone is calling *The Optician* has taken her."

"We don't know that."

"But that's what you think, isn't it?"

"I want you to be totally honest when you answer my next question," Smith said.

"I'm always honest," Ronnie said. "Lies are for fools."

"I couldn't agree with you more. Is there a chance that Dr Sweetman has faked her own disappearance? Is this something she's capable of?"

"No," Ronnie replied without hesitation. "It is not something she's capable of. Why would she do something like that?"

"Perhaps she wants the publicity. Maybe she's timed her disappearance to coincide with the second instalment of the podcast."

"Absolutely not. Vanessa is all about the ratings, but she wouldn't stoop to that level in order to get them. She doesn't need to – the numbers speak for themselves."

"If you hear from her," Smith said. "I'd like you to give me a call."

He took out one of his cards and placed it on the coffee table.

"Any time," he added.

"Of course."

"Just one more question before we go," Smith said.

"Go on," Ronnie said.

"Do you know if Dr Sweetman was acquainted with Gemma London or Casey Plant?"

"I couldn't tell you," Ronnie said. "I'm there for the makeup – what Vanessa gets up to away from that is nothing to do with me."

"What about Rachel Gold?" Bridge said.

Ronnie's expression changed. There was sadness in his eyes.

"Are you saying that she's been found?"

"I'm afraid so," Bridge said. "Do you know if Dr Sweetman knew Rachel?"

"I really can't help you. You'd be better off speaking to Steve. He lived with her, so he'll be able to answer your questions better than me."

CHAPTER THIRTY NINE

Steve Brown was a tall man with thin arms and legs. He had to be at least six-five, and he reminded Smith of a stick insect. His neck was unusually long, and his eyes were full of suspicion. Smith explained who they were, and he invited them in.

"I've been worried sick," Steve said in the living room. "Do you have any news?"

"It's still early days," Bridge said.

"It's not though, is it? I know that the first twenty-four-hours are crucial in a missing persons case, and we've almost reached that stage already."

"I assume you've tried calling her," Smith said.

"Of course. She's not answering her phone, and she hasn't been seen on WhatsApp since last night, shortly after the podcast went out."

"Do you have any idea where she could be?" Bridge asked.

"What kind of dumb question is that? If I knew where she was, I would go to her. You're not exactly filling me with hope here."

"We appreciate that you're worried," Smith said. "We're going to do everything we can to find Dr Sweetman. The CCTV footage from the camera over the front entrance of the station showed her getting into a black car just after eight last night."

He decided to leave out the fact that he'd watched it drive away.

"We've since learned that the car is a VW Passat. Do you know anybody who drives a car like that?"

"I don't think so," Steve said. "Hold on... That's the same car *The Optician* drives. I saw the thing on the podcast. Are you telling me he took her right under your noses?"

"We don't know that," Bridge said. "Are you sure you don't know anyone who owns that particular make of car?"

"I just told you I didn't."

"What car do you drive?" Smith said.

"It's a Ford Focus. A black one. It's in the garage if you don't believe me."

"That won't be necessary," Smith said.

"He's got her, hasn't he?" Steve said. "Vanessa has been taken by *The Optician*."

"We'll find her," Smith said.

He was still convinced that the celebrity psychologist had staged her own abduction.

"How long have you and Dr Sweetman been together?" he asked.

"Four years," Steve said. "We met at a conference in Paris."

"Are you also a psychologist?" Bridge said.

"Hardly. I'm an otolaryngologist."

"What's that?"

"It is a bit of a tongue twister," Steve said. "ENT surgeon is a bit easier on the lips. Ear, nose and throat."

"You're a surgeon?" Smith said.

"I specialise in the diagnosis and treatment of conditions affecting the ear, nose, throat, head and neck."

"And you and Dr Sweetman met at a conference of surgeons in Paris?" Smith said.

"She wasn't one of the conference delegates," Steve said. "Obviously, but she happened to be in Paris that weekend and we hit it off. What has this got to do with her disappearance?"

"We have to ask all sorts of questions at times like these," Bridge said.

"Do you know if Dr Sweetman is acquainted with Gemma London or Casey Plant?" Smith said.

"The first two victims?" Steve said.

Smith nodded. "Have you ever heard their names before?"

"I don't think so."

"Are you and Dr Sweetman friends on Facebook?" Smith said.

"We are, yes."

"It's possible that she's friends with them on there," Smith said. "Could you check for us please?"

Steve picked up his phone and swiped the screen. It didn't take him long to find what Smith was looking for.

"Vanessa has more than four thousand friends," he said. "But Gemma London and Casey Plant aren't among them."

"What about Rachel Gold," Bridge said.

A quick check confirmed that Dr Sweetman wasn't friends with Rachel either.

Smith thought of something else. It was a long shot, but it was worth a try.

"One more name," he said. "James Norton."

Two seconds later Steve shook his head.

"Who is James Norton?" he said.

"Just someone who has come up during the course of the investigation," Smith said. "It was a bit of a wild stab in the dark."

The phone in Steve's hand started to ring. After a quick glance at the screen, he rejected the call.

"Press," he explained. "They've been phoning non-stop since Vanessa disappeared. I don't even know how they got my number."

"They have their ways," Smith said.

"They're turning it into a soap opera," Steve said. "My girlfriend has gone missing – there's a chance that she's been abducted by a serial killer, and the press is exploiting it. I suppose it's ironic in a way, considering what Vanessa does for a living. Have you seen some of the pages that have sprung up on social media?"

"I don't spend much time on social media," Smith said.

"There's even a page where people can report sightings of her. Can you believe it? There are photographs on there with supposed sightings of Vanessa. Most of them look nothing like her."

"It's the world we live in," Smith said. "Unfortunately. Just a couple more questions. Does Dr Sweetman have somewhere she likes to go for a bit of peace and quiet?"

"Not that I'm aware," Steve said.

"I take a drive across the moors when I need time to think," Smith said.

"Does Dr Sweetman have a place like that?"

"I would know if she had."

"And you can't think of anyone she might have gone to stay with for a bit?" Bridge said. "The buzz around *The Optician* is reaching fever pitch and Dr Sweetman has put herself right in the middle of it with her podcasts. Is it possible she's taking some time out somewhere?"

"That's not her style," Steve said. "She prefers to keep the momentum going, and she loves the limelight. Something terrible has happened to her."

"Did you and Dr Sweetman have plans last night?" Smith said.

"Nothing special," Steve said.

"Could you elaborate on that?"

"We hadn't planned on doing much."

"She doesn't drive, does she?" Bridge said.

"She's never got her license."

"Did she mention anything to you about how she was going to get home after the podcast?" Smith said.

"Probably in a taxi."

"Just before she left," Smith said. "Her phone beeped, and she said that it was her ride. She didn't check to see if it was in fact her lift. Don't you think that's a bit strange?"

"Not really. It sounds like something Vanessa would say. Can't you check her phone records? I thought the police were able to do that these days."

"We can," Smith said. "But it's time consuming."

"What's that supposed to mean?" Steve said. "Aren't you paid to spend time doing everything you can to find someone who has gone missing?"

"That wasn't what my colleague meant, Mr Brown," Bridge said. "Getting phone records from a service provider isn't a quick process. There are procedures that need to be followed, and that can take days, if not weeks."

Smith was ready to wrap things up when his phone beeped to tell him there was a message waiting for him.

"Excuse me," he said.

He checked his phone. It was a message from DI Smyth. The body of a woman had been found close to Clifton Moor. It hadn't yet been confirmed, but the description of the woman matched that of Dr Vanessa Sweetman.

CHAPTER FORTY

Smith's mind was working overtime on the drive to Clifton Moor. He wasn't thinking about Dr Sweetman. Until it was confirmed beyond a shadow of a doubt that the body was the celebrity psychologist's it was pointless dwelling on it, and he compiled a mental list of other things they needed to look at instead.

They hadn't considered who the woman claiming to be Gemma London's housemate was. She'd called herself Hillary Twain and Smith didn't think she'd given her real name, but they hadn't contacted her since the beginning, and they should have done. The fact that she'd given them false information ought to have sounded warning bells, but the team had ignored them and Smith made up his mind to do something about that.

Dr Sweetman's boyfriend was a surgeon. This was extremely interesting, and Smith decided that they needed to take a much closer look at Steve Brown too. He didn't get the impression that Steve had lied to them, but he'd become increasingly aware that people were becoming a lot more adept at deception than they used to be.

"Are you away with the fairies again?"
It took Smith a while to react to Bridge's words.
"What?"
"You were miles away," Bridge said. "I'd offer to drive, but someone might see me behind the wheel of this piece of junk, and it wouldn't be good for my street cred. Besides which, you seem to be doing perfectly well on autopilot. What's on your mind?"
Smith told him and Bridge agreed with him. They still had a lot of loose ends to try to straighten out.

"This case has been full of loose ends," Smith said. "And I hate loose ends."

"Do you think the dead woman is Dr Sweetman?" Bridge said.

"I don't think it's her," Smith said. "I just get a feeling that Dr Sweetman is alive somewhere. She's going to pop up, safe and sound as soon as her popularity has soared high enough for her. It's just a gut feeling."

"That gut of yours is usually pretty reliable," Bridge admitted. "We'll soon find out. And speaking of which, the DI has confirmed that it was Superintendent Smyth who invited Dr Sweetman to the party. Your gut was wrong there."

"You can't win them all," Smith said.

* * *

"And then there was one," DC Moore said.

He and DC King were ticking names off a list. So far, all of the registered owners of Black VW Passat SE Business TDi cars had been ruled out, but there was one owner that was proving to be difficult to locate. Greg Cooper wasn't answering his phone, and when uniforms went to see if he was home, there was no sign of him or his car.

"According to what I can find about him on social media," DC King said. "It looks like he's a doctor."

"He'll probably have access to drugs," DC Moore said. "Worth digging a bit deeper then."

"He doesn't look like a serial killer."

DC King showed her colleague the photographs of Dr Cooper.

He was a middle-aged man with thinning hair. In most of the photographs he was in the shot with two boys who looked to be in their teens.

"Appearances can be deceiving," DC Moore said. "Do we know where he works?"

"City Hospital."

"Do you fancy a drive over there?" DC Moore asked. "I don't know about you, but I could really do with a change of scenery."
"It's worth a shot."
"We'll go in my car."
"Do we have to?"
"You haven't lived until you've experienced the joys of a Subaru BRZ," DC Moore said.
"DS Bridge always moans that it gives him backache for weeks afterwards."
"The DS is getting old."

Fifteen minutes later, DC King was performing stretching exercises in the car park of the hospital. Something cracked in her lower back after one particularly vigorous stretch, and she made a mental note never to get into DC Moore's car ever again.
"That car should come with a health warning," she told him.
"Nonsense. You just have to learn about the right posture. I've been driving her for years, and there's nothing wrong with my vertebrae."

They went inside the hospital and walked up to the front desk. A woman with a nasty cut on her cheek was complaining that she'd been waiting for over two hours. A man behind the desk asked her to take a seat. He assured her that she would be seen as soon as possible.
"It's ridiculous," the woman said. "I pay more taxes than most people. I pay your wages."
"Please," the receptionist said. "Take a seat and someone will attend to you soon."
"That's what you said two hours ago."
"What happened to your face?" DC King asked her.
"I fell up the stairs," the woman said.
The stench of stale alcohol on her breath caused DC King to take a step back.

"You fell *up* the stairs?" she said.

"Smacked my face on a broken bottle I'd forgotten was there. It probably needs stitches, but these idiots don't care. I pay enough in taxes. Do you know how much tax this government slaps on booze these days?"

"I don't," DC King said.

"More than enough to pay for a doctor to fix my fucking face. I don't know why I bother. Perhaps I should stop drinking – that'll teach them, won't it?"

DC King didn't get the chance to reply, and she was glad. DC Moore pulled her aside and told her that he'd found a colleague of Dr Cooper's.

"She was a bit of a live wire, wasn't she?" he said.

"I thought I'd heard everything," DC King said. "She thinks she's a model taxpayer because she drinks like a fish. Where are we going?"

"Apparently Dr Cooper works on the paediatric ward," DC Moore said.

"Do we know if he's here today?"

"That's what I'm hoping to find out," DC Moore said. "The woman I spoke to doesn't know him that well, but she's pointed me in the direction of someone who does."

Larry Wood was the ward manager. He was a gruff man with the air of a sergeant major about him. DC King wondered why he'd chosen to work on a ward dedicated to children.

"Make it quick," he said after they'd explained the nature of their visit.

"We're looking for Dr Greg Cooper," DC Moore said.

"You're not going to find him here."

"I thought he worked here," DC King said.

"He does, but he's not here now."

"Do you know where we can find him?" DC Moore said.

"Try Mauritius," Larry said. "He's on a two-week holiday there with his kids."

"How long has he been away?"

"At least a week. Look, I have a lot to do, so if there's nothing else."

"That's everything," DC King said. "Thank you for your help."
Larry Wood grunted and walked away from them.

"That was a waste of time then," DC Moore said.

"Not at all," DC King argued. "At least we can confirm that Dr Cooper isn't *The Optician*. Hold on…"

"You really need to stop spending so much time with Smith. What is it?"

"Where is his car?"

"The uniforms that went round to his house didn't find a car there," DC Moore said. "Perhaps he left it at the airport."

"Perhaps. It'll be easy to find out."

CHAPTER FORTY ONE

"It's not her."

Smith was smoking a cigarette a few metres away from the outer cordon. DI Smyth had just arrived on the scene.

"It's not Dr Sweetman," Smith said. "There's a slight resemblance, but it's definitely not the celebrity psychologist."

"Do we know who she is?" DI Smyth said.

"I only had a quick look," Smith said. "For once, I got here before the Forensic team, and I didn't want to piss Webber off by disturbing her. It looks to me like she's the same age as the first three – early twenties, and she was probably a stunning looking woman when she was still breathing."

"You really need to work on your descriptive language. Is it definitely the work of *The Optician*?"

Smith nodded and exhaled a large cloud of smoke. "No doubt about it. Her eyes have been mutilated. We'll know more when Webber and the team eventually get here. Where is he, by the way?"

"I have no idea," DI Smyth said.

"It's not like him to be late for a party."

"We've had a breakthrough with the vehicle," DI Smyth said. "Harry and Kerry spoke to the registered owners of all the black VW Passats in the city and after ticking all the names off the list they were left with one - a doctor called Greg Cooper."

"A doctor?"

"Don't get too excited. Dr Cooper has been sunning it in the Indian Ocean since last week."

"How is that a breakthrough?" Smith wondered.

"When uniforms went round to his house, there was no vehicle there and that's because Dr Cooper used it to drive to Leeds Bradford airport."

"It's not there anymore, is it?" Smith said.

"Got it in one. Harry spoke to someone at Leeds Bradford, and Dr Cooper had reserved a space for long stay parking. He booked for two weeks, but the vehicle disappeared on Monday."

"*The Optician* began his killing spree on Wednesday," Smith said.

"I thought you preferred not to call him that."

"It's what everybody else is calling him," Smith said. "If you can't beat 'em, join 'em. We've found the car, haven't we?"

"It looks like it. We're liaising with Leeds Bradford, and it's possible that he was caught on CCTV."

"I thought airport parking was supposed to be ultra secure," Smith said.

"Nothing is ultra secure," DI Smyth said. "Hopefully we'll get lucky with the cameras at the airport. We've got the registration number, but it's possible that he's already dumped the vehicle."

"I'd say that's highly likely."

Their conversation was cut short with the arrival of Grant Webber's Suzuki. Smith watched as the Head of Forensics parked and got out of the car. Billie Jones got out of the passenger side, and their body language told Smith that neither of them were happy. Webber retrieved his bag of tricks from the boot and marched ahead of Billie.

"I'd give them a wide berth," DI Smyth said.

"I agree," Smith said. "Webber looks like he's grumpier than usual, and I'm not in the mood for that right now. I did some thinking on the drive over here. We still have a load of loose ends that need tying up."

"Don't we always?" DI Smyth said.

"We haven't given any more thought to Gemma London's phantom housemate, and we dropped the ball there. Why did she come in and claim to live with Gemma when she must have known we'd find out the truth eventually?"

"She could be a crank," DI Smyth said. "This city is full of them."

"No," Smith said. "The identity of the first victim wasn't common knowledge when she came to report Gemma missing. And she knew exactly what Gemma had been wearing that night."

"Are you suggesting she's involved somehow?"

"I don't know what to think, boss," Smith said. "But her presence at the station so soon after Gemma disappeared is suspicious, and we need to spend more time on it."

"We will. If only to make you happy."

"Dr Sweetman's boyfriend is a surgeon," Smith said.

"What was your impression of him?"

"He didn't strike me as serial killer material, but I have been known to be wrong in the past. He's some kind of ear, nose and throat specialist, and he needs to be considered. He'll have access to drugs, and he'll definitely have the skills necessary to carry out the operations on the victims' eyes."

"What else did you get out of him?" DI Smyth said.

"He believes that Dr Sweetman has been taken. He doesn't think she's staged her own disappearance and he's certain she hasn't just gone away for some peace and quiet. It's not like her. The makeup bloke said the same thing."

Billie Jones walked over to them. She nodded to DI Smyth and gave Smith a smile.

"I've got an ID for you."

"Excellent," DI Smyth said.

"According to the driving license we found in the bag next to her body," Billie said. "Her name is Stacy Ladd and she's twenty-one."

"Same age as the first three," Smith said. "Is there anything else you can tell us about her?"

"It's too early to say, but the level of violence on display is different to the others."

"I only had a quick peek," Smith said.

"Her eyes have been mutilated," Billie said. "But the damage to the surrounding tissue looks more pronounced. Pathology will be able to tell us more, but I don't think he liked this one very much."

"You're stealing my lines, Billie," Smith said.

"I'm just giving you my initial impressions. He showed a certain tenderness with the first three, but he was far from careful with Stacy Ladd. It might not be important."

"It's important," Smith decided. "Perhaps he was interrupted and wasn't able to work in peace."

"Or maybe he really didn't like her," Billie said. "I'd better get back."

"What's wrong with Webber?" Smith asked.

"It's that time of year," Billie said.

"Shit," Smith said. "I'd forgotten all about that."

"Time of year?" DI Smyth said.

"DI Brownhill," Smith explained. "It was around this time that she was murdered. Webber always gets morbid at this time of year."

"He needs to snap out of it," Billie said. "If I didn't like my job so much, I'd tell him the truth."

"Which is?" Smith said.

"It's obvious," Billie said. "He needs to get laid."

CHAPTER FORTY TWO

"Where's the urn?"
If Harold Whitton had the strength to do so, he would have shot up in his bed. As it was, he opened his eyes wide and took a few deep breaths. There was a bad smell inside the room and Harold realised that it was coming from him. He'd woken with such a fright that he'd accidentally expelled some of the gases that had built up in his small intestine.

He'd had the dream again, only this time there had been a slight twist to it. He'd been a witness to his own incineration, and he'd found it oddly fascinating. He'd watched as his body, bones and all had been reduced to nothing more than a pile of soft ash.

The process was more involved than Harold expected it to be. His body was placed inside the cremation chamber and heated to more than nine hundred degrees Celsius. After two hours of intense heat, what remained was cooled and any obnoxious bone fragments were removed. Then the coarse ash was processed into a fine powder. This was transferred to the dreaded urn, ready for the family to take possession of it.

Harold couldn't understand where his subconscious had found the information it needed to produce such a dream, but he imagined he'd watched the cremation process on television sometime and now it was all coming back to him. He wished it wasn't. He wished more than anything for this recurring dream to leave him alone.

The door to the room opened and woke Harold from his reverie. It also resulted in another noxious emission, and he sighed deeply.
It was Whitton. "Did you call out?"
"I was dreaming, love," Harold said. "Sorry about the smell."
Whitton smiled. "I've got a Bull Terrier, Dad. The stench in here is nothing compared to what Theakston is capable of. Are you OK?"

"I'm dying, love. There's no way to sugar coat it – I'm not getting out of this room alive."

"You need to be in a hospital," Whitton said.

"I won't have this conversation again," Harold said. "I won't."

"OK, Dad. I won't mention it again."

"Jason has his birthday next week, doesn't he?"

Whitton wasn't expecting this.

"It's his fortieth. He'll be forty on the fifth."

"Then I'll hold on until after that before I leave this mortal coil," Harold said.

"Dad. Don't talk like that."

"That lad needs one day to call his own," Harold said. "He can't do that at Christmas, so the least I can do is let him have his birthday."

"Please, Dad," Whitton said. "No more of this talk."

"He deserves one day for himself. I won't deny him that."

Before Whitton could argue further her father's eyes closed and she felt a tear in her eye when she realised the expression on his face had changed. She hadn't seen this face for a long time. Her dad looked content. He was breathing calmly, and she was sure he was smiling. More tears came and she needed to leave. She glanced at her dying father once more and left him to his dreams.

* * *

"How's Whitton doing?" DC King asked Smith.

"She's staying strong for her mum," he said. "But it's taking its toll on her. Harold hasn't got long left, and we all know it."

"You and he are close, aren't you?"

"We never used to be," Smith said. "But I suppose we've grown on each other in the past few years."

"My Nan died of cancer," DC King said. "She had it in her lungs. I was in my early teens, but I still remember how it seemed to eat her from the inside out. She was a big woman, but in the end, she weighed no more than a child."

"It's a horrible disease," Smith said.

"I sometimes wonder if it would be better to die in a freak car accident or something like that. Something sudden and unexpected. Knowing that it's going to happen is ten times worse."

"I suppose death is a part of life," Smith said. "Nobody escapes it. I wouldn't mind talking about something else, if that's alright with you."

DC King obliged. "Stacy Ladd also did a lot of modelling. Her social media consists of not much else."

"Those four women are connected somehow," Smith said.

"They were all incredibly beautiful."

"It's something more than that, and I've got a feeling that he's finished."

"*The Optician?*"

"No, Kerry," Smith said. "The Boston Strangler. Sorry, that was uncalled for."

"Apology accepted," DC King said. "Why do you think he's finished?"

"I'm just reading the damage inflicted on the victims. Gemma, Casey and Rachel were all treated tenderly. We know at least two of them were administered drugs during the operations and when Dr Bean has examined Rachel Gold, he'll confirm that she was given anaesthetic too, but Stacy Ladd's injuries look like they were born of fury. He showed no care with her, and that's got me thinking."

"Perhaps he was interrupted."

"That was my first guess too," Smith said. "But he's too careful for that. He carries out the operations on their eyes somewhere private. He makes damn sure that he does not get interrupted."

"How do you explain Stacy's injuries?"

"In one word," Smith said. "Hatred. And if we consider the positioning of her body at Clifton Moor it only reinforces this theory. There was nothing staged about the way she was left there. It's as if the disposal of her body was necessary but that's as far as it goes. She was dumped – literally. Cast aside like a broken toy. *The Optician* really did not like Stacy Ladd."

CHAPTER FORTY THREE

"How are you feeling?"
Dr Vanessa Sweetman couldn't feel anything. Her entire body from her toes to the top of her head was numb. She was also unable to speak.
"The anaesthetic will wear off soon."
Dr Sweetman could hear the voice but there was something wrong with it. Her mind had worked quickly – her situation had been processed and the conclusion that her brain had come to was the only logical one to make – she'd been taken by the man the city had dubbed *The Optician*.

But if that was the case, why was the voice talking to her now the voice of a woman?
"I'm not going to harm you."
Dr Sweetman's mind wasn't playing tricks on her – this was not a side-effect of whatever drugs she'd been given; there was a woman only a few feet away from her. Dr Sweetman could smell her – her scent brought with it a memory that was hidden by mist. She couldn't break through the fog to pinpoint the moment she'd come across the aroma before, but she was sure it had been recent.

"We've got a lot to do."
Dr Sweetman had no idea what she was talking about.
"I'll give you some time to pull yourself together. We want you at your best for this."
Dr Sweetman moistened her lips and tried to find her voice.
"What do you..."
That was as far as she got.
"Shh. You must rest now. I'm not going to harm you."
"Where am I?'
"You're safe. I need your face. I need you wide awake for this."

"I don't understand."

This was an understatement. Dr Sweetman was utterly confused.

"Rest now. I have a story to tell, and I want you to be the one to tell it. Everything is arranged. Soon, you're going to tell the world everything it wants to know about *The Optician*."

* * *

Smith had prepared a list. It was a mental list, and it was somewhat garbled. It was for this reason that he started scribbling on the whiteboard as soon as he entered the small conference room. There were a lot of things to discuss, and he didn't want to leave anything out.

DI Smyth came in with Bridge and DC Moore. DC King arrived shortly afterwards.

"Good news," DI Smyth announced. "The Super's crime stats presentation has been postponed."

"I presume this is a tactical postponement," Smith said.

"You presume correctly," DI Smyth confirmed. "To quote Superintendent Smyth, *this Optician nonsense is severely scuppering my hopes of a whitewash of Jack Jones in Leeds*."

"The man's a buffoon."

"I couldn't agree more."

"When is it happening?" Smith said. "When do we have the pleasure of the presentation?"

"It's been scheduled for a week today."

"A Saturday?" DC Moore said.

"Isn't that your birthday?" Bridge asked Smith.

"It'll be a birthday present I'll look forward to," Smith said. "Can we get down to business? As much as I'd love to talk about Uncle Jeremy's vital statistics all day, I'd prefer to discuss something else."

"I presume this is your doing?" DI Smyth tapped the whiteboard.

"I wanted to write it down while it was fresh in my head," Smith said. "First things first – I've been wondering about the vehicle. We now know that *The Optician* has been using the car belonging to Dr Greg Cooper. The vehicle was parked in the long stay car park at Leeds Bradford airport while Dr Cooper was on holiday in Mauritius. It was stolen on Monday, and I'm wondering if Dr Cooper and *The Optician* are somehow acquainted."

"Do you think he could be involved?" DC Moore said.

"No," Smith said. "He's been sunning it in the Indian Ocean the whole time this has been going on, but the fact that the car was stolen from an airport thirty-odd miles away makes me wonder. Why not steal a car in York?"

"Jurisdiction," DC King suggested.

"It's possible," Smith said. "A car stolen on Leeds's patch wouldn't necessarily come up as flagged in York, but I think there's more to it than that. What if *The Optician* knew that Dr Cooper would be away for a couple of weeks?"

"You're doing your *what if* thing again," Bridge said. "But you could be onto something. Dr Cooper wouldn't be aware that his car had been nicked until he got back, and that gives *The Optician* two weeks of leeway."

"What do we know about Dr Cooper?" DI Smyth said.

"He works on the paediatric ward at City Hospital," Smith said.

"Hundreds of people work at the hospital, Sarge," DC Moore said. "Any one of them could have heard about the doc's holiday."

"True," Smith agreed. "It's a lot to check, but it needs to be done."

"What else do you have on this list of yours?" DI Smyth said. "I can't understand a word of what you've written on there."

"I wrote it in a hurry," Smith said. "Hillary Twain. If that's even her real name. She came here claiming to be Gemma London's housemate and we've subsequently learned that Gemma didn't have a housemate, and she certainly didn't live at the address this phantom housemate gave us. Where does this mystery woman fit into all this?"

"She's not some kind of crank," DI Smyth said. "As Smith has pointed out, she knew about Gemma's disappearance before the news was made public, and she also knew exactly what Gemma was wearing on the night she disappeared."

"Who the hell is she?" Smith said.

"We have a photo of her," DC Moore said. "For what it's worth."

"What about an appeal?" DC King said. "Put her picture out there and ask for more information."

"If she's involved in all of this," Smith said. "She's hardly likely to come forward."

"Put her face out there anyway," DC King said. "Someone must know who she is. We're asking for help in locating her. We don't have to elaborate."

"I hope you're not suggesting a press conference," Smith said.

"I wouldn't dream of it. We've got a decent presence on social media – it's about time we used it to its full potential."

"Good idea. Can you organise that? Speak to the press liaison officer."

"Will do, Sarge."

"Stacy Ladd," Smith said. "She's the fourth victim of *The Optician,* and her murder was very different to the first three in many ways. Her eyes were mutilated, but that's as far as the similarities go. The level of violence on display with her suggests a high degree of fury. To quote the fulsome Billie Jones, *he really did not like this one.*"

Bridge glared at him. "Watch your mouth, mate."

"Take it easy," Smith said. "What's different about Stacy Ladd? Why didn't he like her? It's yet to be confirmed but I know for a fact that Dr Bean won't find any traces of sedatives in Stacy's system. He wanted her to suffer, and we need to ask ourselves why that is. Her body wasn't left on display – it was discarded like a piece of rubbish. Everything about this murder makes me wonder if he's finished."

"How did you come to that conclusion?" Bridge said.

"Just a feeling I get. He wanted them all dead – he needed to carry out the surgeries on their eyes, but Stacy Ladd was the one he wanted to punish most. That's where our focus needs to be right now. Why did he hate Stacy so much?"

The sound of Sting telling people not to stand so close to him interrupted the proceedings. DI Smyth let the classic Police song carry on for some time while he searched for his phone. He eventually found it in the pocket of the jacket on the back of his chair. A quick glance at the screen caused him to get to his feet.

"Carry on," he said and left the room without further explanation.

Soon afterwards the door opened, and PC Neil Walker came in. The press liaison officer looked agitated.

"Sorry to interrupt but I've just received a very concerning email."

He produced a memory stick.

"What's on that?" Smith said.

"Something you all need to watch," PC Walker said. "It was sent anonymously but the content doesn't leave much room for interpretation. Dr Sweetman is scheduled to broadcast a podcast tonight, and from the taster I was sent, she's not doing it voluntarily."

CHAPTER FORTY FOUR

DC Moore set up his laptop so the footage from the memory stick was sent to the screen at the back of the room. He tapped the keypad and a grainy image appeared. The screen grew brighter, and everyone gasped when they realised who was in the film.

"She's bound to a chair," DC King said.

Dr Vanessa Sweetman had seen better days. Without a trace of makeup, the lines on her face made her look older. Her eyes looked tired, and Smith wondered if she'd been drugged. She licked her lips and her eyes looked straight at the camera.

"I have a story to tell."

Her voice sounded different, and Smith was convinced that she'd been drugged with something. Her eyes found something off to the side and the subtle nod of her head and movement of her lips was puzzling. She went on to announce that she would be broadcasting live at 9pm tonight. That was it. There was a brief close-up of her face, and the screen went blank.

"He's there," Smith said. "He's the one filming."

"Bloody hell," Bridge said. "Is there any way to trace the email?"

"I've handed it over to the tech team," PC Walker said. "But I think he used a VPN."

"Untraceable," DC Moore said.

"What about the footage itself," Smith said. "There might be something there to give us a clue about where she is."

There wasn't. The team watched the short film five more times and all they could make out was the celebrity psychologist and the chair she was tied to.

"She could be anywhere in the city," Smith said. "Fuck it."

"Do you think he's going to kill her?" DC Moore said.

"I don't think so," Smith said. "I think he took her for the sole reason of telling his story."

"Why couldn't he just tell it himself?" DC Moore wondered.

"It will have more of an impact coming from the celebrity shrink," Smith said. "I could be wrong."

"And he's just going to let her go afterwards?" Bridge said. "I very much doubt he'll leave her alive now that she's seen his face."

DI Smyth returned to the room.

"I heard about Dr Sweetman. We've got every officer in the city looking for the car."

"He doesn't have the car anymore, boss," Smith said. "He'll have dumped it soon after taking Dr Sweetman."

"What do you think he's got planned for her?"

"He's using her reputation. And her fame. He wants his story told, and he wants the whole world to listen. It's going out at nine tonight, but I don't understand how he plans to advertise the fact. Hold on…"

Bridge cast him a glance, but he remained silent.

"The next instalment of the podcast with me and Dr Sweetman is due to be broadcast at eight this evening," Smith said. "*The Optician* is aware of this, and he's going to air Dr Sweetman telling his sick fuck story straight afterwards."

"I don't think there will be many people in the city who won't be tuning in," Bridge said.

"Not just the city, Sarge," DC Moore said. "This is going to be massive. We've got a celebrity shrink who's been abducted by the serial killer the whole country is talking about. This is incredible content. Her ratings are going to soar."

"I doubt she's going to thank him for it," Bridge said.

"It's getting late," DI Smyth said. "I suggest we all get some rest. We'll reconvene back here first thing."

"We still have a lot to get through," Smith said.

"I've got a suspicion there will be something in *The Optician's* story that will get us closer to catching him," DI Smyth said. "We're all running on fumes, and we need a break."

"I'm not going to argue with that," DC Moore said. "I'll be sure to tune into the broadcast later."

He got up and left the room with Bridge and DC King behind him.

"I want to watch the taster video again," Smith said.

"There's nothing in it," DI Smyth said.

"I think there is. The moment where Dr Sweetman turns to face someone else in the room is bugging me."

"We don't know that there was someone else in the room with her."

"Someone had to film it," Smith said.

"A camera can be set up and operated remotely," DI Smyth pointed out.

"I think he was with her the whole time," Smith said.

"I'm off home."

"What was the phone call about earlier?" Smith asked. "You got up so quickly I thought your house was on fire."

"It's nothing like that," DI Smyth said. "It was just something I needed to sort out."

"Fair enough. What's with the ringtone? I didn't have you down as a Police fan."

"It was Porter's idea of a joke."

"The Police thing?"

"Not just that," DI Smyth said. "Porter believes I suffer from a mild form of avoidance anxiety."

"What's that when it's at home?"

"It's a personal space issue."

"Don't stand so close to me," Smith said. "Brilliant."

"It's not funny. I didn't ask him to do that, and I have no idea how to change the ringtone."

"Ask any teenager," Smith said. "Don't stand so close to me. Love it."

DI Smyth gave him a smile. "I'll see you in the morning."

Smith took a step closer and opened his arms wide. "No hug?"

"Don't push me now."

DI Smyth left the room with the smile still on his face.

    Smith started the footage of Dr Sweetman from the beginning. She really did look like she'd been drugged. Her usually bright eyes were dull, and her eyelids drooped. Smith watched up to the part where she shifted her gaze to the side, and he paused the footage.

"Who are you looking at?"

He was convinced that *The Optician* was there with her. He had to be.

    He watched the footage another three times and on the third viewing he found what he was looking for. He got up and raced out of the room. He stopped at the front desk.

"Has everybody left already?" he asked Baldwin.

"You've just missed them," she said.

"Come with me. I need a second opinion on something."

    "What is it?" Baldwin asked in the small conference room.

"I want you to watch this," Smith said. "And tell me what Dr Sweetman is mouthing when she turns her head to the side."

He started the footage and told Baldwin to wait for it.

"Well?" he asked after the crucial part of the film.

"She's definitely moving her lips," Baldwin said.

"What is she saying?"

"What do you think she's saying?"

"I don't want to influence you in any way," Smith said. "Watch it again."

They watched it a further five times. Baldwin nodded thoughtfully and did her best to mimic the shapes Dr Sweetman had made with her lips.

"Woman," she said after a while.

"That's what I see too," Smith said. "I think she's trying to tell us that *The Optician* is a woman."

CHAPTER FORTY FIVE

"I'm really not in the mood," Whitton said.

"Come on," Smith said. "We won't stay long."

"It's been a draining day, Jason."

Smith pulled her closer to him and wrapped his arms around her.

"All the more reason to go to the Hog's Head. We can have a few pints and forget about stuff for a bit. You need to eat, and what's better than one of Marge's steak and ale pies?"

Whitton had come home alone. Her mum had told the girls that they were more than welcome to stay the night, and Laura and Fran didn't need to be asked twice.

"We don't have the girls to worry about," Smith said. "We can have a quiet night at the pub, just the two of us."

"You're not going to take no for an answer, are you?"

"Nope," Smith said. "Is your mum OK looking after the girls?"

"I think it'll help to take her mind off things. And Laura and Fran have been brilliant. Those girls are a lot stronger than we give them credit for."

"I know they are. Do you want a beer?"

"I do," Whitton said.

Smith got a couple of beers out of the fridge.

"*The Optician* is a woman."

He opened the beers and handed one to Whitton.

"How did you come to that conclusion?" she said.

Smith brought her up to date on the developments in the investigation. He told her about Dr Sweetman's revelation.

"Are you sure that's what she said?" Whitton said. "You've never been much of a lip reader."

"That's why I asked Baldwin to watch it," Smith said. "She saw the same thing."

"Why Baldwin?"

"She was the only one around," Smith said. "The rest of the team had already left. We're looking for a woman. I suspected it, and now I know I was right."

"Can you do me a favour?"

"Anything. Anything within reason I mean."

"Can we forget about the case for one evening?" Whitton said.

"I won't mention a word about it," Smith promised. "Sup up – I can almost taste that steak and ale pie."

* * *

The Hog's Head was quiet, and Smith was glad. He was hungry and he wouldn't have to wait long for his pie. The table by the fire was free so he grabbed it before anyone else could. Marge came to the table.

"It's lovely to see you." She turned to Whitton. "How's your dad, love?"

"Not great, Marge," Whitton said.

The owner of the Hog's Head didn't comment further, and she didn't need to. The expression on her face spoke more than words could.

"I could kill for one of your steak and ale pies," Smith told her.

"Make that two," Whitton said.

"And a couple of pints?" Marge said.

"You're a legend, Marge," Smith said.

"I imagine you'll be tied up with this Optician thing?"

"You don't know the half of it," Smith said. "We've never come across anything like it before."

"You'll catch him," Marge said.

Her, Smith thought. *The Optician is a woman*.

He kept this to himself.

"The Super's crime stats thing has been postponed," Smith said when Marge had gone to see to their order. "The public-school dipshit wants to wait for us to wrap up the investigation first. Can you believe it?"
"He's confident," Whitton said. "How long have we got?"
"A week. His presentation is scheduled for my birthday. Something to look forward to, I suppose."
"My dad said something really sad earlier. He told me he's going to hold on until after your birthday before he leaves us."
"What?"
"I know. I don't think he was thinking straight. He wants you to be able to celebrate your birthday without him spoiling it by dying."
The smile that appeared on Smith's face was somewhat inappropriate, but he couldn't stop it.
"It's not funny, Jason," Whitton said.
"I'm sorry. He's a special man. Has he told you the story about the urn?"
"I don't want to hear it."
The drinks arrived and Smith drained half of his pint in one go. He looked across at Whitton and smiled.
"You'll be alright, you know."
She nodded. "I'm worried sick about my mum."
"She's a tough old bird. And she's got us. Tell me something about your dad."
Whitton thought for a moment, and her eyes became animated.
"He once thought he had a promising career as a ventriloquist."
"You're kidding me?"
"I'm not," Whitton said. "He used to make his own dummies. He had this one in particular – Fat Sally, he called her. He would stuff her face with fake cakes during the act."
"And he did this in public?"

"He performed in Blackpool one year," Whitton said. "Me and Mum were forced to watch and I've never been so embarrassed in my life. I must have been about eight, so we're going back to the mid-nineties, and the world wasn't so politically correct back then. Probably for the best. A Yorkshireman with his hand stuffed up the arse of a fat Yorkshire lass probably wouldn't go down too well these days. And some of the jokes he made were downright crude. Fat Sally didn't go down too well anyway. My dad reckoned the boos and choruses of *get offs* were because they were a bunch of Lancashire pansies. The truth was, he just wasn't very good. He gave up on that dream shortly afterwards."

Smith finished his beer and shook his head.

"Do you know if he still has her? Fat Sally, I mean?"

"Probably," Whitton said. "But mum made him promise never to take her out in public again."

"I would have loved to see that. I wonder if he'll perform a final show for us."

"Don't you dare," Whitton warned.

"I reckon it's just what the doctor ordered."

The pies arrived and Smith finished his in record time. Whitton left half of hers uneaten and Smith soon made light work of that too.

"That's better," he said. "I feel almost human again. I know I promised not to talk about the case, but I can't get it out of my head. We've missed something – something obvious, and it's doing my head in."

"OK," Whitton said. "If it's something obvious, we need to go right back to the beginning."

"It started with Gemma London. She was picked up from *The French Connection* on Wednesday night, and she was driven away to her death. We're sure that *The Optician* was monitoring the Uber bookings, and he got there before the genuine driver did."

He finished his beer and caught the attention of the waiter to order some more.

"Casey Plant was next," he carried on. "She was abducted outside a night club. Casey had also spent some time at *The French Connection* that night."

"That pub is the connection," Whitton said. "If you'll excuse the pun."

"At the scene of the third murder, there was a scrap of fabric cut into the shape of the map of France. We know it was left there intentionally because it came from the shirt that Gemma London was wearing when she was taken."

"He wants us to know about *The French Connection*."

"She," Smith corrected. "*The Optician* is a woman."

"I'm still finding that hard to believe."

"It doesn't matter. Where does France come into the equation?"

"I don't know," Whitton said. "But it does. What do we know about that pub?"

"It's owned by an American called James Norton. The man also owns the gym where Gemma London worked, and he just happens to be friends with all four victims on Facebook. But it's not him – he's not *The Optician*."

"How can you be sure?"

"Apart from the fact that he's in possession of a penis," Smith said. "He doesn't fit the profile."

The drinks arrived and Smith took a moment to consider what it was they could have missed. Nothing occurred to him.

"Do you think it's possible that *The Optician* frequents *The French Connection*?" Whitton put forward.

"The place has only been open five minutes," Smith said.

"Gemma London was abducted on opening night," Whitton said. "And Casey Plant was taken shortly after she left the pub the following night. There's something there."

"Cameras," Smith said. "The CCTV at *The French Connection* hadn't been set up yet, and the ones at the night club had been recently vandalised. We're not going to get anything from them but the very fact that we're not going to get any footage tells its own story."

Whitton stretched her arms and yawned.

"I get the hint," Smith said. "Tomorrow's another day."

"Why don't I believe that?" Whitton said.

"OK, I might just tune into Dr Sweetman's broadcast later. Shall I ask for the bill?"

"Please," Whitton said. "I really need some sleep. This has been nice."

"We'll be alright, Mrs Smith."

"I know we will, Mr Smith. Can you ask for that bill?"

CHAPTER FORTY SIX

Dr Sweetman looked considerably more awake than she had earlier. She was wearing makeup, and her eyes were more alert. Smith was watching the broadcast on the screen on his laptop, and he was watching it alone. Whitton had gone up to bed and she'd fallen asleep within seconds. Smith looked closely at the face on the screen. There was still five minutes to go before the live broadcast would be aired and the still shot of the celebrity psychologist was eerie. Here was a woman who had been abducted and taken somewhere for the sole purpose of telling the story of the most depraved serial killer Smith had ever come across and the expression on Dr Sweetman's face didn't tell that story. If Smith wasn't aware of the context involved, he would think she was about to record one of her regular podcasts.

He got up and opened the back door. He had time to smoke a quick cigarette. He wondered what *The Optician's* story would sound like, and he hoped there would be something in it that would help them. He'd never encountered anything like it, and he couldn't understand the reasoning behind it. In every murder investigation, without exception, the motive behind the killing was the key element and it was possible that *The Optician* was about to give them that on a plate. It made no sense whatsoever. There had been occasions in the past when serial killers had reached out to law enforcement in the hope of getting caught but those instances were few and far between, and Smith didn't think that *The Optician* would fall into that category. He didn't know why, but something felt very wrong about the broadcast. He finished the cigarette and went back inside to see what Dr Sweetman was going to tell him.

* * *

"Ninety seconds."

Dr Sweetman was no stranger to cameras but the sinister red dot three feet away from her face was making her feel sick.

"I'll refresh your memory of the rules again. You will stick to the script, and you will not deviate from the script. Should you break the rules, pain will follow. I will not hesitate to hurt you while the camera is still rolling."

"Why are you doing this?" Dr Sweetman said. "I'm nothing to you."

"You're everything to me, Vanessa."

Dr Sweetman winced at the sound of her name.

"I'm not going to hurt you if you follow the rules."

"Why me?" Dr Sweetman said.

"Thirty seconds. We wouldn't want to disappoint your fans by keeping them waiting."

Half a minute later, Dr Sweetman took a number of deep breaths and stared at the blinking eye of the camera.

"My name is Dr Vanessa Sweetman."

She paused there, as she'd been instructed.

"I'm a doctor of psychology, and tonight I have something different for you."

The story *The Optician* wanted her to tell was handwritten in block capitals on a sheet of paper next to the camera. Dr Sweetman cringed when she read the first few words. The script had been written as if it were a twisted fairy tale, and she didn't know if she was going to be able to go through with it.

She was prompted by the glare of *The Optician* and the scalpel she was holding. The steel shone brightly, and the blade was razor sharp.

"There was once a beautiful young girl."

This was the first time Dr Sweetman had seen the words on the page, and she spoke slowly.

"She had nothing but the promise of joy ahead of her."

The Optician's eyes were boring into hers and the sensation was deeply unpleasant.

"She was loved by everyone," Dr Sweetman continued. "Men, women, boys, girls and cats and dogs. The air changed when she was around. Flowers grew where she walked, and butterflies followed like minions."

What absolute drivel, Dr Sweetman thought. *This woman is seriously deranged.*

"Three days before she turned fourteen," she read from the page. "Everything changed. Summer in France. What could possibly go wrong in France in the summertime?"

Dr Sweetman read what was coming next and her eyes found those of *The Optician's*. The scalpel was held up again and Dr Sweetman knew she had to carry on.

"What indeed? Things did go wrong that summer. Things went seriously fucking wrong. There are more characters in this tale. Enter the witches. Four of them, hiding their true intentions behind false smiles and promises of allegiance. Gemma, you were weak. Such is life. Casey played the devil's advocate. You were the voice of reason that nobody chose to listen to. Rachel opted for the role of first mate on this ship of fools."

Dr Sweetman paused again. She wasn't sure how much longer she could carry on reading this nonsense.

She decided to take a chance and deviate from the script slightly. "You're probably wondering where this is leading."

A glance at *The Optician* told her that her sudden ad-lib was acceptable. "There is tragedy to come."

Dr Sweetman assumed that this was the case. She turned back to the script and when she read what was coming next, she wished she hadn't.

"Stacy was fair as a princess and rotten to the core. She was rancid inside. I killed her slowly. She died in unbelievable agony."

Dr Sweetman stopped again. This was not right. It was possible that Stacy's family and friends were watching this, and Dr Sweetman couldn't carry on much longer. *The Optician* was wielding the scalpel again. She was making a show of running the blade across her face.

"Her eyes were plucked like ripe cherries," Dr Sweetman managed. "She was aware of every touch. She screamed and begged, but she deserved no mercy. The beautiful star of the story received none. Her eyes were burned and blistered. *Use this*, Stacy told her. *Your eyes will gleam like the stars in the heavens. Try it.*"

Dr Sweetman was feeling sick. A nod from *The Optician* told her to keep reading.

"The bottle was raised, and the drops fell, one by one. The burn took time to arrive and when the first heat came, both eyes had been contaminated. The eyeballs melted and with the loss of one sense, the others were heightened. This was true pain, and nothing helped. Stacy watched and laughed."

Dr Sweetman looked straight at *The Optician* and shook her head.

"I'm done," she said. "Do what you want with me – I'm not reading any more of this nonsense."

The Optician seemed to be mulling this over. She nodded thoughtfully and tapped the piece of paper containing the script.

"No," Dr Sweetman said, and moved her face closer to the camera. "I'm somewhere in Heworth. There's a basement. *The Optician* is a young…."

That was as far as she got. The camera was swung with astonishing strength. There was a crack as the bones in her nose shattered and blood started to pour out. The second blow knocked out two of her teeth and the third smack of the camera turned off every light inside her head.

CHAPTER FORTY SEVEN

Smith's phone started to ring thirty seconds after the broadcast ended. He'd expected to hear Elvis Costello singing about Oliver's Army and he wasn't wrong.

"I watched it," he told DI Smyth. "We need everyone we've got over to Heworth."

"I'm already onto it," DI Smyth said. "Dr Sweetman mentioned a basement. I don't think there will be many properties with basements."

"It'll be easy to check. Why the hell did she do that? She all but signed her own death warrant by doing that."

"We'll find her. Even if we have to search every house in Heworth."

"That's a densely populated part of the city," Smith reminded him. "There are hundreds of houses in Heworth."

"We have no choice."

"It's possible that *The Optician* has moved her somewhere else," Smith said. "But we still need to look at Heworth first. I can be there in ten minutes."

"Have you been drinking?"

"I had a few pints at the Hog's Head earlier," Smith said. "But I feel fine."

"No," DI Smyth said. "Heworth is going to be swarming with journalists after the broadcast. The last thing we need right now is a story about a drunken detective."

"I'm not drunk. I'm heading over to Heworth now."

"You'll do no such thing, and that's an order."

"Fair enough," Smith said.

He ended the call and composed a short message to Whitton. Then he grabbed his phone and car keys and left the house.

As he started the engine, he did some quick mental arithmetic. He'd had a beer before he and Whitton set off for the pub and he had another four pints in the Hog's Head. When they got home, he'd opened another one. He was a practiced beer drinker, quite a few hours had passed, but he realised that he was probably still over the limit. He switched off the ignition and took out his phone.

Bridge was the first name he came to in his contacts. His colleague answered straight away.

"Where are you?" Smith asked.

"Just about to head over to Heworth," Bridge said.

"I need a lift."

"Has your car finally given up the ghost?"

"There's nothing wrong with my car," Smith said. "I'm a bit pissed, that's all."

"I'll be there in five."

Smith used the time to smoke a cigarette. He tried to make sense of why Dr Sweetman had done what she did. She'd shown great courage, but it could have got her killed. Smith wondered if she was already dead. The attack had been frenzied, and it had all happened quickly, but there was no way to tell if the blows from the camera had been fatal.

The headlights of Bridge's Toyota appeared, and Smith stubbed out his cigarette. Bridge stopped the car, and Smith got in the passenger seat.

"The boss is going to have a hernia if you show up stinking of beer," Bridge said.

"I've already had that lecture," Smith said. "I'll try to steer clear of the press that will no doubt be all over the place."

"What do you think?"

"I think she's still alive," Smith said. "She's going to be bloody and bruised, but I don't think she's dead. I told you we were looking for a woman."

"You also suspected Dr Sweetman at one stage," Bridge said. "And we still have no concrete proof that *The Optician* is a woman."

"Dr Sweetman was on the verge of telling the world. She was about to say that *The Optician* is a young woman. I know it."

Heworth was lit up like the illuminations in Blackpool. The flashing lights could be seen from as far away as Tang Hall. Smith's phone started to ring. It was the ringtone for DI Smyth, so he asked Bridge to do the talking and activated the speakerphone.

"We're heading north on Tang Hall Lane," Bridge said.

"We?" DI Smyth said.

"Me and Smith."

"Is Smith driving?" DI Smyth said.

"We're in my car. Do we have any news?"

"It's chaos," DI Smyth said. "The broadcast has brought every rubbernecker in the city to Heworth. We're fighting a losing battle just trying to keep the public away."

"What about the press?" Bridge said.

"Already camped out on the streets. It's a logistical nightmare."

"Do we have the manpower to cordon off the area?" Smith said.

"I thought I told you to stay at home," DI Smyth said.

"I'm wide awake, boss and Bridge is driving."

"We cannot cordon off an area this size," DI Smyth said. "Even if we had ten times the bodies we do, it would be impossible. There are dozens of roads in and out of Heworth and *The Optician* could have left via any one of them."

"Where are you?" Smith asked.

"Just up from the roundabout on Malton Road. It's pretty central and it's as good a place as any to set up a temporary incident room."

Bridge was forced to stop on the corner of Heworth Road and Stockton Road. The road up ahead was blocked with vehicles.

"Do you have emergency lights?" Smith asked.

"In the glove compartment," Bridge said. "But they're not going to help. The street is gridlocked. What the hell is wrong with people these days?"

"They're looking for their five minutes of fame. We'll have to walk. The boss is only a few minutes away from here."

The walk to Malton Road passed without incident. There were plenty of people on the streets but none of them paid Smith and Bridge any attention. The roundabout was packed with cars and most of them seemed to be trying to exit on the road leading to Heworth. Two police cars had blocked off the entire road, preventing anyone from coming in or going out.

"Too little, too late," Smith said.

"Do you think he's already gone?" Bridge said.

"She," Smith corrected. "*The Optician* isn't stupid. She'll have known what the reaction to Dr Sweetman's outburst would be and she'll have done a runner straight away, with or without the celebrity shrink."

The temporary incident room that DI Smyth had spoken about was no more than a few cars surrounded by a ring of police tape. Smith ducked underneath the tape and made his way towards DI Smyth. He was poring over a map on the bonnet of his car with the DCs Moore and King.

"You stink like a brewery."

Smith ignored the DI's words. "What's the plan?"

"There are more than seven-hundred residential properties in Heworth," DI Smyth said. "We also have to consider Heworth village and the surrounding areas. A lot of people refer to the houses on the outskirts of Tang Hall as Heworth, so all in all we've got over a thousand buildings to look at."

"Do we know how many of them have basements?" Smith asked.

"We're still waiting for that information."

"We don't have time to wait," Smith said. "I've got a feeling that Dr Sweetman is still alive, but that might change soon. What's the delay?"

DI Smyth's eyes narrowed. "Delay? Have you taken a look around? Dr Sweetman's crazy stunt was only broadcast an hour ago, and already we have possibly the biggest police presence we've ever seen in the area. This is a massive operation, and coordinating it is a fucking nightmare."
DI Smyth rarely swore, and Smith knew better than to push him.

"Do we have someone monitoring the backlash from the broadcast?" he asked instead. "It's possible we might get some info from someone who watched it."
"Seven thousand comments and counting, Sarge," DC Moore informed him.
"We've got a couple of uniforms looking at it," DI Smyth said. "But we simply do not have the manpower to do something like this quickly."
Smith understood this perfectly well. "OK. It's possible that something might come of the comments about the broadcast, but right now we need to think strategically."
"Do you have any suggestions?"
"I think *The Optician* is gone, boss," Smith said. "But I don't think she had time to make arrangements to take Dr Sweetman with her. It would be too risky, especially if someone in one of the neighbouring houses had been watching the broadcast. And I think she will have left on foot."
"If that's the case," DI Smyth said. "She could be anywhere by now."

Smith took out his cigarettes and lit one. He exhaled a cloud of smoke and looked skywards.
"She didn't get to the end of the story."
"What?" DI Smyth said.
"Dr Sweetman. She freaked out before the end, and *The Optician* wasn't expecting it. Her story wasn't finished, and she's going to want to do something about that."
"How is that going to help us?" DC Moore said.

"I have no idea, Harry," Smith said. "All I know is we haven't heard the last of *The Optician*. She went to a lot of trouble to take Dr Sweetman, and she did that because her story is important to her."

"You're not helping," DI Smyth said. "Go home. You're half-drunk and there's nothing you can do here. We've got an extensive door-to-door underway and that's probably going to take all night. Go home and get some sleep."

"She's not finished, boss," Smith said. "She needs to have her story heard and that's not going to happen anytime soon. That gives us a bit of time."

"Time to do what?" DC Moore said.

"To find out what the story is, Harry. Dr Sweetman did us a favour tonight. I don't want to crack this one because some twisted psycho has given it to us on a plate. I'm going to find out what that story is before she tells it to us."

CHAPTER FORTY EIGHT

Smith had slept badly. He knew he would. By the time Bridge dropped him off it was past midnight, and he'd made the mistake of drinking two cups of strong coffee. The broadcast of Dr Sweetman telling the story of *The Optician* had played out on repeat inside his head, and he couldn't get it to stop. There was something in the narrative that was going to get them closer to *The Optician*, but Smith still hadn't figured out what it was.

He admitted defeat just after six. It was still pitch-black outside, but he couldn't lie in bed any longer. Whitton was fast asleep. She hadn't even stirred when Smith had got home in the early hours of the morning, and he left her where she was. It was clear that she needed the rest.

He switched on the kettle to make some coffee and opened the back door. The dogs were still fast asleep in the living room and when Smith felt the gusts of icy wind on his face, he didn't blame them. The wind had to be blowing almost gale force, and it took four attempts to get his cigarette lit. He turned his head away from the wind and shivered. He wondered if there had been any developments overnight. He didn't think there would be. The operation in Heworth was a mammoth task, and it had been chaotic last night. He didn't dwell on it – if the door-to-doors had turned up anything, he would find out soon enough.

He went back inside and made the coffee. He checked his phone for messages and saw that there were three new ones. The first two were from DI Smyth. They consisted of a short bollocking for turning up to a potential crime scene stinking of beer and it made Smith smile. The first message was brief.

Consider this your last...

That was it and Smith assumed that DI Smyth had pressed send before he intended to. It didn't matter – the second message left no doubt about what

DI Smyth was telling him. Smith forgot about it as soon as he moved onto the next message.

It was a WhatsApp, and the sender wasn't in his list of contacts.
I think I might know something. Can we meet? I have to work, but I can see you afterwards. The Golden Hen on Malton Road. 6pm.
Smith closed his WhatsApp and opened Google. The Golden Hen was a rough looking pub not far from where the action had been last night.

He tried phoning the number, but it went straight to voicemail. He sent a short message asking who he was speaking to, but the message went unread, and according to the 'last seen' time the sender of the message hadn't been on WhatsApp since just after midnight. Smith decided to try again later. It was early Sunday morning after all.

He went upstairs to check in on Whitton. She was still in bed, but her eyes were open.

"What time is it?"

"Almost seven," Smith said. "You missed the action last night."

He told her about the operation in Heworth.

She sat up in bed. "Is there any news?"

"Nothing," Smith said. "I'm just about to head off."

"Do you think Dr Sweetman is still alive?"

"I really don't know. What she did was stupid, but it was also extremely brave. I never thought she had it in her. We'll find her."

"I feel bad for not being at work," Whitton said. "We need everybody we've got on this."

"Don't even think about it. Work is work, and family is family."

"What about Dr Sweetman's family? Whatever kind of person she is, she still has people who care about her. What about them?"

"Forget about them," Smith said. "I'm going to catch this bastard. I'm going to make sure I catch her."

"You've got six days."

"Don't remind me. That's my motivation."

"You're motivated by the Super's crime stats presentation?"

"Fuck that," Smith said. "In six days, I'll be forty and I may be considering early retirement."

"You're an idiot."

Smith kissed her on the cheek. "I love you too."

He fed the dogs and left the house. The wind was blowing harder now, and he was glad to get inside his car. He started the engine and turned on the heater, even though he knew it wasn't going to help much. It hadn't worked properly in years. Darren's brother Gary had done a lot of work on the car to restore it to its former glory, but he hadn't bothered with the heater. Smith was used to it, and it wasn't a long drive to the station anyway.

The roads were quiet. It was a Sunday morning in late January and very few people chose to be out and about unless they had to. Smith made it to work in record time. He could see from the vehicles in the car park that he wasn't the only one making an early start. DI Smyth's car was there as was the Toyota belonging to Bridge. DC Moore's trauma inducing Subaru was parked next to it.

Smith's first port of call was the canteen. He'd let the coffee he'd made at home go cold and he needed some caffeine in his system before he could consider a plan of action for the day. Bridge and DC Moore had had the same idea. Smith got his coffee and joined them.

"The door-to-door gave us sweet FA," DC Moore informed him.

"It's still early days," Bridge said. "We've got uniforms working on it this morning."

"What do we know about the properties with basements?" Smith said. He took a sip of coffee.

"Last night, we worked on what we could find on the Internet," DC Moore said. "A lot of it hadn't been updated in years, but we should have a more accurate idea of the building plans today."

"Is Kerry in yet?" Smith said.

"She's having car trouble," DC Moore said. "She won't be long."

"Where's the boss?" Smith asked. "I saw his car in the car park."

"Where do you think?" Bridge said.

"Meetings?"

"Got it in one."

"It's half-seven on a Sunday morning."

"And the operation last night was the biggest one in years," Bridge said. "You know what it's like. Questions are going to be asked about budget allocation justification."

"You sound like a politician," Smith said. "I couldn't give a fuck about that. We've been given a helping hand in the form of that broadcast last night. We've got a lot more information to look into."

"Very true. It's possible that this has all been about revenge. The celebrity shrink spoke about a young girl who was wronged. And it looks like our four victims were responsible."

"Who do you think they hurt?" DC Moore said. "Do you think it was *The Optician*?"

"No," Smith said. "Unless she likes to talk about herself in the third person, I think she was referring to someone else."

"Illeism," Bridge said.

"Do what, Sarge?" DC Moore said.

"When someone talks about themselves in the third person it's known as illeism. It's actually a proper psychological condition."

"That's good to know," Smith said. "But I think *The Optician* was referring to someone else – someone close to her."

"A sibling, perhaps?" DC Moore said.

"Could be, or it could be a close friend. We find out what *The Optician's* victims did, and we find our Optician."

"How are you proposing to go about that?" DC Moore said.

"We go back and speak to the families of the dead women, Harry. It's now quite clear that those women share something in common, and the people closest to them are going to tell us what that is."

CHAPTER FORTY NINE

DI Smyth insisted on having a briefing before anything else and Smith hoped it would be what its name implied. They didn't have time to waste. It was possible that Dr Sweetman was still alive somewhere and the more time that passed, the more the chances of getting to her before that changed.

"First things first," DI Smyth said. "The car that we believe *The Optician* used to abduct his victims has been found."

"Her, boss," Smith said. "*The Optician* is a woman."

"*Her* victims," DI Smyth obliged him.

"Where was it found?" DC King said.

She'd arrived two minutes before the briefing.

"Would you believe it's back where it was taken from?" DI Smyth said.

"Leeds Bradford?" Smith said. "You're joking?"

"Unfortunately, not. It was parked in its original parking spot at the airport."

"Why go to the bother of returning it?" DC King wondered.

"That's the least of our problems," DI Smyth said. "The location of the vehicle is causing no end of problems. Webber is keen to get started on it, but he's being held up by jurisdictional red tape."

"What the hell?" Smith said. "That car is a vital piece of evidence. What's the hold up?"

"Jack Jones."

"Uncle Jeremy's nemesis?"

"Superintendent Jones and Uncle Jeremy as you refer to him were rivals at school," DI Smyth said. "And it appears as though Jones is making life difficult for us for that reason only."

"We don't have time for public-school territorial pissing, boss," Smith said. "This isn't a fucking game – a woman's life is at stake."

"Don't worry," DI Smyth said. "Superintendent Smyth has a few aces up his sleeve. Webber will have the car back in York before the end of the day."

"Any news from the door-to-doors last night?" Bridge said.

"Nothing," DI Smyth said. "Which in itself is unusual. Uniforms prioritised the properties with basements, but there are still a lot of houses to check. This is going to take time. And Smith, before you remind us that we don't have time, I'm on the same page as you. We cannot physically work any faster."

"Then we have to work smarter," Smith said. "Dr Sweetman gave us some clues last night in the form of *The Optician's* story. It hints on a definite connection between the victims and that's why we have to speak to the families of the dead women before we do anything else. We haven't found anything that links the victims, but something definitely does."

"Does anybody have any objections?" DI Smyth said.

The silence inside the room told him that nobody did.

"Very well. I'll leave it up to you to sort that out. I'm scheduled to attend yet another damn meeting in twenty minutes."

"What's this one about?" Smith said.

"God knows," DI Smyth said. "They all merge into one non-stop blur of bullshit after a while."

Smith decided that it would be beneficial to kill four birds with one stone, and he suggested they take a victim each. It would save a lot of time that way, and nobody disagreed. Something about Casey Plant's father's reaction to Casey's murder told him that he was someone he could relate to. Whitton had told him that Bill Plant had exploded and threatened to kill *The Optician* with his bare hands, and Smith thought he would be able to speak to him, one father to another.

He hadn't warned the Plants that he was coming but that was intentional. Often a surprise visit proved beneficial. With no time beforehand to rehearse what they were going to say, the information was more truthful, without any embellishments. Smith parked outside the house and turned off the engine. His phone beeped to indicate that he'd received a message. He took it out and swiped the screen. It was from Whitton and all she'd sent was a photograph. Harold Whitton was in the middle of the shot. Flanked by Laura and Fran, Whitton's dad had a beam on his face that made Smith smile. There was no escaping the fact that he was terminally ill, but the grin reached his eyes, and it caused Smith mixed emotions. Harold didn't have long left and the girls were going to miss him terribly, but the photo proved that there was still a bit of life in the old dog yet. He turned his attention to the task at hand. He got out of the car and walked up the path to the front door of the house.

Smith knew that Bill Plant was a short man, but he didn't realise how diminutive he was. He had to be at least a foot shorter than Smith and he was slight with it. Smith didn't think he weighed much more than Laura. He explained the reason for the visit, and apologised for arriving unannounced and Bill Plant invited him in.

A woman who looked to be in her early forties was sitting in the living room when Smith went in. Bill introduced her as his wife Janice.
"He's from the police, love," Bill told her.
"Detective Sergeant Smith," Smith said. "I hope I'm not interrupting anything."
"Nothing," Janice said. "I was about to make some tea. Can I offer you anything?"
"Coffee," Smith said. "If it's not too much trouble."
Janice nodded and left the room.

"We're still numb," Bill said. "Is there any news?"
Smith wondered if he'd seen Dr Sweetman's broadcast, but he decided not to ask.

"Some new information has come to our attention," he said. "Did Casey ever go to France?"

"France?"

"It might not be important," Smith said.

"France, you say? I don't recall ever going to France. Me and our Janice are not very adventurous. A week in Scarborough is about as far as we like to go."

Smith's heart sank.

Janice returned with the drinks. She handed Smith a cup containing something that resembled dirty dishwater.

"Thanks," he said anyway.

He put the cup on the coffee table.

"The detective was just asking if Casey ever went to France," Bill told his wife.

"Oh my," Janice said.

Smith thought she was going to cry.

She wiped her eyes. "Casey was so looking forward to that trip."

"What trip?" Bill said.

"The beauty thing," Janice said. "Remember, she won the school pageant. She got to go to the competition in Northern France."

"I'd forgotten all about that," Bill said.

"She wasn't the same afterwards," Janice said.

"What do you mean?" Smith said.

"I don't know how to explain it. She changed, that's all."

"Did she talk about the pageant much?"

"She didn't," Janice said. "She refused to discuss it."

"And we didn't press her," Bill said. "Whatever happened over there – Casey didn't want to talk about it."

"I think I've got some photos somewhere," Janice said.

"Could you dig them out please?" Smith said. "I'd really like to see them."
"Could you get them?" Janice asked Bill. "I'm feeling a bit tired. I think it was about six or seven years ago. The albums are all labelled."
Smith knew that he was onto something now. He recalled a snippet from *The Optician's* story.
Three days before her fourteenth birthday.
The timeline fit. If the reason for *The Optician's* killing spree was about to turn fourteen when whatever happened to her, happened it would make her the same age as all of the victims.

Bill was gone for quite some time.
"What was the competition?" Smith asked Janice.
"It was a school thing," she said. "Casey was picked to represent the school in a pageant in France. There were a whole load of other girls taking part – girls from schools all over Yorkshire."
"And this took part in France?" Smith said.
Janice nodded. "I forget the name of the place. It was one of those La something names."

Bill came back inside the room. "Found it."
He placed a photograph album on the table. He opened it up somewhere in the middle.
"Le Havre," Smith read. "2015."
Janice tapped a finger on one of the photographs. "That's our Casey there."
The tears came now. Bill placed a hand on his wife's shoulder.
"Now now, love. We need to hold it together."
"She was so beautiful," Janice sobbed. "And so so kind."
"She never argued," Bill said. "Our Casey. She had an old head on her young shoulders. Always the voice of reason."
Devil's advocate, Smith recalled from *The Optician's* story. *The voice of reason that nobody listened to.*

"Do you know any of the other girls?" he asked.

"They were from schools all over," Janice said. "Only one girl per school was picked."

Smith looked closely at the photograph, and he instantly recognised two of the other girls. This was the break they'd been waiting for. The photograph had been taken almost seven years ago, but the faces of Gemma London and Rachel Gold were unmistakable. And when Smith's eyes fell on one of the other beauty queens there was another spark of recognition. It was a much younger Stacy Ladd.

"Do you mind if I take a photo of this?" he asked.

"You can borrow the album if you promise to return it," Janice said.

"Is this something to do with Casey's murder?" Bill said.

"Yes," Smith said. "I think it is. I'll get the album back to you as soon as I can."

CHAPTER FIFTY

Smith called Bridge as soon as he got outside.

"Where are you?"

"I'm still busy with Rachel Gold's parents," Bridge said.

"I've found our link," Smith told him. "All four victims were selected to take part in a beauty pageant in Le Havre in 2015."

"Bloody hell," Bridge said. "Do you think *The Optician* was there too?"

"It's possible, but something happened in France that summer and whatever it was is the catalyst for the recent murders."

"I'll ask Mr and Mrs Gold about it."

"I'll let Kerry and Harry know," Smith said and ended the call.

Thirty minutes later, the team were gathered once again in the small conference room. The photograph of the girls who took part in the beauty pageant in France in 2015 filled the screen at the back of the room.

"That photo is right at the heart of the recent murders," Smith said. "All four victims were In Le Havre that summer."

"According to Stacy Ladd's mother," DC King said. "Stacy travelled there with her dad. John and Paula Ladd divorced in 2018 and unfortunately John passed away the following year so we're not going to get anything from him."

"What did you get from Gemma London's parents?" Smith asked DC Moore.

"They remembered it well," the man from London said. "They didn't go with her, but they remember it. Apparently, Gemma was different when she returned home."

"Different, how?"

"They couldn't really explain," DC Moore said. "But they thought that Gemma had changed somehow."

"Whatever happened there changed her," Smith said. "Casey Plant's parents told me something similar. Something definitely happened in France, and the girls were reluctant to talk about it afterwards. In the broadcast of *The Optician's* story, it mentioned Gemma being weak. I get the impression that Gemma went along with whatever happened because she wasn't strong enough to object. Casey Plant's parents described Casey as being the voice of reason. It was almost word for word how *The Optician* described her. Gemma was weak, Casey was the devil's advocate, Rachel was the first mate and Stacy Ladd was the queen bee – the girl who called the shots. That's why her injuries were a lot more severe than the others. Stacy orchestrated whatever happened and the other three played their own roles in it. We're getting close."

"I want the names of every girl who attended that pageant," DI Smyth spoke for the first time.

"I had a quick check on the Internet," DC Moore said. "And all I could find was a Facebook group. It hasn't been updated in three years, and it looks like not all the girls who took part are members. Gemma London's name isn't there."

"There must be other ways to find out who was in Le Havre that summer," Bridge said.

"Find out," DI Smyth said. "Someone had to organise it. I want that list before we do anything else. My presence is required in another meeting."

"Skip it," Smith suggested. "Tell them you're not feeling well."

"That's not far from the truth," DI Smyth said. "All these meetings are giving me a serious headache. It can't be helped. Get cracking with those beauty queens."

"Who's the admin on the Facebook page?" DC King asked DC Moore.

"Someone called Belinda Bowton," he said.

"Get hold of her," Smith said. "She might be able to give us the list of entrants in the pageant."

"Where did the participants come from?" Bridge said.

"Casey Plant's mother told me they were selected from schools all over Yorkshire," Smith said.

"Don't you think it's odd that all the victims lived in York, but they didn't keep in touch?" DC King said.

"Perhaps what happened in France meant they couldn't be friends anymore," Smith said. "And if they went to different schools, it's possible they didn't hang around with each other."

"I know what you did last summer," DC Moore said.

"What the hell are you going on about?" Bridge said.

"Sorry, Sarge – I was just thinking out loud."

"That's my thing, Harry," Smith reminded him. "And it was a terrible film."

His phone beeped with a message. It was from Whitton again and this time it consisted of text.

Dad is in fine form. He seems to be getting better.

Smith read the message again and he was overcome with a sudden sadness. He'd heard of this phenomenon. It was known as terminal lucidity or *the surge*, and it was characterised by sudden bursts of energy and increased alertness. Smith wondered how long Harold had left. When *the surge* showed its ugly face, it usually meant that the time was near, and Smith knew that he had to prepare himself for the worst. He tapped out a short message telling Whitton to enjoy the time with her father and his gaze fell on another message in his list. It was from the unknown number suggesting that they meet at *The Golden Hen* on Malton Road. It had slipped Smith's mind.

He told the rest of the team about it.

"Have you tried calling the number?" DC Moore said.

"Of course, I've tried calling it," Smith said. "Voicemail every time."
He checked the 'last seen' time and it hadn't changed since he'd last checked. Whoever the mystery person was hadn't used WhatsApp since just after midnight. Smith remembered that they said they had to work so he assumed that was the reason for the WhatsApp silence.

"We need to find out the names of everyone who took part in that beauty pageant in Le Havre in 2015," he said. "One of those girls is going to lead us straight to *The Optician*."

CHAPTER FIFTY ONE

"This is going to hurt."

Dr Vanessa Sweetman was aware of cold fingers on her nose.

"On three. One, two..."

Dr Sweetman didn't hear anything more. The crack as her ethmoid and vomer bones were put back into position was accompanied by an explosion of pain that resulted in a blinding white light in front of her eyes.

"The bones will need to be reset properly." *The Optician*'s touch was gentle as she stroked the cheek. "But that should make breathing easier." The rag that was yanked out of Dr Sweetman's mouth was soaked in blood. Three fingers lifted her top lip to inspect the teeth.

"It could have been worse. Your upper central and lateral incisors are gone, but they've been dislodged cleanly. Have you been overdoing it with the mouthwash? The enamel has worn away on the second premolar and the first molar. Certain mouthwashes are caustic – were you aware of that?"

Dr Sweetman didn't reply. Who was this psychopath? Was she an optician or a dentist?

"You'll have a shiner very soon. Why did you do that? That was a mistake."

"Let me go," Dr Sweetman said.

"Do you remember me?"

"I've never met you before."

"Oh, but you have. I'll help you out. *The French Connection*. Wednesday night."

Dr Sweetman had been there for a short while for the opening of the pub, but nothing about the place explained what was happening to her now.

"Still nothing?" *The Optician* said. "How about Le Havre, in the summer of 2015?"

This caused Dr Sweetman to open her eyes wider. "I was there."

* * *

"You need to see this."

DC King had found Smith in his office. He was staring at something on the screen of his laptop. He turned around and saw that DC King was holding a sheet of paper.

"What have you got there?"

"I found this on the Facebook page for the beauty pageant in 2015. I printed it out."

She handed him the photograph.

"What am I supposed to be looking at?" Smith said.

"This was taken on the first day of the pageant, Sarge. All of the contestants are in it and so are the judges. Look at the woman second from the right."

"What the hell was she doing there?"

Even though the photograph had been taken almost seven years ago, Dr Sweetman hadn't changed a bit.

"She was one of the judges, Sarge," DC King said. "I got that from one of the posts on the page. Dr Sweetman was there for the pageant."

Smith scratched his forehead. "What does this mean, Kerry? What does this mean in terms of the investigation?"

"It's baffling. Is she a victim of *The Optician*, or is she an accomplice?"

"The violence on the broadcast looked pretty real to me," Smith said. "This information has thrown a whole heap of confusion into the mix. Do we know how the celebrity shrink ended up as a judge at a teenage beauty pageant in France?"

"I did some checking there too," DC King said. "She was a student back then, and she did quite a bit of modelling in her spare time."

"I can believe it," Smith said. "She's a beautiful woman. What do we do with this information?"

"You tell me, Sarge. If we assume that *The Optician* was at that beauty pageant, it means that she's no stranger to Dr Sweetman, but I still don't know what the celebrity psychologist's role is. Is she a victim or is her part a more sinister one?"

"Do we have any news from the door-to-doors in Heworth?" Smith said. "Not that I'm aware of. And if Dr Sweetman is involved with *The Optician* somehow, we have to consider the fact that the officers involved in the door-to-door could have been sent on a wild goose chase."

"We have to work on the assumption that she's a victim," Smith decided. "She could be in grave danger right now, if she's still alive, that is."

"What's the plan?"

"We need to speak to everyone who was at that pageant in 2015," Smith said. "Whatever happened there was big, and somebody must remember it. Do any of the names on the Facebook page ring any bells?"

"Apart from three of the victims," DC King said. "None of them has come up during the course of the investigation."

"That could be intentional. It's possible that this murder spree has been in the planning stages for some time, and *The Optician* wouldn't want to draw any attention to herself. Joining a Facebook group would have been pretty stupid."

Bridge came in with DC Moore. Smith filled them in about Dr Sweetman's presence at the beauty pageant.

"That's only added to the confusion," DC Moore stated the obvious.

"We're still not sure what it means," Smith said. "It's possible that the celebrity shrink is in cahoots with *The Optician*, but I don't get the impression that she is. This one is a solo artist."

"A solo artist?" Bridge repeated.

"Think Madonna," Smith said. "Prince, Elton John if you like that kind of crap. They work alone. *The Optician* is the same. She doesn't need anybody else. We need to find everybody who was at the pageant that summer."

"I've found a few more names, Sarge," DC Moore said. "And I managed to get hold of the woman who set up the Facebook group. Belinda Bowton is the mother of one of the entrants, and she's promised to get back to me with the entire list of entrants."

"Put some pressure on her," Smith said. "We don't have time to wait."

"She was driving, Sarge," DC Moore told him. "On her way back from Scotland. We can't expect her to recall the names of the girls off the top of her head after almost seven years."

"Who the hell goes to Scotland in January?" Bridge wondered. "Sorry – I'm starting to think out loud too."

"Keep hounding Belinda Bowton," Smith told DC Moore. "That list of entrants is important."

CHAPTER FIFTY TWO

By five that afternoon the list that Belinda Bowton had promised to send still hadn't materialised and Smith was annoyed. It was possible that the identity of *The Optician* was there in black and white, but Mrs Bowton wasn't answering her phone and there was nothing they could do but wait.

DI Smyth had been occupied by meetings for most of the day and Smith was about to hear all about them. The DI looked weary, and Smith didn't envy him. There had been a time when the DI position had his name all over it, but a series of unfortunate events had put paid to that possibility, and Smith was glad. He was quite happy where he was. He would be a detective sergeant the day he retired, and he had no regrets about it.

"Thank God that was the last one," DI Smyth said.
He sat down opposite Smith.
"Was anything achieved in these meetings?" Smith asked.
"Sweet FA. The CC is pressing for a quick resolution. It appears that *The Optician* has captured the attention of the entire country and York is under the spotlight."
"Did you point out that wasting time in meetings isn't how psychopaths are caught?"
"What do you think?"
"We'll catch her, boss," Smith said. "The information we need is within our grasp, and we will find her. I've got an appointment with someone who claims to have some info, and I'm confident that something will come of that. Harry is waiting for the list of participants in the pageant, and I believe *The Optician's* name will be on that list. It's just a matter of time."
"What time are you meeting this mystery informant?" DI Smyth said.
"Six. At a dodgy pub not far from where you set up the temporary incident room last night. I've got a good feeling about this."

"I hope you're right," DI Smyth said. "Because if I have to sit through another meeting, I may just say something that could end my career."
"Permission to have a sneaky smoke?"
"Will you stop with that nonsense?" DI Smyth said. "But permission granted, as long as you've got one for me."

The sun had said its goodbyes to the city a couple of hours ago and the moon still hadn't risen in the black sky. It was bitterly cold, and Smith shivered as he took out his cigarettes. He offered the pack to DI Smyth.
"How's Whitton bearing up?" DI Smyth said.
He lit a cigarette and handed the packet and lighter back to Smith.
"It's a waiting game now," Smith said.
He lit his own cigarette.
"Harold is experiencing the surge," he added. "Which means that the time is near."
"My mother died of cancer," DI Smyth said.
"I didn't know that," Smith said.
He realised that he really didn't know much about his boss at all. DI Smyth was a very private man.

"Mercifully, her suffering was relatively brief," DI Smyth said. "It was a matter of weeks between her diagnosis and her passing."
"It's a horrible disease," Smith said. "I reckon when it's my time to leave this world, I want it to be as quick as possible. A bullet to the brain, or a head-on collision with a bus. Instant death."
"What a morbid conversation," DI Smyth said. "You'd better get to your appointment. I find that it pays to get there early to these things."
"You sound like you have experience."
"I spent ten years of my life in military intelligence."
"Isn't that a famous oxymoron?" Smith said.

DI Smyth smiled. "When you're gathering intel, reconnaissance work is key. It pays to get the lay of the land beforehand."

"Are you suggesting I scope out the pub before the mystery informant arrives?" Smith said.

"It can't hurt. *The Golden Hen* is a stone's throw from Heworth and that might be relevant."

"The thought had occurred to me," Smith said. "But I'm struggling to figure out how it's relevant."

"Just be careful."

"You know me, boss."

"Precisely," DI Smyth said. "Thanks for the cigarette. I'm off home before the idiots with the pips come up with another reason to have a meeting. Porter is cooking his famous Eisbein this evening, and you haven't lived until you've tasted it."

"He's a good bloke."

"He is," DI Smyth said. "I'm lucky to have found him."

"Even though he likes to make you look like a tit when your phone rings?"

"I managed to change the ringtone," DI Smyth said.

"I'll let you know how the meeting goes," Smith told him. "Enjoy the Eisbein."

    He walked to his car and opened the door. He sat down and slotted the key in the ignition. His phone beeped before he'd turned the key. Smith swiped the screen and tapped on the WhatsApp icon. The message was from the same number that had sent him the message that morning. It was short and to the point.

At The Golden Hen now. I'm wearing a purple jumper and black jeans.

Smith replied with an even shorter message telling the person that he was on his way.

    Purple jumper and black jeans, he thought.

He didn't think a man would wear a purple jumper, but he could be wrong. Anyhow, he sensed that the person he was on his way to meet was a woman. It was just the feeling he got. He started the engine and drove out of the car park.

CHAPTER FIFTY THREE

It was a woman, and she wasn't difficult to find. *The Golden Hen* was quiet, with only a couple of the tables occupied. The woman wearing the purple jumper looked to be in her early twenties – she was very attractive, and Smith wondered if she'd been at the pageant in Le Havre in 2015. He ordered a beer from the bar and walked over to her table.

"Can I get you a drink?"

"I've got one, thanks." The woman nodded to the glass of wine on the table. She introduced herself as Vicky. She didn't offer a surname.

"You look older in real life," she said.

"Thanks," Smith said.

"Not in a bad way," Vicky added.

"What is it you want to tell me?" Smith said.

"I think I know why those women were murdered."

"What makes you think that?"

"I was there."

"Are you referring to the beauty pageant?" Smith said.

Vicky nodded. "I was one of the participants. Do you mind if I pop to the Ladies?"

"No worries," Smith said.

He watched her go. She didn't walk with the grace of a model. Her head was bowed and Smith thought she looked like a woman with a lot on her mind. His phone started to ring. The screen told him it was DC Moore and Smith made a mental note to assign him a ringtone. He knew the perfect song - *London Calling* by the Clash.

"Harry," Smith said. "You've got the list."

"Not quite," DC Moore said. "But I'm on my way to Belinda Bowton's place now. There was a pile-up on the A19, and the traffic was backed up for miles. Mrs Bowton got caught up in it."

"You called me to tell me that?" Smith said.

"No, Sarge. I was going through the people on the Facebook group and one of them told me something interesting. Something happened in France that summer."

"We know that something happened, Harry," Smith said. "It was something that culminated in the deaths of four women. I'm a bit busy right now so could you just spit it out."

"Sorry, Sarge. The woman I spoke to didn't know the details, but one of the models suddenly disappeared. She took part in the initial stages of the pageant, but she wasn't there on the last day."

"Could this woman elaborate?" Smith said.

"She reckons the disappearance was hushed up by the organisers, but there were rumours of an ambulance and some kind of accident."

"Interesting," Smith said. "Dig deeper. I have to go."

Vicky sat back down.

"Where were we?"

"You think you know something about the recent murders in the city," Smith refreshed her memory.

"I vaguely remember the women," Vicky said.

"Why didn't you come forward sooner?" Smith asked.

"Because I didn't twig until I saw the broadcast last night. Is she alright? Is Dr Sweetman alright?"

"I don't know," Smith admitted. "We've got every available officer looking for her."

"I hope she is. I liked her."

Smith's phone started to ring again. Once more it was DC Moore. He rejected the call.

"What is it you want to tell me?" he asked.

"Like I said, it only came back to me during the broadcast. When Dr Sweetman talked about what the four girls did."

"Who is she?" Smith said. "Who was Dr Sweetman talking about?"

"Her name was Ivy something."

Smith recalled the conversation with DC Moore.

"She didn't take part in the last day of the pageant, did she?"

"No. She just disappeared, but I saw the ambulance. I saw the French paramedics and the organisers running around like headless chicken."

"Do you know what happened to Ivy?"

"It must have been something bad for her to be rushed to hospital."

"Tell me everything you remember about Le Havre in the summer of 2015," Smith said.

"Some of the girls were nice," Vicky said. "But there were some bitches too. There always are at things like that. I'd done a few pageants before and you're always going to get the divas who think they're Kate Moss."

"Was Stacy Ladd one of these?"

"She was horrible. A proper madam. She was gorgeous, but she was a really nasty piece of work."

"How long was the pageant?" Smith said.

"It took place over four days."

"Long enough for friendships to form."

"We were a bunch of teenage girls away from home," Vicky said. "Some of the parents came along, but most of us were unsupervised. You can imagine what sort of stuff went on. We were in France – the attitude to alcohol there is totally different to here, and we made the most of it."

Smith was getting an idea of what went on at the pageant, but he still didn't know what had happened that set off the spate of murders in the city."

"What do you think happened to Ivy?"

"I think Stacy and her minions did something to her," Vicky said.

"Why would you think that?"

"Because they were the last ones I saw Ivy with."

"Are you referring to Stacy, Gemma, Rachel and Casey?"

"The broadcast brought it all back. Those four formed some kind of alliance. They were inseparable. And Stacy was definitely the boss."

Smith's phone started to ring again. DC Moore was persistent, and Smith knew he had something important to tell him.

"Excuse me," he said. "I have to take this."

He walked away from the table and answered the phone.

"Sorry to bother you, Sarge," DC Moore said. "But I know who the victim was that summer in France."

"Ivy?" Smith said.

"What? How did you know that?"

"It's not important. What have you found?"

"Ivy Grogan was on the list of girls at the pageant," DC Moore said. "She was the one who was rushed off to hospital. Ivy wasn't part of the Facebook group that was set up and there's a very good reason for that."

He stopped there.

"I'm not in the mood for theatrical pauses, Harry. I don't do suspense."

"Sorry, Sarge," DC Moore said. "I lost signal for a moment. Ivy Grogan isn't on that Facebook group because she's dead. Has been for a good few years. She committed suicide in the autumn following the beauty pageant."

Smith went outside to smoke a cigarette before he returned to the table. He needed a moment to process what DC Moore had told him. He was starting to get a picture of what took place in Le Havre in 2015. Stacy Ladd and her acolytes did something to Ivy Grogan – something that resulted in her taking her own life shortly afterwards. He decided to ask Vicky if she had any theories about that.

He went back inside and ordered another beer. He was halfway back to the table when he stopped. The woman called Vicky was gone.

CHAPTER FIFTY FOUR

Ivy Grogan's parents still lived in the city. Smith and DC King were standing outside the house, shivering in the icy breeze. Smith had picked DC King up after leaving *The Golden Hen*. He'd donated his second beer to a grateful elderly man reading a newspaper. Vicky's sudden disappearance was baffling, and Smith wondered why she'd suddenly decided to up and leave.

The door opened and a man who looked to be around Smith's age looked them up and down.

"Can I help you?"

Smith took out his ID. "DS Smith and this is DC King. Can we have a word?"

"What's it about?"

"Could we speak inside?" DC King said. "It's Baltic out here."

Mr Grogan invited them in and told them to call him Henry. He didn't offer them anything to drink.

"Is Mrs Grogan home?" Smith asked in the living room. "We'd like to talk to her too."

"My wife passed away five years ago," Henry said.

"I'm sorry about that," Smith said.

"What is it you want? Is it something to do with that Optician?"

"It is," Smith confirmed.

"I watched that damn thing last night. Is the doctor alright?"

"We can't discuss that," DC King said.

"I appreciate that this might be difficult to talk about," Smith said. "We'd like to ask you some questions about your daughter."

"I thought as much," Henry said.

"What happened to her?" Smith said.

"Before she sliced open her wrists in the bath you mean?"

Smith could only nod his head in reply.

"I can't talk about it."

"I understand it must be painful for you, Mr Grogan," Smith said. "But this is important."

"I mean *I can't talk about it*," Henry said. "I signed a piece of paper saying so."

"I'm not following you."

"I think he's referring to some kind of NDA, Sarge," DC King said.

"That's right," Henry confirmed.

"Who made you sign it?" DC King said.

"I can't talk about that either."

"Mr Grogan," Smith said. "Henry. This is extremely important. A woman's life is in danger, and you have my word that nothing you tell us today will be repeated."

"Is his word worth anything?" Henry asked DC King.

"It is, Henry," she confirmed. "He's painfully honest."

"Who made you sign the NDA?" Smith said.

"I wasn't thinking straight," Henry said. "Ivy was our whole world. She was my baby girl, and I sold her soul for a few pieces of silver."

"Who paid you, Henry?"

"The people who organised the pageant. They promised me that they would cover the costs of everything. Ivy would get the best medical treatment that France had to offer, and they would fix what needed fixing. But I couldn't tell anybody about it."

"What happened, Henry?" Smith said. "What happened to Ivy?"

"Acid."

That was all he said. Smith thought back to the broadcast and Dr Sweetman's words came to him again.

"Her eyes were damaged, weren't they?" he said.

Henry nodded. "They said it was a horrible accident. There was alcohol involved, Ivy picked up the wrong bottle, and squirted acid in her eyes."

"And you believed that?" DC King said.

"It was a terrible time in our lives," Henry said. "My thoughts were muddled, and we needed the money. You must think I'm a terrible person."

"Not at all," Smith said. "None of it was your fault."

"When I saw the broadcast last night it all came back. Ivy's pain, her suicide and Nelly's death a year later."

"Nelly was your wife?" DC King said.

"She went downhill fast after Ivy did what she did," Henry said. "Her nerves gave up."

"Was Ivy blinded by the acid?" Smith said.

"Not completely," Henry said. "She lost the sight in her left eye – the acid totally destroyed everything in and around the socket, but she had partial sight in her right eye. Looking back, I often think it would have been better for her to have been rendered totally blind."

"Why would you say that?" DC King said.

"Because then she wouldn't have been aware of what she looked like."

"We won't keep you much longer," Smith said.

"It was when the bandages came off that the dark clouds appeared," Henry said. "That was when she spiralled into her depression. Let me show you something."

He got up and left the room.

"Who the hell signs an NDA after their daughter has been maimed?" Smith whispered.

"We don't know the full story," DC King said.

"I've got a good idea. No amount of money would make me keep quiet about something like that. What kind of father does that?"

"He's coming back."

Henry had a photograph in his hand. He passed it to Smith.

"She was beautiful."

Smith had to agree. Ivy Grogan was a classic beauty with flawless skin and a bone structure that any fashion brand would kill to have on their books. Her eyes were a striking shade of green, and they were full of life.

"The top half of her face was destroyed," Henry said. "Her beautiful eyes were ruined, but she still had partial vision in one of them and that's why she did what she did. She took a look at herself in the mirror one night. She ran a bath and got in with a razor blade in her hand. Nelly was the one who found her."

CHAPTER FIFTY FIVE

DC King intercepted Smith as soon as he'd got inside the station the next day.

"We got something from the appeal for the woman claiming to be Gemma London's housemate, Sarge."

"You can tell me on the way to the canteen," Smith said. "I need coffee. We've run out at home."

"I don't think I've ever run out of coffee."

"It's been a hectic few weeks," Smith said. "Out with it then."

"Two people phoned in convinced that they saw her at *The French Connection*."

"Did they say when they saw her?"

"On opening night."

"The place was packed on opening night," Smith said. "And if the mystery housemate is involved with *The Optician,* it makes sense that she would be there – it's the last place Gemma London was seen alive. Casey Plant was also there on Wednesday. Did they give us anything else?"

"Just that she was at the pub that night. It's not really going to help, is it?"

"I don't know, Kerry. Do you think the woman who called herself Hillary Twain could be *The Optician*?"

"It's possible. It's not unheard of for serial killers to taunt law enforcement in that manner."

"Webber pulled an all-nighter with the doctor's car," Smith said. "So hopefully he's got some new info for us. We're close – I can feel it."

"Do you think Dr Sweetman is still alive?" DC King said.

"I really don't know. Nothing came up during the door-to-doors and that makes me wonder if I was wrong about *The Optician* working alone. I got thinking about the night that Dr Sweetman was abducted. I watched the whole thing. She got into the car voluntarily. There were no Uber stickers on it, and Dr Sweetman had arranged for someone to pick her up earlier. What if she knew who *The Optician* was but she wasn't aware that she was a serial killer?"

"If we had her phone, we would be able to check to see who sent her the message telling her that her lift was there."

"We could ask her service provider for the info," Smith said. "But we don't have weeks to waste."

"Do you think it's possible that she kept in contact with any of the girls from the pageant?" DC King said.

"She was a good few years older than them, but stranger things have happened. And she got into that car as if she'd got a lift with the person driving it before."

"It was stolen earlier that week," DC King reminded him.

"I know. It's bugging the hell out of me."

Bridge came in with DC Moore.

"Briefing in ten," Bridge said. "Webber has found something."

"I was hoping he would," Smith said.

"I managed to get the list of all the girls who took part in the pageant," DC Moore said and held up a sheet of paper.

"And?"

"None of the names have come up in the course of the investigation."

Something occurred to Smith.

"Is there someone called Vicky on the list?"

DC Moore ran his finger down the list of names.

"Victoria Lamb. Who is she?"

"The woman I met at the dodgy pub on Malton Road. She was the one who told me about Ivy Grogan and when I got back after speaking to you on the phone she'd done a runner."

"Why would she do that?" DC Moore said.

"I have no idea, Harry. Perhaps she got cold feet. Maybe she'd told me everything she could and didn't want anyone to see her talking to a police detective. I don't know."

He picked up the piece of paper and looked at the names on it. There were eighteen girls at the pageant. Four of the names were very familiar – all of them were now dead, but, apart from Victoria Lamb, none of the other names meant anything.

Smith tapped the paper. "One of these girls knows who *The Optician* is."

"Tracking them all down will take time," DC Moore said.

"Remind me again what it is you get paid for, Harry."

"I was just saying."

"We shouldn't keep Webber waiting."

Smith got up and left the room. He hadn't touched his coffee.

"What's wrong with him this morning?" DC Moore said.

"There's nothing wrong with him," Bridge said. "There's a serial killer out there and until she's caught, Smith won't stop. You should know him well enough by now."

"I think Whitton's dad's illness is affecting him too," DC King said. "He's got a lot on his mind."

"He's right about one thing though," Bridge said. "The answers we're looking for are on that piece of paper somewhere. One of those girls knows something more than we've managed to find out."

DC Moore glanced at Smith's untouched coffee. He picked it up and took a sip.

"Christ. No wonder the bloke is wired all the time – there's enough caffeine in there to keep an army awake for days. That stuff should come with a health warning."

"If you're going to drink coffee," Bridge said. "You might as well do it properly."

He dared to taste the coffee too.

"Bloody hell. I can hear my heartbeat in my ears."

"We'd better get to the briefing," DC King said. "At least you and Harry will be wide awake for it."

CHAPTER FIFTY SIX

Webber had come alone. The Head of Forensics was sitting next to DI Smyth at the table. In front of him was a thin file and Smith didn't think it boded well. It was clear that he hadn't found much in Doctor Greg Cooper's VW Passat. Webber nodded to Bridge and the DCs King and Moore and opened the file.

"I'll keep this brief. We went through the vehicle with a fine-toothed comb. Fortunately for us, Dr Cooper cut short his holiday in the Indian Ocean and volunteered his fingerprints for elimination purposes."

"Did you find traces of the victims?" DC Moore asked.

Webber sighed. "Do you want to hear my findings, or not?"

"Of course."

"Please be quiet then. These are the preliminary findings, but I can confirm that three of the victims were inside that car at some stage. There were a lot of fingerprints and we've matched some of them to Gemma London, Casey Plant and Rachel Gold."

"Not Stacey Ladd?" Smith said.

"I would have told you if we'd found anything."

"Fair enough."

"There were numerous hair strands," Webber continued. "But we haven't finished analysing them all. I can confirm that many of the strands were bleached blond."

"Stacey Ladd had blond hair," Bridge said.

"And it's likely that the hair came from her," Webber said. "Moving on to the driver's side of the vehicle, and this is interesting. *The Optician* was not especially careful."

"She left prints," Smith guessed.

"Dozens of them," Webber said. "On the steering wheel, dashboard and window."

"They're not in the database," Smith decided.

"Obviously," Webber said. "If they were, I wouldn't be sitting here, getting interrupted every five seconds."

"I'll shut up."

"Makeup," Webber said without elaborating.

He looked around the table.

"Was that a cryptic clue?" Smith asked.

"According to Dr Cooper," Webber said. "He's a single parent. His wife passed away a few years ago and he's brought up his two boys alone. The glove compartment was full of eyeliner, lipstick and various other cosmetic products that women like to cover their faces in. So, unless the good doctor was some kind of closet drag queen, we can assume that these products did not belong to him. I would suggest that your Optician liked to wear a lot of makeup."

"It's possible she used it to change her appearance," Smith suggested.

"Very possible."

"Why leave it in the car?" DC King said.

"And why go to the trouble of taking the car back to where she stole it from?" Bridge said.

"That's not my department," Webber said. "But I'm going to offer my opinion anyway. She wanted the car to be found, and she wanted the contents of the glove compartment discovered also."

"You're dead right," Smith said. "It's pretty obvious that she's finished. Her mission was to eliminate the four women who were responsible for Ivy Grogan's injuries and subsequent suicide and that mission is complete. But she has another agenda."

"She's obsessed with the concept of beauty and how superficial it is," DC King said.

"For what it's worth."

"Nothing in that car is going to get us any closer to her," Bridge said. "All the fingerprints in the world are useless without something to compare them to."

"Then we do just that," Smith said. "Forensic evidence is only as good as the people who know what to do with it."

"I think you need more coffee, Sarge," DC Moore said.

"He's right," Webber said. "We're only as good as the other cogs in the machinery."

"I knew you loved me really," Smith said.

Webber got to his feet to indicate that he didn't have anything else to discuss. He nodded to Smith and left the room.

"Ivy Grogan," Smith said.

He walked up to the whiteboard and wrote her name in huge block capitals. He then circled it twice.

"Ivy is at the heart of this. We now know that she was maimed that summer in France. Her eyes were destroyed by acid, and *The Optician* believes the four women who have been murdered this week were responsible. What does that tell us?"

"She was close to Ivy," DC King said.

"Correct. Close enough to risk everything by abducting and killing four women. You do not do that if you're merely a passing acquaintance. *The Optician* did this out of love."

"Love?" DC Moore said.

"It's an age-old motive for murder, Harry. One of the classics. Ivy killed herself in the autumn after the pageant and her mother joined her a year later."

"Does she have any family?" Bridge asked.

"Just her father," Smith said. "She was an only child, and he's not involved in this."

"Friends then," DC King said.

"Definitely worth looking into," Smith said.

"I'm finding it hard to understand why this is happening now," Bridge said. "The pageant was over six years ago, as was Ivy's suicide. Why did *The Optician* wait so long?"

"That's a very good question," Smith said. "It's possible that this has been in the planning stages for a long time. Perhaps *The Optician* wanted to wait until she was absolutely certain that she could pull it off."

"The operations require certain skills," DC King said. "It's not something you learn overnight."

"We'll keep on trawling through that list of entrants in the pageant," Smith said. "We're going to find the answers there – I know we are."

CHAPTER FIFTY SEVEN

By four that afternoon, the team was no further ahead than they were that morning. The four detectives had worked their way through the list of entrants of the pageant in Le Havre, and nothing new had come up. A few of the women were no longer living in the city but the majority of them still called York home, and none of them could give them anything different from what they already knew. Ivy Grogan just disappeared. All of the models were aware of some kind of accident, but none of them could offer any details.

Smith was still certain that one of the models from 2015 had some answers and he wasn't giving up. His tired eyes pored over the names on the list again. They'd managed to ascertain that two of the women were dead. One of them was involved in a fatal car crash in 2020 and the other had taken her own life shortly after the beauty pageant. Smith focused on her. Catherine Grove had taken an overdose of sleeping tablets at her home in Bootham. According to the records, Catherine's parents were both dead, but there was a sister. Heidi Grove was precisely sixteen minutes older than her twin sister.

Smith couldn't find any trace of her on social media. There was no Heidi Grove on Facebook, Twitter or Instagram and Smith thought that was odd. She was in her early-twenties, and it was unusual for someone her age not to use social media. She had never claimed benefits and there was no record of her ever paying tax. Smith sensed that Heidi Grove was worth looking into, especially in light of her sister's suicide. Catherine had overdosed on pills just weeks after Ivy Grogan took her own life.

Smith found DC King in the canteen.

"I was just taking a break, Sarge," she said.

"No worries, Kerry. I think I've found a promising lead."

He told her about Catherine Grove's suicide.

"It does sound promising," DC King said. "It can't just be a coincidence that Catherine killed herself so soon after Ivy did."

"She has a sister," Smith said. "Heidi. I can't find any trace of her anywhere, and that makes me suspicious. She's not on social media, and there are no employment records for her."

"She could be a student," DC King suggested.

"It's possible."

"What about the parents?"

"Both dead," Smith said. "Where do we start looking for someone who clearly does not want to be found?"

"Are there any other siblings?"

"Not according to the records," Smith said. "It was just the twins. Any suggestions?"

"Speak to the other girls who attended the pageant again," DC King said. "Ask them about Catherine. See if anything connects her to Ivy Grogan."

"It's worth a shot," Smith said. "First I need to smoke a cigarette."

It was dark when he got outside. He lit the cigarette and ran through a number of possible scenarios in his head. The series of events was bothering him. Ivy Grogan had been left severely maimed by the acid in her eyes and she'd taken her own life shortly after returning from France. Catherine Grove had joined her a couple of weeks later. The two suicides had to be connected. Smith didn't know the statistics for teenage suicides, but he did know that the suicides of two fourteen-year-old girls in the space of two weeks was not common, especially taking the fact that they knew one another into account.

"Was Ivy's suicide the catalyst for Catherine taking her own life?" Smith wondered out loud.

It was plausible, but Smith wanted to know more.

"I don't even find it strange when you talk to yourself anymore."
Smith turned round to face DCI Chalmers.
"Afternoon, boss," Smith said. "What's new?"
"I'm giving emigration some serious thought," Chalmers said.
He lit a cigarette and exhaled a cloud of smoke.
"What's brought this on?" Smith said.
"I don't know. It's the time of year, I suppose. Months of darkness and crap weather get to you after a while."
"Where were you thinking of relocating?"
"Somewhere warm," Chalmers said. "I had thought about Spain, but what with the Brexit bollocks, that's not really an option anymore. I've heard Australia is nice."
"You heard wrong," Smith said.
"Anyway," Chalmers said. "I'll never get Mrs Chalmers to agree to it. She'll never move away from her tosspot of a brother."
"It'll soon be spring," Smith said.
    "Where are you at with the Optician thing?" Chalmers said.
"We're getting closer," Smith said. "We know why she's doing it, but her identity is proving to be elusive."
"Between you and me, top brass is hoping for a quick result."
"What's new?"
"And you know what the Super is like when his crime stats thing is approaching."
"I couldn't give a fuck about that," Smith said.
"None of us could."
"I've got five days. Five days to find the most twisted woman this city has ever seen."
"No pressure then," Chalmers said and stubbed out his cigarette. "That's me off home."

"It's only just gone four," Smith said.

"Perks of the job," Chalmers said. "Normal hours and no overtime."

"You miss it really."

"Not likely. See you around."

Smith watched as he walked towards his BMW.

DC King came outside and the expression on her face told Smith that she was about to tell him something important. He wasn't wrong.

"Catherine Grove and Ivy Grogan were more than just friends, Sarge."

"Go on," Smith said.

"According to more than one of the models from the pageant, they were involved with one another."

"As in a relationship?" Smith said.

DC King nodded. "And there's more. Catherine's twin sister still lives in the city, and we've spoken to her more than once during the course of the investigation. I think I know who *The Optician* is."

CHAPTER FIFTY EIGHT

Smith's heart was pounding in his chest as they drove to *The French Connection*. He'd made DI Smyth aware of what was happening, and after a brief discussion, he'd managed to persuade the DI that backup wasn't required. He didn't think *The Optician* would be at work, but he was hoping to get some answers from the other people who worked at the pub.

"It's funny, isn't it?" DC King said. "When you suddenly click about the identity of a killer, you wonder why you didn't see it sooner."
"A cryptic crossword puzzle is a piece of cake when you're given all the answers, Kerry," Smith said. "But then there's no point to it. A murder investigation is the same. If it was so easy, we'd all be out of a job. I met the fucking woman. She was there right from the beginning."

When they'd compared the CCTV still of the woman who called herself Hillary Twain with a recent photograph of the bar manager from *The French Connection* Smith had cursed himself. Hillary's glasses and lack of makeup had given her a plain Jane look. Holly's makeup had masked her true identity beautifully and when Smith compared the two photos, taking what they now knew into consideration it was blatantly obvious that they were looking at the same woman.

"Holly," he said. "Hillary and Heidi. She didn't even try to disguise her name too much."
"She was Catherine's twin sister," DC King said. "Catherine and Ivy were in love and when Ivy killed herself after the acid did its thing with her eyes, Catherine's reaction was to follow her to the grave. Heidi somehow found out about what happened in France and planned her revenge. But we still have to ask – why now?"
"That will become apparent when we find her," Smith said. "I know it will."

The French Connection was quiet when they went inside, and Smith was glad. A young man was replenishing the optics behind the bar. Smith coughed to get his attention.

"What can I get you?" the barman said.

"Is Holly in?" Smith asked.

The barman shook his head. "She's off sick."

"How long has she been off?"

"She hasn't been in since Saturday night."

Smith knew they were on the right track.

"Is Mr Norton here?"

"He's busy with some paperwork in his office."

"We'll find him," Smith said.

The barman nodded and turned his attention back to the bottles of spirits.

James Norton shot up when Smith and DC King went in without knocking.

"You can't just barge in here."

"We need to talk to you," Smith said.

James sat back down. "Make it quick. I was busy with the staff wages."

Smith watched him bundle piles of cash into a metal box.

"Do you pay your employees in cash?" DC King said.

"That's not important," Smith said.

He sat down opposite the owner of the pub. DC King remained standing.

"What's this all about?" James asked.

"Holly Grove," Smith said. "Were you aware that Holly isn't her real name?"

"What? No, of course not."

"Her name is Heidi," DC King said.

"I'm surprised you didn't know that," Smith said.

"Why would she lie about her name?" James said.

"That's not important either. I believe she's been off sick for a while."

"She called in yesterday morning," James said. "She's got some kind of stomach bug. It's no big deal."

"How long has Holly or Heidi worked for you?" DC King said.

"About a year," James said. "She worked at the *Norton* for a bit. That was part time. She was a student, but she agreed to take a year away from her studies to run the bar here."

"That's what she told us," Smith said. "She's studying Dentistry, isn't she?"

"That's right."

"We're going to need her address," Smith said.

"I don't have to give it to you."

"I'm asking you nicely."

"I don't care if you smother me with gifts," James said. "I know my rights. I don't have to give you anything without a piece of paper ordering me to do so."

Smith's eyes fell on the metal box in the middle of the table. He stood up.

"No worries. Come on, Kerry."

"Sarge?" DC King said.

Smith turned to James Norton.

"This is what's going to happen now. I'm going to make a couple of phone calls. I'm sure you're aware of the concept of an audit."

James remained silent.

"I'll take that as a yes then. In an hour or so, a team from HMRC is going to descend on the pub. It's going to be extremely unpleasant for you. They're a bunch of nasty bastards, and they're going to audit the fuck out of this place."

James Norton's mouth opened wide.

"It's going to take time," Smith said. "It's a lengthy process and the pub will have to close for the duration. HMRC's finest are going to find irregularities and when they do, they're going to take a closer look at your other business interests. To be honest, I couldn't give a fuck about that. I'm not interested in tax fraud. All I want is the address you have on file for your bar manager."

James Norton looked like he was going to cry. "I don't have her address."

Smith sighed. "We're wasting our time here, Kerry."

"I don't have it," James said. "I really don't. I pay Holly in cash – that's been the agreement since the beginning. She was more than happy with it."

"Heidi Grove doesn't officially work here, does she?" DC King said.

James shook his head. "I don't want any trouble."

"Nobody wants trouble, Mr Norton," Smith said.

"Paul might know where Holly lives. They sometimes go for drinks after work."

"Paul?"

"He's one of my bar staff. He's behind the bar now."

Smith tapped the tin full of money. "Let's hope for your sake that Paul can help us."

CHAPTER FIFTY NINE

The barman was very helpful. He'd given them the address for Heidi Grove, but when Smith and a team of uniforms went in hard, it was clear that the house hadn't been lived in for quite some time. There was a musty smell inside that Smith knew all too well. It was the odour of neglect and the absence of human occupation. Grant Webber and his team were busy checking the place over, but Smith didn't think they were going to get any answers from the house.

"Heidi Grove's face is out there for the whole world to see," DI Smyth said.

It was early evening but nobody on the team had any objections when the DI suggested they carry on working.

"A reward is being offered for any information that leads to her arrest," DI Smyth added.

"How much?" DC Moore said.

"Who cares?" Smith said. "Her identity is out there, and it's going to be extremely difficult for her to come and go."

"Are we a hundred percent sure that she is *The Optician*?" Bridge said.

"Positive," Smith said. "She had motive, and she had opportunity. The barman at *The French Connection* cleared up a few things for us. Wednesday night was busy as hell at the pub. The place was packed, and he couldn't recall seeing Heidi for part of the night. Gemma London was picked up in an Uber around ten. We believe she was drugged and taken to somewhere in Heworth. The pub is five minutes away from Heworth. It would have been possible for Heidi to disappear for half an hour without anybody noticing. Casey Plant was taken from the nightclub in South Bank. She and her friends spent the first part of the night at *The French Connection*, and Heidi Grove was working that night. I think Heidi took a keen interest in Casey –

she was aware that she would be heading over to *Blast*, and she waited. Heidi Grove is *The Optician*."

"Our main priority is to find the location of the property in Heworth," DI Smyth said. "The house the bartender told us about hasn't been lived in for weeks, so Heidi must have access to another place."

"We don't even know if it is really in Heworth," DC Moore said. "We only have the celebrity shrink's word for that, and it's possible that she made a mistake."

"She didn't," Smith said. "Dr Sweetman risked a hell of a lot doing what she did. She wouldn't have mentioned Heworth unless she was certain."

"Uniforms have been busy there since the broadcast went out," DC Moore argued. "They've come up with nothing. All of the properties with basements have been checked and Dr Sweetman isn't in any of them."

"It's only a matter of time before we find her," Smith said. "We know who she is now, and she cannot hide forever."

"Let's go through what we know about Heidi Grove," DI Smyth said.

"She was telling the truth about the Dentistry degree, sir," DC King said. "She was taking a year out after her third year."

"She has no family," Smith said. "We know what happened to her twin sister, and her parents are both deceased. Hold on…"

Bridge looked over at him and grinned.

"Find out when her parents died," Smith said.

Bridge nodded. "I think I know what you're getting at."

"Could you do that now please, Kerry?" Smith asked DC King.

"No problem," DC King said.

"Have I missed something?" DC Moore said.

"We've been here before, Harry," Smith said. "Heidi Grove has no living siblings. Her parents are dead."

"Inheritance," DC Moore said.

"Got it in one. Heidi is the sole heir. I've got a strong suspicion that she's been carrying out her work in her parent's old house."

"It shouldn't take long to find out," DI Smyth said.

"Do you think the celebrity shrink is still alive?" Bridge said.

"I think she is," Smith said. "I don't know why, but I've got a feeling that Dr Vanessa Sweetman is still breathing."

* * *

"Are you still with us?"

Dr Sweetman opened her left eye. Her right eye was swollen shut. Her nose was throbbing in time with her heartbeat, and she could taste blood in her mouth. She ran her tongue over the gaps where two of her teeth once were and focused on the young woman standing over her.

"I need you to change heads."

Dr Sweetman had no idea what this meant. Her vocal cords wouldn't oblige her, so she shook her head.

"I want you to lose the celebrity podcast head. I need your advice as a psychologist. Can you do that?"

Dr Sweetman managed to reply in the affirmative.

The Optician placed a hand on Dr Sweetman's forehead. "You have a fever. You're burning up. I'm going to give you something to bring your temperature down."

Dr Sweetman barely felt the needle as it entered the skin of her lower arm.

"This should work quickly. I'm not a monster. Do you think I'm a monster?"

"No," Dr Sweetman said.

She mustered some saliva and licked her lips.

"I think you're ill."

"Can I be cured?"

"I believe you can," Dr Sweetman said. "But first you need to acknowledge what you did. You need to own your actions."

"Own my actions," *The Optician* repeated.

"You've been hurt. You have wounds that are deep, and they haven't been allowed to heal. With help, this can be fixed."

"Do you think what I did was justified?"

"It's not what I think that matters," Dr Sweetman said. "You can only begin your path to recovery when you figure out the answer to that question yourself. I can't assist you with that."

The Optician picked up a tablet from the table and tapped the screen. "Look."

She thrust it into Dr Sweetman's face.

"I'm more famous than you now. Do you think I look better with or without makeup."

"It doesn't really matter. Beauty is what's inside you."

"You do talk a lot of nonsense sometimes." The words were sung rather than spoken.

"They will find you," Dr Sweetman told her. "I think you should help them."

"Why should I do that?"

"Because you want to get caught. You've finished what you set out to do. You did it, and now it's over, you have to take the next step."

The tablet was replaced on the table.

"Did you know?" *The Optician* said. "You were there. Did you know what they did to Ivy?"

"I didn't," Dr Sweetman said. "I was just one of the judges. I wasn't given any details."

"Do I believe you?"

"It's the truth. I wasn't involved. You need to do the right thing."

The Optician started to laugh. "Nah, I thought it would be harder than it was. Have you ever killed someone?"

"No," Dr Sweetman said.

"Are you scared of me?"

"Yes. Your erratic behaviour frightens me. You're unpredictable and that's unsettling."

"I could kill you right now."

"I understand that," Dr Sweetman said. "But I don't think that would achieve anything, would it?"

The Optician nodded thoughtfully.

"I have to go out," she said after a few seconds.

"Where are you going?" Dr Sweetman said.

"Somewhere important. If you die before I get back, I'm sorry. I really am – I want you to know that."

CHAPTER SIXTY

"I want every officer who isn't drunk or away on holiday over to this address now."

DI Smyth shot up his chair.

"Hold your horses," Smith said.

"That's my line," DI Smyth reminded him.

"If *The Optician* is there," Smith said. "Dr Sweetman could still be in grave danger. We can't risk storming the place. We need to do it subtly."

"When have you ever been subtle?"

"Since the reality of reaching the age of forty has dawned on me."

"What do you suggest?"

"Just me and you, boss," Smith said. "We knock on the door and take it from there."

Smith's hunch had been spot on. Heidi Grove's parents had died within a year of one another. Her father had gone first and nine months after his fatal heart attack Heidi's mother had suffered a stroke and died in hospital two days later. Mr and Mr Grove owned a property between Heworth and Tang Hall. The three-bedroom semi-detached house was on Fourth Avenue and even though there was nothing in the plans to suggest that there was a basement, Smith was convinced that they had the right place. The property had been transferred to Heidi Grove three months ago, and he knew it was where *The Optician* had carried out her macabre operations.

It was after nine when they parked down the street from number 34 Fourth Avenue. Smith got out of the car, lit a cigarette and looked up and down the road. Number 34 was on the corner of Fourth Avenue and Tang Hall Lane. The house was larger than most of the others in the street and, according to the plans it was on a much bigger plot of land. DI Smyth had insisted on backup, of course and a short phone call told him that everything was set up around the corner in Melrose Close. Smith had wanted an ambulance nearby too but that wasn't going to happen. He was informed that it wasn't viable to tie up medical personnel on the basis of a *possible* emergency.

"Ready?" DI Smyth said.

Smith put out his cigarette. "We're going to get her tonight."

"There's a strong possibility that she's seen the media frenzy surrounding her," DI Smyth said. "Her face has been staring out from every news site in the country and it's likely that will make her unpredictable."

"What woman isn't unpredictable?" Smith said.

DI Smyth scratched his cheek and walked in the direction of Tang Hall Lane.

Smith took a moment to study the house. There were no lights on inside, and it didn't look like there was anybody at home. He knocked on the door anyway. DI Smyth reached inside his pocket and pulled something out.

"What the hell are you doing?" Smith nodded to the Taser.

"I'm not taking any chances," DI Smyth said.

"You do realise that just by taking that thing out of your pocket, you're obliged to file a report when this is all over."

"Only if someone saw me draw it."

"Are you suggesting I turn a blind eye?"

"What's got into you?" DI Smyth said. "I much preferred the pre-midlife crisis Smith. You were much more fun to work with before you got old."

Smith knocked again and waited. When nothing happened for ten seconds, he placed a hand on the door handle and turned it. The door was unlocked. DI Smyth indicated with a finger to his lips that they were to keep quiet. A couple of other hand signals followed, and Smith had no idea what DI Smyth was trying to tell him.

DI Smyth rolled his eyes.

"Go in slowly," he whispered. "According to the plans, there are three rooms downstairs – a living room, a dining room and a kitchen. The dining and living room are on the left, and the kitchen is at the end. Keep your eyes left and ahead. There shouldn't be any surprises from the right-hand side."

"And you told me all that with a few hand signals?" Smith said. "Is that the sort of crap they teach you in the army?"

"Idiot."

"It's pitch black in there," Smith said. "I'm going to turn on a light. Is that OK?"

DI Smyth nodded.

"Do not point that taser anywhere near me," Smith told him.

They went inside. Smith found a light switch on the wall just inside the door. It took a moment to adjust to the sudden light but when he was able to see properly, he realised something immediately. The building plans they'd seen for number 34 Fourth Avenue were inaccurate. According to the floor plan the house was a mirror image of the adjacent property. The doors to the living room and dining room were wide open but there was a third door further along the hallway that was closed, and this door shouldn't be there.

After making sure that the first two downstairs rooms were empty Smith and DI Smyth scanned the kitchen with the same result. They stood outside the mystery third door and Smith turned to face DI Smyth when there was a sound from behind the door.

"Backup," Smith said.

DI Smyth realised that it wasn't a question when Smith swung the door open wide and a strip of light lit up half a dozen stairs.

"Another fucking cellar," Smith said and started to walk downwards.

"I'll keep watch up here," DI Smyth said.

"We need that ambulance now," Smith shouted up.

Dr Vanessa Sweetman was slumped over in a chair in the middle of the room. Her hands were taped to the arms of the chair and there was a tube attached to her wrist. An IV bag containing a clear liquid was hanging crudely from a nail on the table next to the chair. Smith could smell blood. He freed Dr Sweetman's hands, carefully raised her up and felt for a pulse. "She's still alive," he screamed. "We need a fucking ambulance now."

He held onto Dr Sweetman's hand and took in her injuries. One of her eyes was swollen shut and there was swelling on and around her nose. There was no blood on her face. Her lips were cracked and slightly open. Smith could see that some of her teeth were missing.

"Hold on," Smith said. "Help is on the way."

He felt pressure on his hand and Dr Sweetman's good eye opened.

"Is she still here?" Smith asked her.

Dr Sweetman shook her head, and it obviously hurt to do so. The pain was written on her face.

"An ambulance is on the way," Smith said. "Do you know where she went?"

Dr Sweetman's mouth opened wider. "Somewhere important."

"She said she was going somewhere important?"

"Yes."

"You're going to be OK," Smith said. "You look like shit by the way."

Dr Sweetman squeezed his hand.

"Don't try to speak," Smith said. "We'll have you out of here in no time."

"Jason," Dr Sweetman said.

"Don't speak."

"What took you so long?"

CHAPTER SIXTY ONE

Smith shivered and rubbed his hands together. It was almost midnight, and the temperature had fallen below zero. He crossed the bridge over Tang Hall Beck and headed for the dim lights in the distance. He stopped when he was halfway. He could hear a woman's voice, and it was a familiar one.

Heidi Grove was sitting cross-legged in front of the memorial wall. Smith stayed where he was and let her talk. After a minute or so, he approached and stood a few metres behind her.

"Do you mind if I sit down?"

Heidi nodded without turning round. Smith knew that he should feel afraid right now – this was a woman who had mutilated and killed four people, but Smith felt no fear as he sat down beside her with his hands on his knees. *The Optician* was gone, and a sad young woman had taken her place.

"We found the diary," Smith said.

Heidi looked at him now. "Did you read it?"

"I read enough. I'll read the rest later. You know you have to come with me now."

"What will happen to me?"

"That's not my department," Smith said and regretted it as soon as the words left his mouth. "I mean – it's not me who gets to decide. You'll be evaluated and then it's up to the people who make the hard decisions."

"Is Dr Sweetman still alive?"

"We got to her in time," Smith told her. "You didn't have to do that to her. She played no part in this."

"I told her I was sorry. I needed her to tell my story."

"She didn't get to finish it," Smith said. "Do you want to do that now?"

"It's all in the diary."

The diary she was referring to was her sister's. They'd found it in one of the bedrooms. Smith had only read a few paragraphs, but he suspected that Catherine Grove's journal would fill in the remaining gaps left in the investigation.

"You didn't know that Catherine kept a diary, did you?" Smith said.

He guessed that Heidi had only stumbled across it when she inherited her parents' house.

He was right.

"I found it when I was clearing some things out of the house," Heidi said. "I didn't know my sister at all."

"I didn't really know my sister either," Smith said. "The diary is behind everything you did, isn't it?"

"I didn't even know. I didn't know how deeply Catherine was hurt by what happened to Ivy. I didn't even see it, and I should have done. What those girls did destroyed her. It tore her apart."

"They were young girls, Heidi," Smith said. "They were drunk and none of them deserved what you did to them."

"I'd do it again if I had the time over again. I'd change nothing."

Smith knew he was probably going to get into trouble for what he was about to do next, but he didn't care. He didn't think Heidi was going to change her story when she was inside an interview room and he needed to hear that story now.

"When did it start?" he asked. "When did you decide to kill them?"

"Not long after I first read Catherine's diary," Heidi said. "I wasn't there for her when she was in hell, and I needed to make things right. You wouldn't understand."

This was an understatement. Smith didn't understand at all.

"You came to see me shortly after Gemma London went missing," he said. "Why did you do that?"

"I wanted you to find her," Heidi said.

"That was important to you, wasn't it? You needed us to see what you'd done."

"Of course I needed you to see. I needed the whole world to see – to really see."

"You took Casey Plant next," Smith said. "Was the order of the abductions important?"

"No. Stacy had to be the last one, that's all."

"Because you think what happened to Ivy Grogan was Stacy's fault?"

"I know it was her fault," Heidi said. "It's all in the diary."

There were still a lot of questions Smith needed answers to.

"How did you manage to steal Dr Cooper's car?"

"It wasn't difficult. Greg and I had a thing for a while, and I knew about the holiday. I also knew where he kept the spare key to the car. I took it one night when I stayed over at his place."

This was probably something they should have looked into, but they didn't even consider a connection between *The Optician* and Dr Cooper.

"How did you get Dr Sweetman to go with you?" Smith asked. "I saw her get into the car, and she did it willingly."

"Uber," Heidi said. "She thought I was an Uber driver."

"She got in even after I'd warned her about Uber drivers."

"It was still when you were under the impression that the killer was a man. She saw me and didn't hesitate."

"It's freezing," Smith said. "Shall we go?"

"Don't you want to hear the rest?"

"Not really," Smith said.

He was feeling a bit ill already. He decided he would read the diary and wait until Heidi was formerly interviewed to see how the rest of the story played out.

He got to his feet and held out his hand.

"Come on."

Heidi got up without his help.

"Are you going to handcuff me?"

"Do I need to?" Smith said.

"I like you," Heidi said. "I liked you the moment I met you. You're one of the good people on this planet, and there aren't many of them left."

Smith didn't think the words of a psychopathic serial killer could really be considered a compliment, and he didn't take them thus.

"There are police officers everywhere," he told her. "If you try to run, you'll be caught within seconds."

"I'm not planning on running," Heidi said. "I didn't do this so I could run when it was finished. Surely, you can see that."

CHAPTER SIXTY TWO

"Thank God that's over and done with."
Bridge sipped his coffee, and it was clear from his face that he would have preferred something a bit stronger.
"I can think of more pleasant things to do on my birthday," Smith said.
   Superintendent Smyth's dreaded crime stats presentation was relatively short this year, but the two hours everyone had had to endure felt much longer. It was two hours that Smith was never going to get back.
"Those specs actually suit you, Sarge," DC Moore said.
Smith had got the phone call yesterday – his glasses were ready, and when he put them on for the first time he was amazed.
"Jeez," he'd said to Stella Read. "I really was half blind."
The optician had warned him that he might experience headaches for a few days, but these should pass. So far, Smith hadn't suffered any.
   "They make you look quite intelligent," Bridge said. "I'm going to have to start treating you with a bit more respect, especially now you're officially bloody old."
"I'm forty," Smith reminded him. "It's not old."
"According to statistics," DC Moore said.
"Shut up, Harry." Smith didn't want to hear the rest.
   "What are you going to do with your certificate?" DC King said.
Everyone on the team had been presented with a certificate of excellence for the work on *The Optician* case. Everybody knew that the gesture stank of an afterthought. It wasn't clear whether the investigation would be cleared up in time to give Superintendent Smyth the edge over his rival in Leeds, and it was definitely a last-minute thing.
"I must have lost mine," Smith said. "Oh well, shit happens."
   "Did you see Dr Sweetman's latest podcast?" Bridge said.

"What do you think?" Smith said. "I've seen enough glorification of murder to last me a lifetime."

"You should watch it, Sarge," DC King said. "She was brilliant. She got up there, looking like she'd done three rounds with Mike Tyson, and her words were really heartfelt."

"What was it about?" Smith said.

"The value of appearances and how society needs an attitude change if it's going to survive. The fact that she presented it with her face looking like that really made her words hit home."

"She attracted more than two times the viewers that she did for the one with you, Sarge," DC Moore said.

"And all of the proceeds have been promised to the family of the first victim," Bridge added.

"Gemma London?" Smith said.

"Ivy Grogan, you berk. Ivy's suicide was what started this. She was the real first victim. It's only her dad left, but I'm sure he'll be grateful for the money."

Smith finished his coffee. "It's time I was off."

"Do you fancy a few beers later?" Bridge said. "It is your birthday, after all."

"I'll give it a miss," Smith said. "I promised I'd pop round to see Whitton's dad."

"No problem. You're off tomorrow, aren't you?"

"That's right. I'll see you all on Monday."

* * *

When Jane Whitton opened the door Smith was aware of laughter inside the house and he hadn't been expecting it.

"What's going on?" he asked.

"Fat Sally is what's going on," Jane said. "Somehow, Laura found out about that hideous puppet, and she wouldn't stop nagging until I dragged her out of the cupboard I stuffed her in years ago."

"That might be my fault," Smith said.

"I thought as much. Do you want a beer?"

"Thanks, Jane. A beer would be perfect."

Whitton appeared from the kitchen. She walked over to Smith and wrapped her arms around him.

"What was that for?" he asked her.

Whitton shrugged her shoulders. "Do I need a reason to hug my ancient husband."

"Thanks. I definitely need that beer now."

"Those glasses suit you," Jane said.

"I feel old," Smith said. "You're the second person to tell me that today."

He grabbed a beer from the fridge and made his way upstairs to the source of the laughter. It was coming from the spare room. Harold Whitton had moved into the room a couple of weeks ago. It had been his idea. He didn't want to disrupt Jane's sleep with his restlessness, and the spare room was also closer to the bathroom. Smith suspected there was another reason for his relocation. He didn't think Harold wanted to die in the bed he'd shared with his wife for more than four decades.

"What's all the noise about?" Smith asked.

"Fat Sally," Laura said in a fake deep voice. "She's got an arse like a couple of badly parked double decker buses."

Smith was glad he hadn't taken a sip of beer yet. He knew it would now be all over the wall if he had.

"Where did that come from?" he asked Laura.

"Sorry, son."

Harold's voice was no more than a croak, and it sounded like the words were a real effort to get out.

"You're supposed to do it without moving your lips," Fran said.

Fat Sally had seen better days. The straw that had been used for her hair had turned brown and a lot of it had fallen out. Some of the stuffing inside the puppet was spilling from her impressive stomach and one of her shoes was missing.

"Tell him the other one," Fran dared Laura. "The one about throwing her in the air."

"I'd prefer it if you didn't," Smith said. "Go and see if Nanna needs some help with the food."

"But Dad," Laura said.

"Please," Smith said. "Granddad needs a bit of peace and quiet."

"Happy birthday, son," Harold said.

"Forty years old," Smith said. "Who would have thought it?"

"You got your man then," Harold said. "Or should I say woman."

"It doesn't make me feel good. It's like we only arrived afterwards. She did what she set out to do, and we didn't change a damn thing."

"I'll have none of that talk on your birthday. Go on down and enjoy yourself. I need to sleep a bit."

"No worries, Harold," Smith said. "What was the other one Fran was talking about? The one about jumping the air."

Harold gave him a weak smile.

"I wouldn't say Sally was fat," he said. "But when you throw her in the air, she gets stuck."

Smith laughed. "Get some rest."

CHAPTER SIXTY THREE

Smith was torturing himself. He was reading Catherine Grove's diary again. He hadn't slept much, and he'd admitted defeat at seven and got up, even though it was Sunday and he had a day off. The birthday celebrations at Whitton's parents' house had been a welcome distraction from everything that had happened in the past couple of weeks, but Smith couldn't switch off from it for too long. He made himself a second cup of coffee and started to read from the beginning again.

When he'd first come across the journal he'd been surprised. He'd expected the diary of a fourteen year old girl to be full of immature teenage ramblings but the words of *The Optician's* twin sister displayed a maturity beyond her years. This was a girl who knew how to express herself and who wasn't afraid to bear her soul on the page.

The earlier entries spoke of Catherine's first meeting with Ivy Grogan. Theirs was love at first sight. In Catherine's eyes, Ivy was someone she wanted to spend the rest of her life with. Smith really couldn't believe that a teenage girl had felt like this. They would meet in secret as often as they could.

The beauty pageant was mentioned a couple of months after Catherine and Ivy first met and Catherine's tone was upbeat. It made Smith feel terribly sad. Neither of them knew what tragedy the pageant would bring with it.

Smith stopped reading when he reached the part of the diary that chronicled the events of the pageant. Catherine Grove hadn't been there during the incident with the acid, but she'd seen Ivy shortly before that. She'd watched her with the other four girls, and she'd reached her own conclusions about what transpired. She outlined these suspicions in her journal.

Smith wondered what had gone through Heidi's head when she read the words in front of him. Catherine had been there when Ivy's life changed forever, and she'd been shunned afterwards. According to the diary, Ivy refused all contact. Catherine didn't give up. She tried everything but nothing worked. And then she learned that Ivy had taken her own life. She'd given up on life, and Catherine made up her mind to do the same.

Smith couldn't read any more. There was a conflict taking place inside his head. Did what happened to Ivy Grogan and Catherine Grove justify what Heidi had done? Four young women were dead. They were no more than children when they played their part in what eventually cost them their lives, but did they deserve it? Smith didn't think so. One thing was certain – he was never going to forget *The Optician*.

Whitton came downstairs with her phone to her ear. Smith couldn't gauge her mood from her face, and he hoped that Harold was OK. He listened as she said her goodbyes and asked if she wanted some coffee.
"We need to get over to my mum and dad's," Whitton said.
"Has something happened?" Smith said.
"My dad isn't responding to anything my mum says. I've phoned for an ambulance."
"Harold doesn't want to die in hospital," Smith said.
"What the fuck do you suggest I do, Jason? Sit back and watch him die because he's a stubborn old man?"
Smith got up and wrapped his arms around her. "I'm sorry. Let's go."

Neither of them spoke during the short drive. Smith parked outside the house and Whitton got out and opened the door without waiting for him. The ambulance still hadn't arrived. Smith looked up at the house. He could see Jane through the window in the main bedroom upstairs. He went inside and walked slowly upstairs. He poked his head inside the room. Whitton was helping her mother pack some things into a small case.

"What can I do?" Smith asked.

"Go and talk to him," Jane said. "He listens to you."

"Is he awake?"

"He is, and he knows exactly what's going on. Talk to him. I will not have my last moments with my husband with him kicking and screaming as he's dragged out of his house."

Smith didn't think there was much chance of that. He left them to it and went to the spare room.

"Harold," he said.

Whitton's dad wasn't moving and Smith feared that it was already all over. His eyes opened and Smith moved closer. He noticed that Fat Sally was sitting on the chair opposite the bed. Her button eyes were staring directly ahead. Smith avoided eye contact with her.

"Harold," he said again. "An ambulance is on the way. You need to go to hospital."

Harold nodded and his lips opened.

"I know, son.'

His eyes closed and a final breath of air escaped from his mouth.

Smith stood outside the main bedroom. His eyes found Whitton's and he gave her a tiny shake of the head. He watched as she put her arms around her mum and both of them fell down onto the bed. Smith left them. He went back downstairs, opened the front door and went outside into the street. He took out his cigarettes and managed to get one lit after three tries. He sat down on the wall and watched as an ambulance approached and stopped outside the house.

THE END

Printed in Dunstable, United Kingdom